"Who did this to you, Brenna?" he asked.

She threw his hands away. Unshed tears of hot shame shone brightly in her eyes now that he had seen the badges of that which she had tried so hard to hide.

"I shouldn't have come in here," she began uncertainly, heading for her own room and cursing herself for not realizing earlier the state of her night attire. But she was not to be so lightly let off, for Nicholas Pencarrow had had enough and he was at the door before she was.

"Now, Brenna," he said softly. "You are going to tell me how a girl well cosseted in a family of unquestionable name came by such abuse."

"I won't tell you!" He would hate her now. Hate her and despise her and expose her. Everything was finished, over. Black despair spiraled inward. "Please, Nicholas, let me go." Her voice was an aching whisper.

"I can't," he returned. "Damn it, I can't."

* * *

Fallen Angel
Harlequin Historical #171—September 2005

Fallen Angel

Sophia James

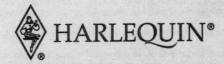

HARLEQUIN®

TORONTO • NEW YORK • LONDON
AMSTERDAM • PARIS • SYDNEY • HAMBURG
STOCKHOLM • ATHENS • TOKYO • MILAN • MADRID
PRAGUE • WARSAW • BUDAPEST • AUCKLAND

ISBN 0-373-30480-3

FALLEN ANGEL

Copyright © 2004 by Sophia James

This edition published by arrangement with Harlequin Books S.A.

® and TM are trademarks of the publisher. Trademarks indicated with
® are registered in the United States Patent and Trademark Office, the
Canadian Trade Marks Office and in other countries.

www.eHarlequin.com

Printed in U.S.A.

To Peter, Karen, Tim and Anne
for their love, patience and expertise.

Chapter One

Airelies, Kent—August 1861

Brenna stood still, stock still, head tilted at the low sounds of a fine summer evening, and listened. The river ran behind her and the plane trees rustled in the light night winds, just as they always did. But something was different; Mars and Bellona, her hunting dogs, stopped with their hackles up stiffly along bony spines as if they had felt it too. Brenna's hand went quietly to her gun before going forward, shaky fingers pushing the flintlock guard up and inserting a steel-tubed charge. The trees were thicker now as they entered into the wooded copse a half a mile from Worsley, bordering on the Northern London Road, and she had to thrust the leafy branches aside to push through towards the sounds which she could now identify with more clarity.

Voices. Men's voices. Low and soft and dangerous. A spurt of fear leapt into her heart, making it beat hard, and she stepped back in retreat, signalling her dogs to do the same, crouching in the undergrowth to get a look at what it was the men were doing before she left.

Two men came into her vision, dragging a third barely conscious man between them, his head bloodied, a blindfold tied roughly across his eyes, the fine linen of his shirt and the cut of his trousers strangely out of place against the rough homespun of the others.

'My God, highwaymen,' Brenna thought, one hand moving unbidden to her mouth as if to stop the words that might come; the other one tightening on her weapon. Mars growled suddenly from behind her and Brenna held his muzzle, willing him into a calmness she herself was far from feeling. She watched the blindfolded man being tied roughly to the thick bough of an elm tree, then the two men walked away.

Listening, she tried to determine their movements. They'd be going back to the coach without doubt, for it was a robbery here in progress. She wondered at the fate of his lackeys or outriders and at the audacity these robbers had to strike on such a well-travelled portion of the road. Creeping forward, almost at his back now, she rounded the tree to his left, watching all the time for the return of the others whose voices she could hear as indistinct rumbles further out of view. Crouching as she reached him, she sensed his knowledge of her being there for his head turned in her direction, bandaged eyes sightlessly looking for the source of sound. She spoke then, quietly, in the lowest whisper that she could manage. 'You have two men with guns, busy now with the spoils from your carriage, I think…'

He stiffened and broke across her words. 'Can you loosen the ropes and this thing across my eyes?' His husky voice was deep with anger.

'I'll get your ropes first. It will be safer if they should return.' He nodded and she fumbled with the cords knotted across his wrists, cursing herself for the time it was taking and watching all the while for the reappearance of the others.

She just had them loose as boots crashed back into the small clearing, and as the man beside her whipped the cloth from his eyes she dropped down to her knees and sighted her gun, shooting it low into the leg of the first robber and ramming the charge into the barrel to take the second shot. Rough arms, however, pulled her behind the protective bough of a tree as a bullet whistled overhead, and she was held down firmly against a broadly masculine chest, the shirt gaping open to reveal all that lay within. Fury and shock hit her simultaneously, along with the echo of a more unfamiliar emotion. For a moment she felt safer than she ever felt before as the hard lines of his body rippled beneath her fingers. Strength, energy and unblemished brown smoothness. And heat. Then her dogs crashed between them, fearful of her closeness to this stranger. Blushing furiously, she pulled away from his grasp and crouched down beside him, careful to leave some space.

'Give me the gun and get out of here,' he ordered. When she did not move, his eyes met hers in question.

'Get out of here, Princess,' he repeated quietly.

'You are practised with weapons…?'

His smile was unexpected as he took the gun and she felt her heart lurch with choking excitement. Instinctively she drew back from him. She must never let anyone close. She knew that. She had always known it.

'I'll keep them at bay until you are safe,' he returned, jamming in the next flintlock and resighting the gun. She noticed the crested gold ring on his little finger and the threads of the same colour in his hair and then she ran, lifting the skirts of her hunting habit and fleeing across the forest into the safety of the fields, glad of the dogs at her side. The sound of gun-shots echoed through the glade behind her: three, four, five and then silence. Biting at her lip, she imagined him falling, gold-green eyes sightless and still, and she was winded by the feeling of loss and worry.

'Please, God, let him live, let him be safe.' The words became a litany tumbling in her breath as she hurried down the paths to Airelies Manor and threw open the door, her heart pounding loudly in her ears as she leaned back against it. Mrs Fenton came from the kitchens to investigate the noise and, amazed at Brenna's appearance, was at her side in a moment.

'What on earth is wrong, love?' she burst out, wiping flour-powdered hands on her large apron.

'There's some highwaymen in the woods. Lock the doors and windows and get the guns from the study. If the gentleman they're trying to rob gets shot, they'll be up at Airelies next. I think they saw me!'

Rose Fenton jammed the brass bolts home, locking the floor catches for further protection. 'My God, Brenna. We're alone here save for Albert and young Stephen. We can't possibly shoot anyone.'

'I just have,' the younger woman answered, horri-fied anew as the housekeeper began to cross herself, uttering holy incantations to a forgiving God.

'You killed someone?'

'Shot his knee off, I think. At least it should slow him down a bit.' She stopped herself from mentioning the other man. The gentleman *would* be safe, she told herself. He seemed strong and fit and the gun in his hand had been reloaded with expertise. She tried to recall the crest she had seen on his ring, a lion rampant across two drawn daggers. Strength and danger. She smiled at the way the image suited him so exactly, the colour returning to her cheeks as she ran to each front window, pushing the locks into place. The feel of her uncle's gun in her hand heartened her further, as did the silence in the valley. Should she go back to help him? She dismissed the thought summarily. Her reappearance would more likely compromise his safety than help him. But still she could not relax as she strode up and down the front hall, eyes glued to the scene outside for any sense of movement.

No more shots had rent the quietness of evening, although they had heard the shouts of men from the village a short time ago. Mrs Fenton's white face brought her back to the moment and she struggled to hide her own worry from the elderly housekeeper.

'Whoever is dead or alive seems unlikely to bother us now,' she said quietly and consulted the clock at the end of the hallway. 'But, to be sure, we will pack in the morning and return to London. And I will ask Albert to send Stephen down to Worsley for any word of the incident.'

Just as she had finished speaking, however, a conveyance turned into the drive, stopping at the front of the house. The door was thrown open and Brenna's heart leapt in shock as she fleetingly saw the man who'd been bound to the tree step out, her gun held firmly in his hand. Without further thought she turned to the housekeeper.

'Tell him I have gone. Tell him, thank you for my gun and tell him…' she called over her shoulder as she ran up the stairs '…tell him I don't wish to see him again.' She disappeared into a top bedroom just as the door knocker sounded.

Smoothing out her apron, Rose Fenton took a deep breath before opening the door with a less than enthusiastic smile, to be confronted by the most handsome gentleman she had ever had the pleasure of meeting, even despite his numerous bruises. He had hair the colour of burnt copper and gold-green eyes. The dark burnous cloak he wore was torn across the shoulder, the gold appliqué fraying badly.

'May I help you, sir?' she enquired breathlessly, her eyes on Brenna's gun, which he suddenly handed to her, bowing in apology, a smile on his lips.

'I have it from the inn at Worsley that a Miss Brenna Stanhope is in residence here and I think this may be hers. I can't be certain.'

The housekeeper cut his words short. 'Yes, sir. Miss Brenna told me what happened and she bade me to thank you.'

'She's here, then?' His glance perused the empty spaces inside. 'Might I speak with her for a moment?'

Rose Fenton blocked off his view by moving in front of him. 'No, sir, she's…she has just gone…' The lie came picked from thin air and with little plausibility.

'Back to London?' he queried uncertainly.

'No, not for now. She's gone south.'

The man leant against the wall outside, a slight frown sifting across his features. 'She doesn't want to see me, let me give her my thanks?'

'No, sir'.

'Could I leave her a letter?'

'No, sir. She just wants to forget the whole incident. It's finished with and she'd rather just have it at that.'

'I see,' said the other, straightening and moving back from the overhanging portico. 'Could you make sure she knows I have come and please do convey my warmest thanks.'

'I will, sir,' Mrs Fenton answered, frowning as the man looked up to a window on the first floor. The movement of a figure flitting back quickly from view behind heavy velvet curtains was easily caught.

'You have other guests here?' he enquired carefully, watching as she answered.

'No, sir.'

Rose Fenton breathed a sigh of relief as she closed the door.

Upstairs, Brenna witnessed his departure, a sense of disquiet permeating her whole being.

He had seen her.

He had even found out her name and where she lived. Could the information harm her? Could the interest she had heard in his voice translate into a menace? Or a damning curiosity?

With a deepening frown, she observed the carriage winding its way from Airelies and out into the darkness of the main road north.

Chapter Two

Nicholas Pencarrow, Duke of Westbourne, Knight of the Realm and owner of half a dozen of England's finest estates, leaned back in his leather chair, feet up on his desk, reading with bemused interest a letter from his lawyer.

'After much searching we can find out very little about Brenna Stanhope. There is certainly no mention of the girl until she was sixteen, making a name for herself on the piano in select gatherings organised by a Sir Michael De Lancey, her uncle. Miss Stanhope appeared briefly in society five years ago as a débutante in one season only in London. Further enquiries have turned up the name of the Beaumont Street Orphanage. It seems Sir Michael and his niece run the establishment together, Miss Stanhope teaching at the school...'

Nicholas frowned. An orphanage? The idea intrigued him as did everything else he had discovered about the elusive Miss Stanhope. Flicking through the remainder of the letter, Nicholas determined it to contain brief mention of Michael De Lancey's reduced family circumstances and little else. 'Damn it,' he cursed under his breath. Why was she so secretive? His mind ran back to the woman he had seen in the woods, hair the colour of ebony, eyes of violet and a body rounded and feminine. 'Brenna Stanhope…' he whispered her name softly into the empty corners of the room, remembering the timbre of her voice, the dimples in her cheeks and the feeling of her warm breath against his bare chest.

And when he had touched her…

A noise from outside pulled him from his thoughts and he rose even as the door opened to admit Lady Letitia Carruthers, all blond ringlets and flashing blue eyes, her fashionable pink redingote day dress shaped to a waist so thin his hands could easily span it. 'Nicholas darling,' she said breathlessly, throwing herself headlong into his arms before perching on a nearby couch and artfully arranging her skirts around her. 'I am exhausted, and this ball you are going to throw will be the culmination of hours of hard work. Even Christopher in his heyday did not contemplate such opulence.'

Smiling at the reference to her long-dead husband, Nicholas poured two generous brandies, one of which he placed in her outstretched hand. 'Your taste is always exquisite, Letty, and I appreciate the time and effort you have invested in the occasion.' Crossing to his desk, he extracted a black velvet jewellery box, and laid it before her. 'This is for you by way of gratitude.'

Letty squealed, throwing open the lid with a hurried delight. 'Rubies, Nicholas,' she whispered, 'and such beautiful ones.' With infinite care she drew the chain of gold and red from its soft bed and, unbuttoning her bodice, presented her back to him. 'Will you fasten them?'

Nodding, he moved behind her, assailed instantly by the expensive perfume that enveloped her in a cloud wherever she went, his hands competent at her back while she waited for him to finish.

'Nicholas, you do know I love you, don't you?'

He turned, caught by the seriousness in her voice, swallowing at her admission and feeling guilty, as he did each time she had said it, for he knew, in truth, that he could not say back what it was she longed to hear from him. A tight smile played around his mouth as he perceived her disappointment. Why did women always want what he could never give them? Why could he not relish the commitment to relationships other men made without recourse to a safer distance? He knew the answer even as he voiced the question.

Johanna. His mother.

His father had married for love and look where that had got him. Widowed at twenty-six with two young boys and a heart as broken as he was, Gerald had finally drunk himself into the oblivion he functioned best in.

At eight Nicholas had tried his hardest to comfort both his father and five-year-old brother Charles, but without Johanna the family centre was gone, dissolved into a strange mix of long silences and unfathomable anger, the remnants of a family who had loved too much and lost everything because of it. And when, thirteen years later, Gerald's liver had finally succumbed to the abuse of a decade and he had died, predicting that his sons would follow the same path as he had, Nicholas had vowed that this prophesy would never come to pass and had spent his life either in the arms of experienced widows or hardened show girls, neither pushing for the state of matrimony that he was determined to escape.

Bending down, Nicholas collected some papers lying in a bundle at the top of his desk. Aye, to him survival marched hand in hand with distance, mere affection containing no real power to hurt. And if sometimes he recognised the flaws in his reasonings, he was also quick to remember the lonely years of his childhood. Never again would he let himself be so vulnerable.

Breaking the awkward silence of the moment with the merely mundane, he turned back to her and said, 'I'll see you out then.' His words came harshly across Letitia's admission and he was pleased when she followed his directive without argument and walked before him, the clutter of servants in the corridor precluding any other more personal talk.

The party after the opera was crowded with people thronging out into the open halls, and it seemed every second one was calling to Nicholas on an urgent and important purpose, invitations offered and congratulations given for some new and successful business venture of his.

They all knew of his Midas touch, the way he made thousands from every concept he believed in and the way his holdings multiplied each year: land, horses, ships and women.

Nicholas Pencarrow, Duke of Westbourne, never went anywhere without every female eye in every room fastened upon him, young and old, and all with the same thought in their minds—how they longed to be the one to tame the lion who stalked in their midst, with copper hair and tawny eyes, the most handsome man in court and the richest to boot.

Tonight, dressed entirely in black, he seemed to prowl the confines of the small room in an unspoken need to be free, though as he stood, glass in hand, a name mentioned behind Nicholas made him turn.

'Michael De Lancey.' A woman was introducing an older man to a couple directly to his left and the name on Brenna Stanhope's file leapt to mind. Her uncle? His eyes raked across this man and Nicholas smiled as he heard the accent, cultured and quiet like his niece's. With care he beckoned a footman stationed across the room, the servant hurrying through the crowd at the summons and waiting as the Duke pulled out a card from his jacket pocket.

'Please inform Sir Michael De Lancey that I would like to meet with him when he finds himself free,' he said politely, returning to his own conversation as the man hurried off.

It was only a few minutes later when he felt the small man's presence at his shoulder. Nicholas held out his hand to the other's uncertainly offered bow, taking Sir Michael's hand firmly in his own and saying with feeling, 'I am very pleased to meet you, sir. Your niece, Brenna Stanhope, has no doubt told you of her part in my lucky escape near Worsley!'

Michael De Lancey started, a frown deep in his eyes as he shook his head. 'No, your Grace, she has told me nothing.'

The admission floored Nicholas. 'You have not seen her in the past three weeks?' he asked in amazement.

'Oh, indeed, yes, Brenna lives with me.'

'And yet she has mentioned nothing?'

'No, I am afraid not!' Grey eyes came up to his

own, honest eyes with all the look of a gentleman, and Nicholas, surmising this man not to be lying, changed tack instantly.

'Would you permit me to call on your niece, Sir Michael?'

'No!'

One word and so unexpected Nicholas could hardly credit the answer. Did he not know to whom he was speaking? Did he not understand the social etiquette due to such a title as his own? He sized up the situation and tried again.

'You won't let me call on your niece?' The query was phrased more in incredulity than anger.

'I'm afraid not.'

'And you have my card?'

'I do, your Grace.'

Perplexed, Nicholas ran a hand through his hair. 'Is she married already?' he said suddenly.

'No, your Grace.'

'Betrothed?'

'No, your Grace.'

'Then you would agree that she's free to make up her own mind about whether or not to see me?'

Sir Michael shifted uncomfortably, giving the impression of a man who was backing himself into a quickly approaching corner. 'Yes.'

'Then please give her this.' Taking out another card, Nicholas wrote on it in haste. 'I would very much like a reply.'

Nodding, Michael De Lancey clutched the paper in his fist and Nicholas watched him call for his coat and hat and take his leave.

Brenna rose the next morning early, dressing in one of her customary dark-blue velvet gowns, then hurried downstairs to the breakfast room, coming to a halt as she saw her uncle already seated and looking very perturbed.

'Good morning,' she said, favouring him with a smile as she took the seat opposite and poured herself some tea.

He cleared his throat. 'Brenna, I need to talk to you.'

'Mmm, what about?' She glanced up as he took a card from the table in front of him, and placed it before her.

'That!' he stammered as she raised the gilt-edged card to her eyes.

NICHOLAS PENCARROW
DUKE OF WESTBOURNE

'Who is he?' she returned quietly, a premonition of disaster seeming to emanate from the words themselves.

'Read the back.' With dread she flipped it over, her heart beating faster as she placed the context of the message: *Would you permit me to say thank you in person for your help at Worsley?*

Unsure eyes surveyed her uncle. 'I didn't tell you. I thought it might make you worried.'

'But you'll tell me now?' he asked softly.

'Yes,' she answered, giving him a blow-by-blow description of the whole episode.

Her uncle was silent when she finished, phrasing his next question only after much thought. 'Did you talk with him at Airelies?'

'No.'

'Did you see him properly, Brenna?' The words came hesitantly.

'No. Why?'

'I think he could be persistent, you see, as well as both powerful and stubborn. The whole of London treads carefully in his wake and it seems he owns almost half of it.'

'The wrong man to rescue, you mean?' Brenna quipped. 'I should have left him to an untimely end, especially now if he's going to harass me.'

Michael De Lancey grimaced. 'I do have a feeling about this man. I think you should at least meet him. Be as dour and miserable as you want. It is the mystery that is making him interested. I know his type. It is only the thrill of the chase that he craves and there are plenty of women in London who will attest to that truth, or so I'm told.'

The words made sense, though already Brenna's heart beat painfully at the thought as his gold-green eyes and dark copper hair came fully to mind. With a rising irritation she stood and pulled at the plait that hung across her shoulder. She knew better than to allow herself such feelings.

'I thought I'd finished with all this, Michael. That season in London was by far enough. I'm twenty-four now, a happy spinster and a woman in my own right and I don't want the Duke of Westbourne to come and call on me.'

Michael frowned. 'Well then, let's get it over with. I'll have Kenneth take over your reply this morning and with any luck we can have him out of our lives by this evening.' He stood then, searching in a drawer on one side of the room for paper and pen. 'Here, write to him and say you could see him at three o'clock. I'll come home at three-thirty and remind you of an appointment we have at four. That way we can have the whole thing finished within under an hour.'

Reluctantly, Brenna took the page and wrote a very brief and very formal invitation to Nicholas Pencarrow, hating herself for having to do it while mentally calculating all the things she'd need to put off till the morrow now that she had him to deal with today.

A reply had come from Pencarrow House by noon: Nicholas Pencarrow would be pleased to call on her at three o'clock p.m.

At half past two Brenna made her way upstairs to prepare her hair in the most unappealing style she could arrange, buttoning her velvet dress up to the collar and placing upon it the shapeless blue oversmock, which she often wore at the orphanage. At five to three she was sitting stiffly in the wing chair near the fire in the small dining room, hands primly in her lap, when she heard his carriage pull to a halt outside. She resisted the urge to go to the window. He'd seen her at the curtains once before and she had no wish for him to think her remotely inquisitive about him. Instead she stood facing the door and waited until it was opened by Polly, the serving maid.

'The Duke of Westbourne, Miss Brenna,' the young girl announced breathlessly, shepherding him in before going out again and closing the door.

Brenna's widening eyes came up to his, all the handsomeness of each reckless libertine who'd ever pursued her across countless nightmares rolled into one. At Worsley with blood on his face and a split upper lip he had still seemed well favoured. Today, dressed in tapered trousers, a double-breasted jacket and silk hat and gloves in hand, he emanated pure masculine grace and style—and something else a lot more un-settling.

He registered her fright and the dress all at once. Today she seemed different and his glance was drawn to her fingers, which turned a handkerchief nervously this way and that.

'Miss Stanhope,' he began quietly as cold violet eyes stole up to his, a flinty hardness in their depths, which he could not comprehend.

She fears me, a warning voice came from deep inside. 'I am Nicholas Pencarrow and I thank you for receiving me.'

'You did not have to come,' she spoke now for the first time, her velvety voice exactly as he had remembered it.

'But I wanted to,' he replied. 'May I sit down for just a moment?'

Nodding, she indicated a chair furthest from where she sat. She seemed older today, her hair bound up into unbecoming braids at each ear and drooping down across her neck. He couldn't recollect ever seeing any-body's hair put up quite like that and wondered why she should have fashioned it in such a way, knowing he was to call. The truth hit him suddenly even as he pondered it. She wanted him to see her like this: the clothes, the hair, the lack of a welcome, they were all mixed somehow in a puzzle he could not even vaguely begin to comprehend.

Nicholas shifted in his seat and began softly. 'I wanted to thank you personally for your help last month outside of Worsley.' Wary eyes flickered briefly to his and then away. 'If you had not come when you did, I am sure I would not be here today.' A frown crossed her face as though she struggled for a fleeing social politeness.

She does not want me here. She wishes she had left me in the woods. Nicholas's mind rebelled at the thought as he continued slowly, 'The man you shot was taken to the doctor and his leg was lost. I'm afraid he knew who you were. The Worsley constable said your name without thinking. I hope that will not be a problem.'

Palpable fear flickered momentarily in Brenna's eyes. 'Yet he's in prison?'

He nodded. 'And I'll make sure he stays there a long time.'

'What happened to the other one?'

'He is dead.'

'Oh.' Silence stalked the room, a heavy silence, uncomfortable and unbroken, and as she sat there he knew she would not speak.

'Do you go out often?' His voice was soft as he tried to lighten the subject and piece together some of the parts of her life of which, as yet, he knew so little.

'No,' she answered quietly, a slight frown forming on her brow.

'Then would you not accept an invitation to my ball next month?'

'No.' The reply came definite and flat, a 'thank you' added afterwards almost in an unconscious notice of manners.

'Is there anything you would like to accompany me to in London? The opera? The ballet? The symphony?' Brenna's head came up at the mention of the last and for the first time he saw interest, though she shook her head even as he thought it.

'You like music?'

'Yes.'

'You play the piano well.'

It was said not as a question but as a statement, and she looked up, puzzled. 'How could you know that?' she asked unsurely, and suddenly it hit her. He had been finding out about her. A giddy spiralling slam of terror crossed her face as she stood.

'Your thanks are acknowledged, your Grace, but I shall now say goodbye. Polly will see you out.' Her words left room for no others as she rang the bell and turned towards the window and Nicholas's perusal of the back of her was abruptly cut off as the young servant bustled in. Amusement creased his eyes at the dismissal. This girl had no notion of the respect normally accorded to him by polite society.

And he liked it.

Gathering his hat and coat, he made towards the door, stopping as he reached it. 'I shall leave my card on the table here, Brenna. If, by chance, you should change your mind and have a want to see the symphony, I would be most willing to escort you.'

She stiffened at the liberty he took in using her Christian name and turned as she determined him gone, catching her reflection in the mirror above the mantel as she did so. White faced and drawn, even her eyes seemed bruised and guarded.

Is this what I have become? she wondered, as her fingers unlaced the ugly plaits and she pulled her thick hair free. Tears stung her eyes and for a second she longed to call him back and be seen even momentarily in the way she would have liked him to remember her by, but common sense stopped her. If people knew even a tiny part of her secret, the patronage of her orphanage would flounder and the protection of the

children would be at risk. With determination she
tucked her hair behind her ears and faced the mirror.

'Forget the Duke of Westbourne,' she told herself
sternly and was disturbed by the dash of anger that
threaded her eyes.

Chapter Three

Nicholas entered the orphanage in Beaumont Street just after eleven o'clock. He'd had his secretary make an appointment for him to view the place in the guise of becoming a financial patron using a secondary title of his, the Earl of Deuxberry. He hoped Brenna Stanhope would forgive him the deception if she saw him, knowing otherwise he may not even get a foot in the door.

The corridor was crammed full of children's paintings, and the sound of a piano and voices could be heard coming from a room towards the back of the house. As he entered he was met almost immediately by a tiny grey-haired woman, who thrust out her hand in introduction.

'I'm Mrs Betsy Plummer, the Matron here,' she said kindly, 'and I presume you are Lord Deuxberry.' She inclined her head as if unsure of the protocol involved when addressing the titled peerage, looking up as a question came nervously to her lips. 'We understand you may be interested in lending your patronage to Beaumont Street? Lord knows we could do with some.' She reddened at the realisation of her blasphemy.

Amusement filled the Duke's eyes and then query as music sifted through the thick walls. 'The music is lovely.'

'Yes. That's Miss Stanhope on the piano. She's the lady who opened the place, you see.'

'May I be allowed to watch the lesson?'

'Well…not normally,' she faltered, frowning heavily. 'But perhaps there is a way around it. If you're very quiet, we could observe from the upstairs balcony. That shouldn't disturb them at all.'

Following the woman up a narrow staircase, he entered a room filled with sunlight, a balcony overhanging the hall beneath them.

'This is far enough. Miss Stanhope is very particular about her privacy.'

Nicholas looked down in the direction of her gesture, and the sight of Brenna, hair down and playing to the children, assailed him with all the force of a salvo fired at close range.

She was beautiful and completely changed from the deliberately dour woman who had greeted him two days ago in her London drawing room. Today, curly dark hair fell in a glorious curtain to her waist and her violet eyes sparkled with playfulness as she rose from the piano and formed the children into a circle, taking a hanky from the sleeve of her navy blue gown and wiping the nose of a carrot-topped toddler who clung to her skirt.

'Oh, my goodness, Tim, I hope it is not you next with the sickness. Laura is quite enough for now.' The boy smiled as she ruffled his hair and joined up all their hands. 'Let's sing "Ring a Ring a Rosie", shall

we? I'll start you off.' Breaking into the circle, she
began to chant the words of the ditty, falling down at
the end just as all the children did.

'Excellent. Only this time let's not fall on me.' A
laughing voice came from the very bottom of the pile
and, reassembling them, she went to begin again.
Nicholas felt a hand pulling him back and reluctantly
drew his eyes away from the sight before him.

'I'll take you to the office now. Perhaps I could
show you some of our hopes for the place and for the
children.'

The door shut behind them as the music faded,
though Nicholas stood still for a second, breathing in
deeply to try to mitigate the effect Miss Brenna Stanhope seemed destined to wreak upon him. God, she
was so lovely and so different from any other woman
he had ever come across. Working for a living, and
here? His eyes flickered to the mouldy ceilings and
rusty pipes, as the reports of Sir Michael De Lancey's
financial problems came into mind. Where was the
music and dancing and laughter with her peers that a
beautiful woman like her should have. She was only
twenty-four and hardly the matron her lifestyle es-
poused her to be. Dark violet eyes and dimples and a
face that should be etched upon the surface of some
ecclesiastical ceiling came so forcibly to mind that he
had to shake his head in an attempt to regain a lost
semblance of reality. With an effort he made himself
follow Mrs Plummer into an office.

'Does Miss Stanhope come here often?' Nicholas
asked, trying to appear indifferent to the answer.

'Yes, indeed. She teaches three days a week and
spends most evenings here. Her uncle has funded
much of it, you see, but has fallen on harder times, so

now we have to put out our feelers, so to speak.' She looked slightly nervous again. 'We try to keep our costs down to the minimum but, as you can appreciate, the whole task is a bit daunting given the age of this building and the needs of this community...' Mrs Plummer was finding her tongue with growing gusto and it was almost ten minutes later when Nicholas was able to interrupt.

'What I have seen has impressed me greatly. If you would like to put your figures together and send them to my secretary, I'm sure we could be of assistance.'

Mentioning a large sum of money, he leaned across the table and wrote down a name and address.

'It has been most interesting, Mrs Plummer.' He could hear that the music in the background had stopped and suddenly he had no desire to have Brenna Stanhope discover him here. Not now. Not yet. 'And I am sure we shall be seeing each other again.' Opening the door, he strode down the hallway to the outside sunshine and was pleased to see his man ready and waiting with the horses.

Betsy Plummer watched as he entered his coach and then she hurried back inside as soon as the conveyance had turned the corner.

'Brenna, Kate,' she called loudly, her voice shrill with unquestioned elation. 'We got it, he's promised us so much.' Two faces came into sight, whooping with laughter and relief. 'And you should see him, girls,' Betsy added slowly. 'He's the most handsome man I think I've ever seen.'

Warning bells rang in Brenna's ears. 'What did you say his name was again, Betsy?' she asked slowly, fearing the answer.

'The Earl of Deuxberry,' crooned the other, and Brenna expelled her indrawn breath with relief.

The months aged into November and the summer weather seemed all but gone. Brenna settled again into her comfortable, untroubled existence now that Nicholas Pencarrow seemed happy to leave her alone, though at nights sometimes, when the business of the day had receded, she allowed herself to daydream about him. Quietly at first and then with more ardour, the Duke of Westbourne's gold-green eyes and lopsided smile invaded her fantasies, leaving her with a feeling of guilty pleasure in the morning and a firming resolution to put him from her memory.

At Beaumont Street things had become more agreeable, for under the patronage of Lord Deuxberry much of the old leaking plumbing had been fixed and the dormitories had been lined to make them warmer as they awaited the onslaught of winter. His chits came with a regularity no one dared to question and all hoped would continue, for, apart from the first visit, they had never dealt with him again directly, but rather with his chief secretary, a dour-faced but competent man called Winslop.

Today Mr Winslop had come to call with invitations in hand, one each for Brenna, Betsy and Kate, asking them to a supper Lord Deuxberry was hosting at his home in Kensington. Brenna felt uneasy as the man spelled out what would be expected of them.

'His Lordship has made it very clear he would like the three of you to come. I think he may be ill pleased were this not to be the case as he has gone to some trouble to assemble an audience whose patronage would be forthcoming should you promote your orphanage well. It will not be too formal. If the weather is kind it may even spill out into the conservatory and, if not, all three drawing rooms will be in commission.'

Kate and Betsy looked at each other as they imagined the magnificence of the house. Brenna stared straight ahead and knew exactly what it would be like. Her one year out in the season had been so indelibly impressed on her mind, how could she not remember? The staff would stand at attention whilst cynical well-dressed men and women would condescendingly dissect their mission, their clothes, their manners and their looks, piece by piece until there was little left. And the worst of it was that she was caught, she would have to go, for to displease this patron could affect the welfare of the children who, after all, had no hand in the realm of these politics.

Mr Winslop handed each of them an invitation, their names printed boldly in black and he spoke quickly as he stood to depart.

'The sixth is the date set, as you can see. I could arrange for his Lordship's carriage to be sent if you should wish it so.'

Brenna shook her head, breaking in across his instructions. 'No, my uncle will lend us his conveyance.' The others nodded at her suggestion, anxious to be able to leave when they wanted rather than to be marooned in such illustrious company and dependent only on the whim of Lord Deuxberry.

Mr Winslop demurred and closed his book, handing over yet another chit to Betsy. 'Very well, then. We will see you all next week.'

* * *

Five days later Brenna, Betsy and Kate found themselves pulling into the drive of a house far bigger than any of them could have imagined.

'He must be one of the richest men in England,' Brenna said as she observed the huge mansion and all the women looked at each other with undisguised apprehension. 'No wonder he can afford to help us.'

'Lord Deuxberry…' The name ran upon her lips as she strove for any recollection of such an aristocrat when she was doing the season and failing in her quest. It was strange that she did not know of him, given his obvious wealth, for such opulence rarely went hand in hand with anonymity.

The carriage stopped outside the front portico, two footmen walking down huge marble steps to help them alight and accompany them to the butler, who stood stiffly at the main doorway.

Nicholas came out a moment later and his breath froze in his throat as he watched Brenna, dressed in simple blue, hair bound simply and face alight, her beauty reflected somehow in the moonbeams that danced across the glass dome above her, isolating her in the silver of an ethereal lightness.

'Ladies,' he said gently, striding forward on long legs, his gaze fastened firmly on Brenna Stanhope, 'welcome to my home.'

Brenna whirled towards the voice, her glance snapping to his face. The Duke of Westbourne! For a second she thought to turn and leave—indeed, took the first step—before reason stopped her, and in that second she knew that this trap had been set most wisely, with patience and stealth. Her heart beat loudly in her ears as she forced her body into a stillness she was far from feeling, fists clenched white at her side as his hand came forward. She did not dare to let him touch her for fear of feeling again the sharp knowledge of his skin and was pleased when he let his fingers fall. The gentleness in his eyes flummoxed her, though, given her obvious insult, as did his next words.

'I watched you from the balcony as you were on the piano playing "Ring a Roses",' he explained softly, his smile touching his eyes.

'Indeed, *Lord Deuxberry*,' she stressed the title and raised her chin, licking her lips in an unconscious message of fear.

'I sometimes use the name, which is also mine by right, for it lets me function more anonymously.'

He looked straight at her and, liking his directness, she smiled.

Her face changed from hard to soft in a second, large dimples gracing both cheeks and liquid eyes dancing with lightness. God, she was so beautiful, how could her season here ever have gone poorly?

'Could I take you through to meet our guests?' he asked quietly. 'I have tried to assemble a group who are the least wolfish that I know and also the most generous.' Kate and Betsy nodded at his words.

Brenna frowned. *Lord, please let there be none amongst them that she might once have known.*

The drawing room was full of guests though the gaslights burned low, almost as candles, evoking a sense of warm friendliness conducive to their cause, and she felt heartened by the half-light. Missing Nicholas's sign to his secretary to take the others, she found herself escorted by the Duke, and, as he introduced her to the guests with an unaffected charm, she noticed the deference he was accorded by all with whom he chatted. He made it easy for her to speak of the orphanage, bridging the way with his own admission of patronage.

In his company, buffered as she was from any more personal queries, she felt herself relax, all the dreads and fears of discovery pushed away.

As she asked for their coats at the end of the night, she could not credit just where the time had gone.

'Would you permit me to show you my home before you go?' Nicholas asked the group as they stood at the front door. Kate and Betsy jumped at the chance, Brenna looked more tentative. 'Just the music room, then?' he compromised and led the three across into the other side of the house to a large glassed conservatory filled with palms and flowers, a fish pond along one end of the windows and a huge grand piano down towards the other. The women gasped in astonishment at the size and beauty of the place, so unexpected and inviting. Betsy and Kate moved to the pond and Brenna to the piano, where her fingers tinkled lightly across ivory keys checking its tone. Nick watched her and stood quietly as she played a simple arpeggio.

'Would you like to play?'

His voice was husky and her eyes expressed her confusion. 'No, thank you. It's very beautiful, but now we have to go.' The words came stilted and formal across her tongue and she sensed his disappointment. 'My Lord…' she began, but he held up a hand to stop her.

'Nicholas, please.'

'My Lord,' she continued more firmly, 'I have no doubt you have patronised our orphanage purely out of a misdirected belief that you owe me something. I helped you at Worsley simply because you were in trouble and now I want to know that you are helping the children of our orphanage simply because they are in trouble. Tonight was an invitation that, had I known the truth of your identity, I would have refused, and in the future I would like you to know that this cannot happen again. You have paid your debt with more than interest, your chits come regularly and with a generosity that staggers us all. But I am not part of the bargain, my Lord. You could never pay enough for me.'

He stood watching her, stepping back slightly, wondering why life held her so rigid and noticing the way her lips turned up at each end, even when she did not smile. She was both beautiful and clever—he had not expected that. He observed her carefully and began slowly, mindful of the other two who looked about to join them. 'May I ask but one small favour, Miss Stanhope?'

Uncertain violet eyes regarded him.

'If I was able to get a private ballet performance of the Christmas version of *La Sylphide* at Her Majesty's Theatre, would you and the children do me the honour of being the audience?'

Brenna gasped at the invitation. 'You could do that?' she asked, amazed that he should think such a feat even possible, her mind running to the reviews she had heard of the pageant made famous by Marie Taglioni herself.

'Money can buy dreams,' he said quietly, watching the smile die in her eyes and perplexed by her answer.

'That is debatable, my Lord,' she whispered distantly, 'for more often it kills them.'

Charles Pencarrow bounded into the southern drawing room of Pencarrow House the next afternoon and

Nicholas stood to greet his younger brother with delight.

'Charlie,' he said, shaking the proffered hand with warmth. 'When did you arrive up from Hertfordshire and why did you not let me know you were coming? Grandmama is not with you, is she?' He looked around behind his brother for any sign of his grandmother, Elizabeth, Dowager Duchess of Westbourne, his eyes coming back to Charles for his answer.

'Grandmama is not here, and I was only coming for the day except the meeting in London went on for longer than I had hoped, so I deemed it safer to wait here and go home in the morning.'

Nick nodded and crossed to the cabinet behind him. 'You want to join me in a drink? Whisky?'

'Brandy, I think. I'd already started on one at the club before I heard the news.'

'News?' Nicholas asked, a puzzled frown across his face. 'What news?'

'The news that a girl dressed like a nun turned down an invitation to the symphony from the highly acclaimed, but perhaps overrated, Duke of Westbourne.'

'Ahh, that news!' Nick laughed. 'The gossips, I fear. Well, they're half right. She did turn me down, but she doesn't look like a nun.'

'Who is she?'

'Brenna Stanhope, the same girl who rescued me in the woods on the London Road.'

'But you said she wouldn't see you?' Charles queried.

'She wouldn't. I had to trick her into coming here. I've become the patron of an orphanage she runs in the East End, and she only accepted an invitation—

and with great wariness, I might add—from that patron, Lord Deuxberry.'

Charles laughed in disbelief. 'She doesn't like you?'
He beamed. 'You must be losing your touch, Nick.'

Nicholas frowned and lowered his voice to almost
a whisper so that Charles had to strain to hear. 'When
Father met Johanna he knew in one moment that he
loved her. "Once and forever", those were his
words…' Raising his glass, he finished his drink, all
layers of urbanity overshadowed by a savage anger.
'And he said it would be the same for us.'

'My God,' Charles retorted, all humour fleeing, 'you
can't be telling me…'

'I'm not telling you anything.' His eyes darkened
perceptibly. 'And don't worry, it's a passing fancy
that's all. In a month she'll mean as little to me as
every other women I've known.' He stalked over to
the window and threw open the sash, enjoying the air
that rolled into the room. Brenna Stanhope made him
restless and uncertain, for she made him imagine possibilities he thought he'd long since dismissed.

'The men at the club called her clever.'

Hearing the question in Charlie's voice, Nicholas
refilled his glass and tried to explain with a stoic patience.

'Brenna Stanhope has a mind that would cut most
men's logic to ribbons; if I had to describe her personality in one word, it would be "formidable". Last
night she told me that she was not a part of any bargain
and that I could never pay enough for her. That was
just before she ordered me to leave her alone.'

Charles began to laugh in earnest. 'What does she
look like?'

'She has dimples.'

'Alan Wrightson claims she is beautiful.'

'Then the man, for all his faults, cannot be accused of having bad taste in women.'

'He claims she has violet-coloured eyes.'

'Those too.' His brother's whoop of delight made Nicholas's heart sink.

'When do I get to meet her?'

'You don't and I'll see you at dinner.' Draining his glass, Nicholas put it down on the table and walked out of the room.

In his own study he shut the door and leaned back against the cushioned header of his favourite chair. For twelve years he had been the quarry of countless feminine wiles and pushy doyennes all eager to marry him off and tie him down. For twelve years the gossips had run his name with this woman or that one until finally they had framed him callous and hardened. The 'Heartless Duke of Westbourne' was how he had heard his name bandied as the cream of each year's débutantes were paraded before him and failed to rouse even the slightest interest. He ran his fingers across his temple and closed his eyes. Letitia Carruthers. Deborah Hutton. Alison Smythe-Finch. His consorts of the moment were all well bred, all well experienced. And all easily left. His father's legacy personified. What stamp, then, did Brenna Stanhope make on him and why? He shifted in his chair and finished his drink.

Beautiful, clever, mysterious and with eyes the colour of Scottish heather after the rain. He shook his head at his sudden predilection for the way of poetry and smiled wryly before bending his head to the figures in a thick ledger on his desk.

Chapter Four

Nicholas spent the next morning at the London Ballet Company's headquarters arranging a private session of *La Sylphide* to be performed as a matinée the following Wednesday. He then hailed his cabriolet and drove straight to Beaumont Street, running into Brenna as he stepped into the place. She was dressed today in a white smock splattered with colour, carrying a tray of spiky paintbrushes. Her hair was bunched up untidily upon her head, curling tendrils escaping down dark against the lightness of the uniform.

'Hello,' she said softly, and he was surprised by the deep blush on her cheeks as he came to stand beside her. Clenching his fists, he jammed them in his pockets just to make certain that he would not touch her.

'You're painting?'

'I'm m…making a mural for one of the dormitories. The children are helping me, which explains the mess.'

She stammered slightly, both from the question and his demeanour. Today he seemed as far from the grand lord as she'd ever seen him.

'May I have a word with you alone, Brenna?'

She frowned, both at his continued familiarity in

using her Christian name and at the implications of a private conversation. She didn't want to be alone with him, but under the circumstances there was little else she could do to prevent it. With feigned nonchalance she opened the door to her study, making sure that he sat before she went around to her desk, having no wish to leave him with the opportunity of shutting them in together.

Nicholas noticed a well-used copy of Alexander Kingslake's revolutionary tract 'Eothem' beside her elbow. Why was he not surprised? 'I have organised the ballet for Wednesday,' he began. 'The performance starts at three, but we'd need to be seated by at least a quarter before the hour.'

Brenna nodded, unsure as to her reaction to the whole thing. A ballet performed privately just for them pointed out to her his privilege, but also she understood, for the first time, the power that lay close to his hand should he choose to use it. It worried her, this sovereignty above others, accorded not merely because of his title but inherently there because of who he was. If he could organise an outing of this magnitude on just a whim, then think of what he could find out should he really set his mind to it. He would make a powerful foe and adversary, and a dangerous investigator should she cross the threshold of his curiosity and cause him to venture into the realms of mystery he might easily wish to dissipate—because of this she would need to be careful. Her uncle's words came back to her from the morning of Nicholas's first visit: *I think he could be persistent… The whole of London treads carefully in his wake and it seems he owns almost half of it.*

She forced her mind back to the present and her eyes

narrowed doubtfully. All the problems of dress and shoes for the children presented themselves as her mind ran fretfully over the number of nights left for the sewing.

Nicholas, for his part, understood none of the reasons for her reticence, placing it, instead, to her fear of public places and he said, less gently than he meant, 'I think, Miss Stanhope, that the children would definitely enjoy it even if you are determined not to.'

She caught his glance and replied coldly. 'My feelings for such an outing hardly need figure here, your Grace—'

'Then why do you hesitate?' he broke in.

Brenna sighed and stood, turning to the window, arms wrapped tightly through each other as she replied, 'It's all so privileged and dreamlike, this world you offer us, and far from the reality that will ever be Beaumont Street.'

'And you think that it's wrong to want to share it?' he countered, watching her with a growing interest.

'I think it is wrong to want it.' She turned to him now, eyes ablaze with intensity. 'It's like the children's bedtime stories, endings that belie all sorts of beginnings, fairytales that only live in books or in a rich man's world, for none of them will ever have what it is you so easily offer, though many here may want it afterwards. You can't covet what you don't know, you see. Ignorance counteracts want, just as knowledge fosters it.'

'And where in your philosophy lies choice, Miss Stanhope?' His words cut deep across her arguments and she was still as she answered him.

'The freedom of choice has never belonged to any

of these children, your Grace. It was gone before they ever had the means to exert it.'

'So now you choose for them. They never had it nor are they likely to with your reasonings.' His voice came louder with his own growing exasperation. 'You think people, once choiceless, can never be empowered; you think opportunity must be dismissed in the face of a chequered past and all in the name of a changeless future. You think people can't drag themselves out of a mire and triumph over adversity and disaster to spite circumstances over which they never had control in the first place?' His fist came down hard upon her table. 'Damn, Brenna, I don't believe you or you wouldn't be here trying to make the difference.'

Brenna jumped at the noise, her eyes large and dark in a paling face as she struggled against his anger, knowing that to lose his patronage would be a disaster and knowing too that his money did buy him the right to order things just as he willed it. Accordingly she withdrew into silence.

He watched her with a frown in his eyes. He wanted to cross the room right there and then and drag her away from all of this: his anger and her fears and a world of parentless children, the poverty of east London, a table of food set only with scraps, and a house that had seen better times. And Brenna herself, this dark-haired lady of mystery, whose world offered no path for friendship or understanding but, rather, buried the gifts he offered under the age-old resentment of privilege. He spread his hands wide in a gesture of defeat and said wearily, 'Think it over and send me word of your decision tomorrow.' With that he bowed his head slightly and left the room, this time shutting the door firmly behind him.

Brenna groped her way to the chair and leant her head against her arms, her mind running numbly over their dispute. 'Oh, God,' she whispered to herself. She was too old to feel like this, like a child who'd been castigated by a righteous and reasonable parent, though one fully ignorant of the very arguments themselves.

She lifted her eyes to the door, knowing the reaction Kate and Betsy would give to even the mention of a privately performed ballet; all the joy and disbelief she herself might have felt had it not been Nicholas Pencarrow who was offering it. In a flash she knew what it was that she would do. The others and the children would go on Wednesday and she herself would depart for Worsley with three of Michael's burliest servants accompanying her, given the recent problems of the road. Her absence would then determine the Duke of Westbourne's true intent. If he continued with these more-than-generous offers, it would be on the basis of his wanting to for the sake of the children and not for some misbegotten sense of indebtedness that their meeting in the woods of Worsley had seemed to inspire in him.

She wanted their personal relationship severed. He was dangerous and she was vulnerable. She wanted Nicholas Pencarrow, Duke of Westbourne, Earl of Deuxberry, completely gone from her life.

Returning to London from Airelies the following Friday, Brenna found her uncle ill and propped up in bed, surrounded by lemon barley drinks and a strong smelling camphor-based inhalant. One look at him, however, told her the problem was one far worse than the common cold he seemed to be attributing his breathing problems to, for he appeared blue about the lips and his chest rose and fell in a motion she found instantly disconcerting.

Gesturing to Dumas, she crossed to Michael's desk, took paper and a pen from the top drawer and addressed the letter to the doctor, asking for his immediate assistance. Folding it and sealing it, she handed it to Dumas.

'Take this to Dr McInnes's house immediately and wait till they give a reply before you come home. Tell him I said it was urgent and that I'd be very indebted if he could come straight away. And, Dumas,' she whispered as she followed him to the door, 'please be as quick as you possibly can. I'm sure Michael is a great deal worse than he realises.'

Dumas squeezed Brenna's hand and she watched him leave, using the small space of time to plaster a smile back on her face. She did not want to worry Michael with her own fear. He nodded at her weakly as she rejoined him, taking the hand he offered and bringing it to her lips. 'Michael, you'd be cross with me if I'd just lain there as you have and demanded no help at all, and at the moment I feel like strangling you for your carelessness.' Fluffing the pillows up behind him, Brenna ordered hot water to be added to the camphor to try to create an inhalant to ease him. The minutes ticked on, each one inexplicably longer, Brenna's ears listening.

At last there was the sound of a carriage drawing up to the front porch, then she heard footsteps upon the paving.

'The doctor's here.' She sighed in relief, leaving Mrs White to watch Michael as she hurried to the front door to let him in, pulling it open in one quick move-

ment, almost colliding as she did so with the Duke of
Westbourne. Frustration and anger veiled manners as
she gave him no greeting. Could she never meet him
without this ridiculous blush?

'I am waiting for the doctor,' she said shortly, stepping outside to peer up and down the street for any
sign of a returning Dumas. Fresh tears of frustration
rushed unbidden to her eyes as she saw the street
empty and Nicholas was both astonished and alarmed.

'What's wrong?' he asked brusquely, pulling her
around to meet him.

'It's Michael,' Brenna answered tightly. 'He's so
sick and a doctor has yet to arrive.'

Hailing his waiting phaeton, Nicholas ordered his
driver to Harley Street for help before returning to the
house. He caught a glimpse of Brenna as she hurried
to the second-floor landing and was beside her in a
trice. Both came at the same time into Michael's room.
His breathing now was erratic, jerkily taken and nois-
ily completed and Nicholas went to his side, loosening
the nightshirt from around his neck and pulling him
from the bed towards the window.

'Get the chair, and bring it over to the balcony,' he
said to Brenna, throwing open the doors to the frig-
idness of the late afternoon. Cold winter air came roll-
ing on to Michael in icy waves and the change in tem-
perature seemed to soothe him for, seated in the
armchair by Nicholas, he regained at least a little measure of his breath, and his colour settled slowly into a
more normal pinkness.

Brenna knelt at her uncle's feet, her hand in his,
tears streaming down her cheeks in relief at his improvement, her trance broken moments later when a
well-dressed stranger appeared in the bedroom.

'Clive.' The Duke of Westbourne strode towards the new arrival, hand outstretched, and Brenna's eyes strayed thankfully to the black medical bag he carried. Nicholas Pencarrow's doctor and here so quickly? She stood with an uncertain gait, wishing Dr McInnes and Dumas present so that she might dismiss this pompous-looking newcomer, but one glance at Michael changed her mind for he still struggled for a normal breath. The man observed it too and quickly took control.

'If you wouldn't mind waiting downstairs, miss, I would like to examine my patient in private.' His eyes moved to the Duke, who came forward and led her out of the room and down to the parlour he'd been in the first time he'd ever come here. His ministrations raised Brenna from the state of shock she'd felt ever since she'd seen the danger of Michael's affliction and she shook free from his arm and seated herself on a chair near the cold and fireless hearth, raising her eyes to Nicholas's as she did so.

'I'm sorry.' It was all she could say; she couldn't even speak any more. She was sorry for herself and for Michael, sorry for all the huge and unsolvable problems that suddenly seemed laid at her door, sorry for Nicholas's help given so freely even in the face of her own secrets, and sorry she could not lean into his strength and sob her heart out. Her chin wobbled and, as her hand came up to hide it, she cast her eyes down towards the floor, willing herself not to cry, not here and not now. She drew in a noisy breath and held it, struggling for a strength she far from felt.

Nicholas watched her efforts and crossed to a drinks' tray, pouring out a liberal brandy and swirling it in his hand to warm it before turning to rejoin her.

Effortlessly he came down on his haunches in front of her and placed the glass in her hands, a little distanced so as not to alarm her, but close enough to be able to speak quietly and try to allay all the fears for Michael he could see reflected so plainly in her beautiful violet eyes.

'Brenna, Clive Weston-Tyler is a thorough physician and Michael already looked a lot better before we left his room.' Her eyes strayed quickly to his, glad of his hopeful words, and she nodded as he continued, 'I'm sure he's seen lots of cases just like this one and he will be more than competent in dealing with your uncle.'

Taking a deep breath, Brenna tried to recover her scattered composure and tried also to still the shaking that seemed to have gripped her since leaving Michael's room.

Seeing this, Nicholas pushed the glass to her lips. 'Clive will be having to come and see you next if you don't drink up.'

The words brought her eyes to his face. 'He looks expensive,' she blurted out before she had a chance to stop herself and Nicholas nodded, a smile in his voice.

'He is.'

Goodness, she thought. I hope he's not too much longer then, the shock of the bill could harm Michael just as easily as his lack of breath. 'He is your family doctor?' she countered awkwardly, trying to fill in the gap.

'Yes. I keep him on a retainer for any medical emergency. Tonight I'm getting my money's worth.' Laughter glinted in green eyes and embarrassment crossed into hers as she turned away. Had he guessed at her thoughts? Was this his way of saying that he'd settle any accounts? First the orphanage, and now in their very home. How far did his indebtedness to her extend? Surely he was beginning to feel the weight of all these unexpected burdens.

She put down her glass, uncertain as to the effects of the brew, for her mind seemed already apart from her body and she always liked to feel in control. Standing, she walked to the window, looking out towards the dusk as it fell over the rooftops, her thoughts racing across the last few months.

With a new resolve in her eyes she began quietly, 'Thank you for your help tonight, your Grace. Michael is dear to me and without him—' She stopped, unable to go on, and he nodded as he saw what it was she was trying to say to him, though she hurried on as she guessed he was about to speak. 'I consider your debt to me paid in full. A life for a life, yours for Michael's. It's a well-fulfilled obligation and I hold you in no arrears…' She hesitated then, unable to phrase the obvious final conclusion, though he stepped forward and did it for her.

'So you're saying that now you want me gone. Is that it?'

Said like that, after all that he had done, it seemed so callous she could barely agree, though when she lifted her eyes to his she was amazed at the wry amusement that had settled there.

'I'll bow out on one condition, Brenna,' he said softly and a frown creased her forehead as she searched without success for his meaning. 'I want both you and Michael to come to my ball.'

Another social gathering! Unsureness knotted in her stomach.

'Why?'

'Your life is too narrow and you're too young to live like a nun.'

'And you think it's up to you to change it?' She coloured, angry now as she tossed her words at him with little care. 'Your title affords you lordship only over your demesne, Nicholas Pencarrow, and lies far from deciding what may be best for me.'

'Then you won't come to my ball?' he countered lazily, a muscle ticking at the back of his cheek, making a lie of his carefully placed indifference.

She felt caught. He always made her feel like that. If she rejected his offer, he still might meddle in her life, and if she accepted, all the old dangers lay very close at hand. A room filled with the game of love, dancing and flirting. Hard violet shards raked across him.

'If I accept, it will be on one condition only,' she mirrored his words and his smile deepened.

'What's that?'

'I won't dance.'

Fresh merriment filled his voice. 'As you wish.' He held out his hand but she failed to take it, angry at his teasing in a way he would never understand.

'I don't have a dress.' The words were out even as she thought them—childish, she knew, but she wanted to diminish some of his pleasure at having cornered her and let him worry about what it was she would wear.

'I'll send you one.'

'You will not.' Shock ran through her body at the intimacy of his suggestion.

'Then come in navy. It always suits you.' His face creased into a wide smile as he continued, 'I'd even be happy with the paint-splattered white smock, just as long as you're inside it.'

She blushed again, her whole body roiling at his unspoken meanings. Nicholas Pencarrow was flirting with her? Her, when he had the choice of every other London female? Without wishing it, she softened her tone, disarmed against the power he was so pointlessly offering, and deep dimples appeared.

'I begin to think it would have made my life more tranquil had I just left you to the mercy of the highwaymen, your Grace.'

'Tranquillity can sometimes be equated with boredom, Brenna. You have to take risks in life to get what you want.' Gentling his teasing when he felt her withdrawal, he added, 'I missed you at the ballet the other afternoon.'

She had the grace to look slightly guilty. 'I had business in Worsley. We're selling Airelies.' She disguised the hurt well, she thought, her businesslike tones hard across the softer sorrow.

'That's the house I came to with your gun?' Nicholas asked.

'Yes, I was brought up there from the age of twelve.' She added, 'It's home,' before she could stop herself.

'More so than this one?' He gestured at the building they stood in.

'Michael brought me there first after York...' Halting in mid-sentence, she realised the extent of what it was she had just revealed to him, and cursed herself for the inadvertent slip of both tongue and mind. The arrival of Dr Weston-Tyler at that moment saved her from any awkward explanations.

'Will he be all right?' she asked, her legs readying

for flight upstairs should his answer prove different from what she hoped.

The older man nodded. 'He's had a severe attack of asthmatic bronchitis, Miss Stanhope, due largely, I gather, from the fact that you were not here to send him off more quickly to a physician.'

Brenna's face crumpled. ''Tis much the same as I told him. I'm afraid he's very stubborn.'

'And no longer a young man.'

'That, too.'

'This condition is worsened, you see, by two things: age and worry.' He gave the prognosis as if he had just read it from a textbook and Brenna paled as she answered grimly.

'He's suffering from both, I fear, and there's not much I can do about either.'

'Then take him on a holiday,' the doctor answered nonchalantly with the universal prescription he meted out to all his rich patients.

Where could they go, thought Brenna, and with what money could they get there? The realisation hit her in that second that neither the doctor nor Nicholas Pencarrow would ever know the curse of dire financial straits. Why, the fee from one consultation alone would probably cover a week at a resort on the south coast beaches and the Duke of Westbourne's legendary wealth was common knowledge amongst all.

'Well,' continued Dr Weston-Tyler as he made much of packing away his gleaming equipment, 'there's nothing more I can do here.'

Nicholas watched, his hands tightening behind his back. God, couldn't Clive understand there was no money? How plain did she have to be? How humble did she need to become, or had Clive tripped so much in the world of luxury that he now failed to understand its other face of hardship? Nicholas interrupted, putting the moment of uneasiness at an end.

'I am sure Sir Michael and Miss Stanhope will find some solution. Are there medicines to be left?'

The practitioner nodded. 'I've made a list...' He went to hand it to Brenna, but Nicholas took it instead.

'I'll get these,' he murmured, tucking the paper into his jacket pocket before Brenna could insist otherwise. 'And I'll give you a ride home, Clive.'

Brenna walked towards the door, ushering them into the small hall and opening the front portal with obvious relief, though Nicholas stopped as he stepped through.

'I will send Thompson back with the medicines as soon as they're made up and I will include the invitations.'

Brenna looked at him uncertainly.

'For the ball,' he enlightened her. 'As you promised, minus the dress and the dances.'

She nodded, little in the mood for teasing. 'Goodbye, your Grace.' She curtsied stiffly, though her eyes softened. 'And thank you for helping Michael and for the doctor...and the medicines,' she added lamely, for it seemed her constant place to ever be the receiver of favours, apart from in the first few moments of their acquaintance.

Nicholas almost began to speak again but, thinking better of it, tipped his hat and walked into the night. How did one offer gifts without also offering an affection he knew she wanted nothing of? How did he, knowing De Lancey's financial problems, balance pride against charity, balance help against interference?

Chapter Five

Nicholas spent the next two days sifting through the records of Michael De Lancey's family, finding, to his surprise, the notice of a brother, Fenton, blessed with six daughters by 1837 and then a long-awaited son born in the same month and year that Nicholas's investigations had turned up as Brenna's birth date. He glanced again at the latest letter from his lawyer, which had uncovered some more facts. Fenton's wife Daphne still lived out of York, mad by all accounts but cared for by the youngest daughter, the others having made respectable, if not grand, marriages. A furrow creased his brow as he copied the country address of the house called Farnley, standing in a borough of the northern city of York. Crossing to a drawer, he pulled out a map, unfurling it on the table before him, trying to plot the exact route he would need to take to reach this place.

Brenna Stanhope was taking over his rational thought, he thought wryly, remembering back to last night's unexpected visit from Deborah Hutton. The opera star at the height of her career and charms had always appealed to him, yet, as he had taken her to

his bed, he had imagined not honeyed tresses but ebony ones, not sky blue eyes but fearful violet orbs, not
light flirtatious banter but a heavily veiled articulate
aloofness that bespoke all of the one he was becoming
increasingly obsessed with. Last night had shocked and
worried him in a way no other incident ever had. He
had to be mad to let Brenna affect him like this and
yet he was completely powerless to change it. 'Keep
your distance, Nick,' he chided himself softly. 'Remember, Brenna Stanhope is just an interesting diversion, nothing more.' He rang for his butler. Burton
appeared less than thirty seconds later, bowing slightly
as he entered the Duke's company.

'You called, your Grace?'

Nicholas smiled, easing the other man into a more
relaxed stance. 'I need to go to York for a few days
tomorrow on business. Could you let the stables know
and have them bring the brougham around at nine
o'clock in the morning?' He stopped, trying to find a
way to phrase the next sentence. 'If my family should
enquire of my whereabouts, tell them that I have had
to go north and I will be home on the Sabbath. If there
is a problem that you feel needs my attention, you may
send word to the Excelsior in York, though I can think
of nothing that could warrant such a need, short of a
disaster.'

Burton nodded, a look of puzzlement crossing the
man's countenance, though if Nicholas saw it, he gave
it no heed.

Farnley was an old house, once grand but run down
and tatty looking, and the farm cottages were in the
same sad condition. Nick was not surprised. He knew

the family to be in straitened circumstances since the
death of Fenton.

The carriage stopped at the front portico and Nicholas stepped out. Without warning, a door swung open
and a young woman appeared. She came out into the
light with a familiar reticence, and in that second Nicholas knew the answer to all his intended questions, for
there could be no doubt that this was much more than
a distant relation to Brenna Stanhope.

'Good afternoon, I seem to have lost my way to
Smail's Mill.' He made mention of a small town he
knew to be a few miles to the west of Farnley, bringing
a map from his pocket to reinforce the statement. 'I
am Nicholas Pencarrow, newly come from London,
and you would do me a great service if you could point
out the direction I must follow.'

'Oh.' The girl blushed, obviously hesitating as to
whether or not it was proper to speak with him, when
a voice came loudly from inside.

'Who is it, Charlotte? Who is there? Who has come
to see us?'

'Excuse me.' Charlotte bowed politely, and disappeared into a side room to return immediately and bid
him enter into the company of Daphne De Lancey.

Even in old age she was a beautiful woman, though
there was a glint of madness in her eyes and a certain
unkemptness about her appearance. Charlotte mirrored
her handsomeness, but Brenna outdid them both, and
a portrait that hung askew upon the wall behind her
showed the six daughters all from the same mould, and
a son thatched blond and freckled. His glance flicked
back to the woman he now knew to be Brenna's
mother.

'Welcome, Mr Pencarrow, to Farnley. I am Daphne De Lancey and this is my daughter Charlotte.'

Nicholas turned and favoured the girl with a smile. She was taller than Brenna, heavier of feature, though much more open to strangers.

'I am very pleased to meet you, sir.' She curtsied as stiffly as Brenna did. That trait must run across all the De Lancey women, Nick thought, for a sense of independence sprang from these two nearly every bit as strongly as it did from the youngest Miss Stanhope. Or De Lancey, he corrected himself.

Brenna De Lancey, born exactly the same day as her brother George and disappearing thereafter for all of twelve years.

Daphne's voice brought him back into the present. 'My daughter tells me that you are lost.'

'I am, and if you could but give me some instruction as to the path I must follow to reach the Mill, I would be most grateful.'

Daphne stood. 'We usually eat here within the next half an hour. I know this is an invitation pushed upon you without much warning and indeed by strangers as we are, but we would deem it an honour if you were to join us.'

Put so humbly, how could Nicholas refuse, and his smile touched his eyes for the first time as he surveyed the two women before him. With a little persuasiveness in the right direction there was much here that he could learn and he could also begin back for London that very same night.

'I would be delighted, Lady De Lancey, though it truly cannot be for very long as I have business matters most pressing to attend to.'

'Hurry then, Charlotte, and fetch Mr Pencarrow a

beverage,' Daphne barked the order and the girl jumped up towards the drinks' table, turning back to him only as she reached it and enquiring of Nicholas what it was he wished to have. His glance raked across the ill-laid trolley chancing on a port he enjoyed, and he gave her his preference.

'Are there just the two of you here?' His eyes flicked to the family portrait behind Daphne.

'At the moment…yes,' Charlotte answered with an open honestness. 'All of my sisters are married. George, our brother, died soon after that drawing was completed.' She stopped, watching Daphne before adding, 'Our father too.' Sadness showed plainly across both faces.

'You were lucky, then, that the land was not entailed,' Nick said quietly. 'Some families could lose everything were the male heir to die.' It was said more in innocence than design, though as he looked up an expression of such guilt was written across Daphne's face it was as if she had screamed, *We lost it way before that*, and taking her drink she finished it in one long and unbroken swallow.

Charlotte glanced around uneasily at her mother, and Nicholas, seeing her uncertainty, raised his glass in a toast.

'Here's to life,' he said slowly.

One begun, one ended. Two babies, born on exactly the same day to two very different women, and a family lost to Brenna.

A coldness began to settle inside of Nicholas, an answer to a puzzle he didn't want to find, a premonition of Brenna's fear, of her secrecy, an understanding of Michael's protection and an explanation for Daphne's madness. He squashed it down, not willing to dissect it at all further, and questioned Charlotte instead. 'Do you ever come down to London?'

'Oh, hardly ever,' she laughed. 'We have a relation there, my father's brother.' She glanced around uneasily. 'He has a house in Camberwell, I believe. A Sir Michael De Lancey—mayhap you know of him?'

Nicholas made light of his answer, unwilling to take the subject any further for he didn't wish to alarm Daphne or inadvertently frighten Michael or Brenna into flight.

'It's a big place,' he replied flatly, his eyes flitting unbidden back to the visage of an unlawful male heir and a family portrait which should have proudly held the likeness of a woman who was becoming increasingly important to him.

The drive back to London was a long one for Nicholas, all his energies spent trying to unravel the puzzle of Brenna De Lancey Stanhope, and, on arriving in town he directed his driver to deliver him to his club instead of Pencarrow House.

Almost the only other occupant of the place as Nicholas walked through the salons was the Earl of Drummorne, Francis Woodhams, sitting ensconced in an armchair by the fire, brandy in hand and lost in thought.

'Penny for them?' Nick chided as he sat to join him, beckoning a passing waiter for a whisky.

Brown eyes rose in greeting, a tepid smile barely lighting them in humour. 'Sit at your peril, Nick, for I warn you today I am not good company.'

'Did your brother abscond with more of the family jewels?' Nicholas quipped without apology, thinking of Bertrand, a known gambler whose excesses seemed paid for only by Francis's good intelligence in business.

'Nay, it's Louisa. She's leaving me!'

'But you only just returned from Paris and, from all accounts that I've heard, the trip seemed more than a success.'

For the first time Francis smiled. 'I thought so too! It seems, however, the life of a well-bred courtesan is not enough for her. She wants her independence.'

Nicholas grimaced. 'Tough to promise,' he said with feeling.

'My thoughts exactly. Seems she has a woman friend in business on the east side of town, someone from her far and distant past. The woman is the epitome of "unconventional femininity", according to Louisa. Together they could rule the world.' He upended his glass. 'Louisa working in an orphanage. Can you even imagine it?'

'Hell!' Nicholas lurched to his feet. 'Not the Beaumont Street Orphanage run by Brenna Stanhope?'

Astonishment raced across Francis's brow. 'Yes. I'm sure that is the name she mentioned…'

'Interesting, indeed.' Nick stood, running his hands through his hair before facing Francis urgently. 'Where's Louisa now?'

'She's at the town house. You want me to go with you right this minute?' Francis groaned and stood. 'This had better damn well be important, Nick.'

'Believe me, it's very important,' came the cryptic reply, and Francis hurried to catch him up.

The walk through Hyde Park to Mayfair was a long one and Brenna paused to look around her, the semidusk of the early afternoon burying the city under a carpet of smoke.

London. It was glorious and dismal, rich and poor, elegant and tatty. Here, in an area favoured by the fashionable and wealthy, the houses changed their coats; larger, spacious, gardened and well to do, and Brenna, walking now into Mount Street, smiled as she caught sight of Louisa waiting patiently at the corner, parasol opened above her to guard against the dampness in the air.

'Brenna!' The girl came forward. 'It seems an age since I've seen you.'

'It has been,' Brenna returned, kissing the offered cheek lightly, her eyes widening with astonishment at the beauty before her. 'And how a year in Paris has changed you, Louisa! You look wonderful.' Her glance fell across the colourful silk bodice of a day gown cut daringly low.

Louisa smiled, tucking errant blond curls beneath a lace-edged cap. 'Francis bought me a whole wardrobe in Paris. He bought me this too.' She pulled forth a necklace, laced in gold and emeralds, and Brenna, holding them, felt the warmth of Louisa's body on the metal.

'And you're happy?'

'I am trying to be, though sometimes…' Her blue eyes darkened as she struggled to continue. 'Sometimes I would like to be more in control of my own destiny, Brenna, and determine my future just as you have yours. But enough of that. The reason I have asked you here today is to give you a gift!'

'Me?'

'Yes, and from Paris no less! You're to come right now and try it on. Francis has just left and won't be back till tomorrow at least and I have the apartment entirely to myself.'

Brenna stepped back, unsure about continuing. They met usually in some anonymous safe place far from the real world of either, and seldom discussed the past that bound them both together. Now, well dressed and pampered, Louisa wanted no recollection of her early years, and Brenna had little want to delve there either. It was as if in this mutual pact of silence something was salvaged, some sense of dignity and honour, some shape of a past that mitigated their guilt and let them stand free and independent.

'I'm not sure,' Brenna hedged, thinking of some reason to leave, but seeing the hurt of disappointment in Louisa's eyes. 'Well, perhaps only just quickly. I really can't be long.'

'Nay, not long.' Louisa wound her arm through Brenna's and excitedly bundled her down the street, stopping at a well cared-for, semi-detached house that lay wreathed in elegant black iron lacework. Finding the key, she pushed the door open and Brenna, stepping inside, was assailed by the unmistakable smell of expensive perfume.

'Up here!' Louisa beckoned, running up steps draped in eastern carpets. 'I want to show you your present.'

Brenna followed, crossing to a bedroom that filled the whole front of the house, French doors spilling out to a balcony and lawn lace curtains shielding it from the view of others. Her mouth fell open with amazement.

'This is your bedroom? You sleep here?' Her eyes noted a bed, easily the largest she had ever seen, and shifted back to the woman beside her, her dimples appearing as unexpectedly as the sun after a long and dingy day. 'Goodness, Louisa, but this is decadent.'

Louisa chuckled and threw open her cupboards. 'Wait till you see the rest, but be warned against criticism, Brenna, for our childhood of otherwise has taught me to enjoy excess.'

The words were said gently and Brenna sobered, running her fingers now through yards of silk and velvet and tulle in the shape of what seemed like a hundred gowns hanging in proud array. 'They're beautiful, Louisa. I think that this Francis must truly love you.'

Blue eyes twinkled. 'He does and one day he'll realise it, but for now…' She went to one end of the cupboard and pulled forth a gown still wrapped in calico to shield it from the light of day.

'This is yours, Brenna. I found it at Bussy's. The madam there said it had been ordered by the daughter of a Marquis who had never come back to claim it and I thought of you straight away.'

Brenna pulled off the drab material that enfolded the garment, and her eyes were filled with wonderment at the sight before her: an evening gown of dark red silk, high backed and square bodiced, the V-shaped front trimmed with wide lace revers, and an overskirt gathered at the waist before falling in scalloped edges to the floor.

'My Lord,' she breathed to Louisa. 'It's lovely… more then lovely…'

'You truly do like it?' Louisa squealed in happy anticipation. 'Try it on!'

'Now?'

'Yes.'

Both girls fell into laughter. 'You're sure no one will come?'

'Positive.'

It was all the encouragement Brenna needed and, peeling off the blue velvet, she reached for the red silk, Louisa fastening the row of tiny buttons at her back.

Intrigued, Brenna went across to the armoire, stretching up on her toes to see the hemline and unpinning her hair, using Louisa's brush to stroke out the shiny heavy mass of curls until they gleamed. 'I can't believe that you bought this for me,' she whispered, trying at the same time to pull up the bodice a little. 'You're sure it suits me?' A tiny niggle of doubt sat in Brenna's mind as she turned towards the mirror, her breasts swelling across the tightness.

'Wonderfully!' Louisa supplied, laughing as the other woman blushed. 'And it's well past time you broke out and wore something apart from navy. The world of men is not at all as you may think it to be, Brenna, and old age can be lonely without a soulmate.'

Brenna was still, caught between the past and the future in a way she often was in the company of Louisa. And the dress of silk and lace felt undeniably luxurious.

'People truly wear the décolletage this low?' Brenna's knowledge of the latest in fashion was, at her own admission, sadly lacking.

'All of them, though this one would be considered tame, even on an unmarried lady.'

Brenna pulled the bodice up for a final time, sighing as she made not a whit of difference to the amount of exposure. 'It almost seems indecent,' she whispered, wishing suddenly that she did have the confidence to be seen in such a gown, given that it was hers to keep.

'Well, it's not, though you may feel happier if I showed you the whole thing. Come downstairs with me and help me bring up the mirror from the front salon. It's usually kept up here, but Francis has just had the hinges mended. We'll find some shoes and a hat and you'll be able to see your dress properly then.'

Buoyed up by Louisa's enthusiasm, Brenna nodded; five minutes later they were in the front hallway, heaving the heavy mahogany piece of furniture towards the stairwell.

'Tip it my way,' Louisa commanded, 'and hold it still. I'll see if I can lever it up on to the banister.' Brenna strained and brought the length across her chest, lowering her arms to try to heave it upwards and feeling the breath leave her body with its heaviness.

'Are you sure we can manage this, Louisa?' she queried doubtfully.

'I've done it before with the maid.' She frowned. 'Or perhaps it was with Francis...' And at that second the front door, not five steps away from them, was flung open, spilling forth an astonished-looking blond man and Nicholas Pencarrow, two pairs of eyes staring at them in disbelief.

'Brenna?' Her name came incredulous and huskily from Nicholas and she almost expected him to reach out and touch her just to ascertain she was not a mirage. Her arms quivered beneath the weight of the mirror, caught in its heaviness so that she could not even adjust the neck of her gaping dress and, as Nicholas came forward to relieve her of its burden, she felt his eyes running across her.

Shock surged through Nicholas's body. Brenna here and in the company of Louisa Greling and shoeless, her hair falling loose across a gown fashioned from lace and silk? Brenna with one of London's most celebrated courtesans and looking just as provocative?

Where were the high-necked blue velvets, the books, Beaumont Street? How could he reconcile one with the other?

The question was forming on his lips as she whirled, racing up the stairs without pause, her face aflame with embarrassment, the dress seen through Nicholas's eyes acquiring only a cheap showiness, which in Louisa's company had not been obvious.

Slamming the door behind her, she hauled off the gown, tears of frustration rising as she tried to unfasten all the tiny buttons. Reaching with shaky hands for the blue velvet, she pulled it on with as much quickness as she could muster, one foot against the door to bar entry given the complete absence of any lock. Once the dress lay in place across her body, she felt stronger, wrenching her stockings into place with fingers more like her own and tying her hair back in one long and customary plait. Wide eyes observed her reflection in the mirror. Lord, what could she say to him? How could she explain away her friendship with Louisa or her reasons for being here?

Honesty!

The word came quiet and true and with a growing resolve, but the newly found confidence completely shattered when she heard a knock on the door and the Duke of Westbourne's voice without.

'Brenna? May I come in for a moment?'

In panic she made for the door, pushing it open and herself out in almost the same movement. She would meet his questions on the landing, not in the bedroom, though with no sign of Louisa or the man she presumed to be Francis, her heart began beating anew.

Nicholas stood, leaning slightly against the railings of an ornate balcony, his gaze softening as he observed the transformation of the woman now before him, laced into the shapeless navy velvet as though covered from head to foot in androgynous armour.

With quiet patience he stood his ground, waiting for her to look at him, willing her to explain what was going on. Finally, an anguished visage tipped up to his.

'It…it…it is not as you may think, your Grace,' she stuttered in her haste to explain. 'The dress was a present from Louisa, from Paris, which she insisted that I try on after making it plain no visitors at all were expected this afternoon.' She stopped, taking a breath in nervousness. 'It's very flimsy and hardly me and far too…too…'

'Revealing?' Nicholas supplied. Green eyes glittered with a hard masculinity. 'You do know what this house is, do you not, Brenna?'

She turned at his question and walked towards the stairs, willing him to keep his distance, willing herself to stand her ground.

Quietly she nodded.

'Then you also realise how damaging it would be to your reputation if another had arrived instead of me? No matter what the reason?'

Again a small shake, the brittle sharpness of unshed tears welling behind her eyes. He could never know how well she understood the danger or how close to the truth he tarried.

'Louisa has been a friend of mine for a long time, though today is the first day I have ever come here. The dress…' she added brokenly, 'I haven't many and thought perhaps for your ball…' She bit back the words as soon as she had said them, cursing her stupidity and waiting for laughter.

None came.

Nicholas stood still, fighting the pain in his heart, fighting the desperate want of her that swept through his body at her confession. In truth the dress looked stunning, but for all the wrong reasons. And she still did not have a dress for his ball.

His mind flicked to the countless clothes most ladies of his acquaintance had the choice of, worn once and discarded, and it was on his tongue to offer again the gift of a more suitable gown, but he kept silent, seeing the intrinsic pride in the lift of her chin and in the anger of her own admission.

'Come, Brenna,' he whispered softly. 'Let me see you home.'

She hesitated, bewildered by his gentleness and her own lack of alternative. 'And the other man with you,' she said. 'You will explain?'

He nodded, watching her carefully, the man in him hard pressed to act the gentleman she expected. God, if he had any sense he'd seduce her here and now and be damned with the consequences. Already he could hear the muffled noises of lovemaking in the salon below. Francis and his mistress seemed to have settled their differences in passion, he surmised, wishing it could be that easy for him. His loins ached with the want of her.

'I think we should leave,' he said huskily, stepping back as she preceded him down the stairs, unwilling to speak further until they were outside, so little did he trust himself.

Brenna frowned and did as she was bid. Suddenly he seemed angry and withdrawn. Would he let it be known that he had found her in such a compromising position, or worse, would he withdraw his money from the orphanage altogether?

Concerned violet eyes raised up to his as they came outside into the drizzle of a late afternoon. Taking a deep breath, she began in earnest. 'I realise my behaviour today was inexcusable, my Lord, and the dress—'

He let her go no further.

'You looked beautiful.' The words came harsh and ragged and hardly like the Duke of Westbourne. In consternation she looked up to find darkened eyes boring down into her own. 'Thompson will deliver you to Greerton, Miss Stanhope,' he said unevenly, opening the door to his carriage to let her in and stepping firmly back as she seated herself. 'And I will see you at my ball.'

She could only nod, watching as he signalled to his driver to leave, watching as he turned back to Louisa's house, a desperate dread beginning to form about her mind as she realised his intentions. Would Louisa be savvy enough to deflect his curiosity? She hoped so. How she hoped so.

Chapter Six

It was the twenty-sixth of November before Brenna knew it and the night of the ball she had dreaded and longed for had finally arrived.

Pacing back and forth across her bedroom floor, she castigated herself anew for not simply refusing Nicholas Pencarrow when first he had given her the choice. This past week, getting a dress made, or rather altered, had been a harrowing and tiring job. Having avoided fashionable society, Brenna had paid little heed to current fashions, but she had finally succumbed to Michael's insistence that the blue velvets would definitely not do, would, in fact, attract her the attention she did so wish to avoid, and the alternative of his mother's cream silk gown was therefore mooted. He'd brought the dress down from the attic enveloped in the smell of mothballs and bade Brenna to put it on. It was a dress from another time, high waisted in the Empire style and appliquéd in lace and velvet. Apart from a slight tear on one puffed sleeve, and a hemline that would need to be lengthened, the dress fitted her perfectly and, matched with a pair of topaz earrings belonging to Michael's aunt, would be every bit suitable for attending a ball of the magnitude of the Duke of Westbourne's.

The afternoon had consisted almost entirely of getting ready, a pursuit so ludicrous and time-wasting according to Brenna that she could barely sit still when, in the final moments before leaving, Polly had put the finishing touches to her hair, curled and caught high upon her head with dark ringlets trailing unbound to her waist.

Standing the instant the process was finished, she snapped on the earrings and slipped into low-heeled golden shoes, then hurried quickly down the stairs.

'I am not certain about the wisdom of this,' she mumbled softly, as she came within her uncle's company, registering the formal dress Michael was in and the invitations splayed large across the table in front of him. Would Nicholas Pencarrow take some notice of her and thus force the attention of the entire assembly upon her personage, or would she see censure on his face after the débâcle at Louisa's? She shook her head and concentrated instead on happier thoughts. At least Michael would be with her; if the worst happened and it all went awry, she had fulfilled part of a bargain that she would never ever strike up again. This would be her first and last taste of the lifestyle of the very rich and her final absolution of any debt she felt regarding the orphanage funding given by Nicholas Pencarrow.

She had not, after all, seen him for well over a week—even his secretary had stayed clear of Beaumont Street. Did that bode well or ill? she wondered, remembering back to the day of Michael's sickness. She had expected the Duke back on her doorstep that selfsame night, carrying the medicines which he had

insisted on paying for, and her surprise had been great
when the servant he had named did indeed come and
very much alone. When the doctor had returned the
following afternoon, she had again looked for Nicholas, expecting to see his face in the window of the
carriage, ready to bait her into the next agreement she
would not wish to make. But still he kept his distance.
Perhaps tonight need not be the quandary she was
making it into. Perhaps Nicholas, tempted by other
riper morsels, had finally taken her help in Worsley in
the spirit she had pleaded with him all along to do. A
frown marred Brenna's forehead as she boarded the
carriage with Michael. Perhaps she gave herself too
much credit in her bizarre imaginings of an attraction
between them. Tonight he would see the ordinariness
in her and that would indeed be the very end of it.

Half an hour later their carriage swept up a drive
festooned with lights and burning torches, and liveried
footmen, and Brenna's confidence washed away, her
body coming forward from the seat to view the house
more closely. Every door that led out on to the front
balconies was decorated with numerous lanterns, and
on guard duty at the columned entrance stood a bevy
of servants dressed in black and white, escorting each
newly arrived guest up the stairs and inside. She recognised the faces of Lord Palmerston and Lord Ten-
nyson, Tory politician and Poet Laureate respectively.
How far and quickly had she strayed from her own
more humble surroundings.

Swallowing, she felt her mouth dry with fear. It was
all as she remembered, though a thousand times more
grand and opulent, for never in the year of her season
had she come near the houses of the *haut ton*, and

Nicholas Pencarrow seemed to sit at the very pinnacle of that.

Music assailed her senses as the carriage door was opened to the lively strains of Strauss and to the smell of gardenias. Gardenias in November? Brenna's eyebrows lifted at just that simple cost. Nicholas Pencarrow must have had them especially nurtured in glass houses, a summer flower to bedeck this wintertime land and all in a gesture that fairly screamed out the never-ending prosperity of the very wealthy.

Her eyes came around to Michael and, unfolding themselves from their carriage, they walked up the stairs to a line that had formed in the drawing room. Ahead she could see the Duke welcoming each guest and Brenna's stomach lurched in nervousness as they waited. She hardly dared lift her eyes to the assembly she could see in front, for she was every bit as exposed as she had dreaded and even the smile that lit up Nicholas Pencarrow's eyes failed to ease her tenseness.

Nicholas had glanced up to find her right there. Dressed in a gown from another era, she looked as if she had crossed the time barrier and walked straight in from 1820. He'd never seen her look so beautiful. The earrings she wore sparkled with violet lights that matched her eyes and her hair hung in a dark thick curtain, curling across her shoulders. Even the apprehension he perceived, as he took her hand, did nothing to diminish her loveliness, her stillness reflecting her dress and setting her apart from every other woman present; compared with her, they looked either overdone or overexposed. Warmth crept into his eyes and a warning came, as if in answer, into hers.

'Good evening,' she spoke primly, almost snatching her hand from his where it had lain too long, and frowning as he drew her towards a woman a few feet away who was also greeting newcomers.

'Grandmama, this is Brenna Stanhope and her uncle, Sir Michael De Lancey. Brenna, this is my grand-mother, The Dowager Duchess of Westbourne.'

Grey eyes came directly up at the mention of the Stanhope name, though as a smile broke out across her face and touched her eyes with a dancing mirth, Brenna relaxed.

'Nick, you are as remiss as your brother, for neither Charles nor you has ever mentioned to me how beau-tiful your mysterious Miss Stanhope really is.'

Nicholas grimaced, softening his countenance im-mediately as he felt Brenna's gaze turned to him. He swallowed the reply he would have liked to have given, as green eyes raked across his grandmother in a silent warning of intent.

And Elizabeth was as intrigued as Nicholas was. Why, the child seemed to hark from an age long past, dressed in a fashion she could remember from years back and with a countenance that belied description. Yes, she could well understand her boys' lack of out-line, for Brenna Stanhope was not at all beautiful in the vogue of this day. No, she harked back to a more mythical and enigmatic time, a time when a woman's beauty lay not in the purely physical but in the char-acter, and strength of purpose, and difference.

Everything she had ever heard of Brenna Stanhope was underscored by other people's ideas of what a proper woman should not do. She was not married, she had had a poor first season, she worked for a living in the East End of London amongst children of the working classes and maintained no connections with the society Elizabeth was used to mingling in. There was nothing in her background that should have endeared her to Nicholas, and yet, on meeting her for the first time, Elizabeth could feel her attraction every bit as clearly as her grandson could. She was the complete opposite to him and the most right, dark against light, stillness against energy.

Letitia Carruthers's voice broke the spell and rudely brought Elizabeth back into the moment. 'The Beauchamps are here, Nicholas, and they would like you to meet their new daughter-in-law.' Nicholas's eyes raked across the never-ending procession of newly arrived guests as he reluctantly let Brenna go.

'Damn,' he muttered to himself. It would be at least an hour before he could be free and time was very precious under a bargain that would deny him further access after this night, should he use it unwisely. In frustration he turned back to his place in the welcoming committee, leaving Michael to take Brenna through.

In the main drawing room Brenna was thankful to see Julia and Thomas Cartwright, a couple already known to them, ensconced in the vicinity. At least in a group they would be relatively safe from the intrusion of others, though the night began to appear more and more untenable.

Her eyes looked at the timepiece gathered on a chain at her uncle's waist. Half past eight. Lord, but it seemed like hours already that they had been here and it had not yet passed thirty minutes? An aching worry built behind her brow as she searched the front vestibule for Nicholas Pencarrow, wishing that if any one should come to harry her it might at least be him. The thought made her clench the beaded velvet of her small bag and draw away her glance from the very one who had landed her in this predicament in the first place. The Cartwrights' greetings centred her attentions away from the gathering group of young men who had formed about her as Julia took Brenna's hand in hers.

'My goodness, darling,' she enthused. 'You seem to be attracting attention already, and out of those infernal blue velvets you favour, I can well see why. Which one has taken your fancy so far?' Her glance went around the room, a frown creasing her eyebrows as she looked over all the young men present. 'If I were young again and looked as you do, I'd be setting my cap at Nicholas Pencarrow or his brother Charles. Though from what one hears, neither of them is an easy catch to land.'

Already more young men had formed a group around them, though a movement at her side caused her to glance up, her eyes widening as she found a man who looked surprisingly like Nicholas Pencarrow standing there, though younger and lighter of hair. He bowed slightly, sweeping his gaze across her in an unconscious gesture of sizing her up.

'Good evening, Miss Stanhope. I am Charles Pencarrow, Nicholas's brother, and I have been sent by our grandmother to fetch you to her.' Brenna's eyes met his, her own uneasiness receding a little as she saw that his presence had dispersed all other hopeful suitors, though returning again when she assimilated the magnitude of the request he carried.

'Your grandmother?' she replied uncertainly, thinking back to the woman in the reception line and clamping down on a growing apprehension as she heard the whispers of the Pencarrow name all about her.

Julia's ravings have substance, she thought suddenly, her own curiosity inspecting the countenance of the man before her, trying to determine just what it could be in some men that made such fools of young women. Her own age and circumstances buffered her against a similar fate and left just plain inquisitiveness, though her regard of him faltered somewhat as his face broke into a broad smile, the corner of his eyes wrinkling into lines of laughter. 'If you will come with me, I will take you to her.'

Brenna's heart sank as she felt Charles's hand on the small of her back, leading her across to a table against a far wall and very near to where the musicians were playing some lilting melody that Brenna could not quite place. Charles saw her seated and beckoned to his grandmother. Elizabeth came over immediately.

'Miss Stanhope—or Brenna, may I call you that? Nicholas told me of your part in his rescue at Worsley and I would like to thank you.'

Brenna's dimples showed deep in each cheek. 'Oh, it was more a case of chance than rescue, your Grace. I just untied your grandson's bondage cords, gave him my gun and ran. In all honesty, he really did rescue himself.'

'Not the way he tells it.' The woman opposite her chuckled. 'Though he did say your aim was no better than mine.'

Brenna blushed anew. 'It was most unladylike, I'm sure. In my defence I would say the options were limited.'

'I do not criticise, Brenna.' The Dowager's voice lowered in tone. 'I only wanted to thank you.' Violet eyes caught grey ones and Elizabeth lightened the subject.

'Are you enjoying the ball so far, my dear? I can see you have more than your fair share of admirers

who will all be hoping that you do dance. Ahh…' She
waved at someone behind Brenna's back. 'Here is my
grandson now. Please do just favour him with one
waltz.'

Brenna started to plead her abstinence from such an
entertainment, drawing back somewhat when she saw
it was Nicholas, not Charles, who came to his grandmother's side.

'Nicholas, I want you to ask Miss Stanhope for a
dance. She seems most reticent and, after all, this is
our ball…' she rapped a fan lightly on the table as if
underlining her words '…and we all have to have at
least one dance. 'It is my wish,' she added more quietly, 'and a favour to me.'

Brenna's eyes shot up to Nicholas in a mute appeal
for help, but he stayed silent, holding out his hand as
if in deference to his grandmother. Having no other
option but to go with him, she stood, allowing him to
guide her on to the ballroom floor for a slow waltz
though, as his arms came around her, she experienced
again the pure breathless heat she had felt in the woods
and the same shock of safety. Disorientated, she stiffened and he sensed it immediately.

'If this is so distasteful, we can stop right now.'

Brenna averted her eyes and forced herself to relax;
to go to pieces now in front of this crowded room
would invite the disaster she so ardently wished to
avoid. With a huge effort she confronted him directly.
'Your family has a way with words and favours, your
Grace. Take this dance, for example—just more than
a request and just less than an order.'

He smiled against her hair, this quick-witted adversary much more familiar to him than the beautiful
frightened butterfly she had suddenly changed into.

'I thought, you see,' she continued, 'that we had a bargain, you and I. No dances, no dresses and four hours at a ball. 'Tis no wonder you are so rich, Nicholas Pencarrow, for your word lies in tatters beneath your wants.'

'It is not normally the case,' he returned cryptically, 'but four hours leaves me little time to convince you once and for all that I am not quite the scoundrel you paint me.'

Her face came up at that. 'And why should you wish me to know otherwise?' The game was begun and she wanted to know all the rules.

Because I want you, Brenna Stanhope. Because I want to run my hand across your skin and through your hair and feel the taste of you on my lips.

Shock at his unbidden thoughts stopped Nicholas from answering as he took a deep breath and tried to harness the growing needs of his own body. 'Because I would like to have you for a friend.'

The words softened her anger and she changed her stance immediately, fishing around for the first thought to come to mind.

'Your house looks lovely, though I think the gardenias were a bit excessive myself.'

'Pardon?' he asked blankly, not following her drift at all. Everything inside him ached in need.

'At the front door, I mean...' She hesitated, suddenly feeling her criticism to be out of place. 'It's winter here, you see, and they bloom only in the summer.'

'Ahh...' His eyes sparkled with frank masculine admiration and he forced himself to relax. 'You think I spent too much?'

She blanched at that. 'I'm sorry, 'twas rude of me

to imply such.' He held out a hand as if to stop her apology.

'No, I'll write them out of the celebrations next year. What flower would you recommend?'

'Holly berries and crabapple sprays. They're cheap and plentiful at this time of the year. The colour would have complemented the candles and you could have paid country folk to collect them. It is difficult at the moment on the land—financially, I mean...' she faltered weakly under his observation, for something in those tawny eyes had changed.

'I like your dress,' he said quietly after a minute. 'It's much nicer than anything I could have sent you, though a lot less imaginative than the creation I caught you in at Louisa's.'

'It was my grandmother's,' Brenna answered his first sentence, ignoring the second completely.

'You've caused a sensation here in it.'

The frown across her eyes deepened. 'I hope not.'

Something in her quietness disarmed Nicholas completely. 'You don't like the attention?' he asked sharply, her answer coming with a mounting blush across her cheeks.

Oh God, how could he protect her from everyone else in the room without standing right next to her all night and drawing the notice to her in the process that she so wishfully decried? Besides, knowing Brenna Stanhope as he did, he also knew she would not even want him there. Suddenly he realised that it was a mistake to have forced her into such a situation. The whole timing was wrong and he could see Letitia bearing down on him as the music slowed and came to an end. She reached out to him, effectively claiming him for the next dance, though Nicholas held her back as he signalled his brother Charles to his side.

'Could you take Miss Stanhope back to her uncle, Charlie, and see that she is not bothered? She does not wish to dance!'

Charles's eyebrows shot up. 'But she just has been, Nick, with you.'

'That's different,' he growled without explanation, a frustration in his eyes his brother could not define.

Charles led Brenna back to Michael and stayed on to talk, reasoning that his presence might do just as Nick had bade him, and, for the moment, it did look as though it was working to that effect as all the young men seemed cowed by his place at her side. Across the room, however, there was a buzz of interest in the fact that if Miss Brenna Stanhope wasn't with one of the Pencarrow boys, then she was with the other one.

Twenty minutes later, having managed to pair Letitia off with an obliging French Count, Nicholas walked through the crowds in search of Brenna, finally finding her standing with his brother and her uncle near the widely opened French doors to one end of the Blue Conservatory. For a moment he could just stand and watch from a distance, caught in this game as he had never been before, fearful to go close lest she rebuff him and fearful to stay away lest the hours drip away minute by minute until nothing was left.

Boldness won over restraint, for either way he was doomed. Fixing a smile on his face, he casually walked across to the small group, helping himself to a glass of cognac from a passing servant, which he downed inside the space of one footfall.

'Would you do me the honour of the next dance, Miss Stanhope? It will be the last set before supper.'

Brenna had felt his presence even before he joined them and her heart thumped wildly. Another dance! The danger of everything was escalating and her fists bunched tautly at her side. She must bury this fear of Nicholas and treat him as she did any other man with whom she had had business dealings, for had they not bargained on this night only, the hours already marking themselves off against midnight, and, apart from two dances that she had not expected, what else had been lost?

Her indifference. Her calmness. Her very quietude, which had given no other man a second glance save for this one.

She bit her lip in consternation, trying to still her fear as Nicholas signalled the musicians to play one last waltz. Taking her hand without any question of consent, he pulled her body into his as the chords of a lilting song began. 'Just for this dance, Princess, do not fight me. 'Tis the bargain between us and almost the ending of it.'

His voice was an aching whisper, a caress across her own screaming denials, a truce between adversaries who, finding the battle lines ill drawn, could still define no other.

And Brenna's guard fell away completely as she relaxed into him.

Just for this dance, just for these minutes, just for once in my life let me be as other women are, let me feel as other women feel and know the touch of a man who would want me.

The music swirled about them, as did the blur of a hundred other guests faceless and nameless in the vor-

tex of a time that could last only one single dance.
And when the music finished Nicholas's duty as host
called him up on to the makeshift stage and Brenna
remained still and alone below, her body swallowed
up by a sea of others, though this time their interest
did not touch her, did not permeate the glow and fear
that budded within.

She saw Nicholas looking for her, but did not try to
move aside into his range of vision, for the moment
of the dance had passed and she stored it merely as a
memory, something given fleetingly as a gift to one
who could never know the permanence. And the
thought did not make her sad—the opposite, rather, for
she would always remember the warmth she had seen
in Nicholas's eyes. She even laughed slightly to herself
as she watched him, his voice rising above the crowd,
welcoming them to his ball and bidding them to feast
at the long tables set out with food of all kinds. Tonight he was hers, not Elizabeth's grandson, not
Charles's brother, not even a Duke reputed to be the
most powerful in all of London. No, tonight he had
existed outside of all his titles and responsibilities, just
as she had, like the dress she wore returned from a
time it could never be a part of.

Michael joined her as the speeches came to an end
and a bevy of waiters carrying hot plates emerged to
add their share to a table already well over-laden. He
indicated above the chatter that they should join the
other guests and partake in the supper; after filling their
plates, they moved to a quieter place near the windows. Thomas and Julia Cartwright joined them almost
immediately.

'We've been looking for you everywhere.' Julia
smiled breathlessly, casting a look at Brenna which

told her clearly that she had seen her dance with Nicholas Pencarrow and now would not be satisfied until she knew all of the details.

Brenna was pleased when Michael shook his head and explained, 'We know Nicholas Pencarrow from the orphanage, Julia. He is a patron of Beaumont Street.'

'And I thought to have a far more romantic tale to tell all my friends, though I have heard it said that Nicholas Pencarrow will marry Letitia Carruthers before the summer is out.'

Brenna frowned, not wishing to be drawn into any discussion of Nicholas's love life, though without meaning to she scanned across the room for his presence, finding him to one side of the piano. Out of an intrigued curiosity she met his gaze and held it, amazed at the intensity her reaction elicited from him. He left the group and strode straight across to her, taking her arm even as he excused her from her surprised uncle and marching her out. In the privacy of an adjoining room he shut the door firmly behind him.

'Brenna, we need to talk,' was all he said, placing himself on the desk and leaning one hip against it to steady his half-seated frame. 'Do you know a man called Redmund Osborne?'

'No.' A small prickle of recognition snaked into her conscience, but she could not quite place the memory.

'You have never met anyone by this name?'

'No. I don't understand why you should ask...' she whispered.

'I don't either,' he said savagely, reaching for her then in an action that bridged no refusal. Pulling her full up against him, his lips slanted across hers with an unmistakable passion. She gasped, eyes wide at his unexpected assault but, as his hand came up against her cheek, stroking away the tension, her mouth opened to his without wishing it so, welcoming the warm wetness of his thrusting tongue. Something new and foreign and completely unknown assailed Brenna and she found herself arching her body and moving against him, her mouth tasting the sweetness of his. The sudden sound of voices outside pulled them apart and she ran the back of her hand across her mouth as if to physically remove the traces of him and her body began to shake so violently she could barely speak.

'This should never have happened. Do I look to you like an easy woman? Is it this dress…these earrings…?' She snatched at the last even as she said it, dragging them from her ears and taking her first steps towards the door.

'Brenna, I *want* you.' The words cut across her tirade, surprising Nicholas almost as much as they did her. Since the waltz they had shared an hour ago he had been trying to keep his distance, his penchant for restraint underscored by a new and unfamiliar emotion.

'Want me?' she shook her head vehemently and turned back. 'Want me for what?' Her eyes met his with such frankness that Nicholas had the grace to smile. He was as vulnerable as he had ever let himself be and she knew too little to capitalise on the fact. Her innocence sent him reeling. She was so unlike any woman he'd ever known, grave, mysterious, naïve, funny and fearful and, at this moment, an amalgamation of every one of them. He capitulated completely.

'Want you to marry me.' He ground the words out stonily, remembering his father's curse that he'd also marry for love but live to regret it, the surprise in his voice as evident to him as it must have been to her.

'Marry you?' Complete and utter amazement coursed through her. Was this the way the very rich procured their paramours, the pretence of convention at least cancelling out any baser notions of guilt?

'Yes.' He pulled himself away from the desk and stood before her. She had to tip her head to see into his eyes, almost golden now.

'No.'

'You won't marry me?'

'No.'

'Why not?'

'I won't marry anyone!'

'Ever?'

She nodded her head

'May I ask why not?'

'No.'

'Then I don't understand.'

Bruised eyes came swiftly back to his and Brenna's chin lifted. She did not comprehend any real truth in what he had said. After all, how could he ask her to marry him in his almost total ignorance of whom she was and without any mention of love? 'There is nothing about me that you need to understand, your Grace,' she answered, her whole stance stiff as if daring him to say different. 'Every other woman in that room would jump at the chance to be married to Nicholas Pencarrow, so I suggest that you go back in there and find the one who most appeals. The choice, I might add, is staggering.'

'Was it my kiss?' he countered wryly, resorting to humour in his hurt. 'It usually has quite the opposite effect.'

She ignored the jibe and went on strongly, 'Letitia

Carruthers is the woman for you, your Grace. She understands the rules of this game as I do not.'

'You see it as such?' Nick's head came up. 'As merely a game?'

'You are the Duke of Westbourne. Titles such as yours accord you the luxury of making up the rules.'

'And on what wisdom do you relegate all I have said to mere sport? When to you have I not been honest? Or fair?' Turning towards the fireplace, he ran his fingers through his hair, perplexed by her as he always was. 'What words tonight have I said to make you believe it's a jest?' He stopped, suddenly more certain of her actions. 'The kiss…it began with the kiss…' He stopped again, watching the telltale redness creep up across her cheeks. 'There is no shame in a kiss, Brenna, only joy, and love as we make it…'

Shame…shame…shame… One word blotted out all the others and she was back thirteen years in a hovel in York. Of a sudden she could take no more. Lifting her skirts, she dashed from the room, giving not a second's thought to the voice that tried to halt her.

Nicholas stood against the half-open portal and watched her flight, but made no move himself to follow, a frown forming slowly. He had upset her badly. There was none of the calm Miss Stanhope on display as she ran from him, none of the measured stillness that she put up like a shutter as soon as the conversation became at all personal.

And her anger had come from the kiss.

Brenna found the ladies' room and went inside, moving to the mirror to reposition her earrings in the reflection of the glass, a wide and pale face staring back at her, her whole mind reeling at the exchange

she'd just been a part of. How had this happened?
What had she done to elicit such nonsensical promises
from a man such as the Duke of Westbourne, re-
nowned across London for his restraint and power?
What manner of man would ask her to marry him in
one breath and then throw it all back to teasing in the
next? And his kiss! She swallowed her panic to breathe
deep of a newly won composure, and with grace she
left to find Michael.

They departed just as another older man was leaving, collecting their coats at much the same time and,
as the greying squire turned to her from the cloakroom,
a spark of recognition leapt coldly certain into his eyes,
and unsurely into her own. *Redmund Osborne*—the
name Nicholas had mentioned. She turned away even
as he uttered her name.

The silence in the carriage was complete, Brenna's
misery overpowered only by Michael's seething wrath.
The worst that they had feared had happened and no
words could ever lessen the danger, though Brenna
spoke quietly of a different matter. 'Nicholas asked me
to marry him tonight.'

'He did what?'

'He asked me to be his wife,' she qualified, needing
the compliment to cancel out the last few minutes.

A light shone quietly in Michael's eyes as he questioned her. 'And what answer did you give him?'

'The only one I could, given my circumstances.'

'You refused him without even an explanation?'

'Yes.'

Their house came into view and Michael bade the
welcoming Dumas to take Brenna in, though Brenna
turned unsurely. 'You are not going out again?'

He shifted himself on the seat, seemingly unwilling to explain. 'Just for a little while. I'll see you in the morning.'

It was so unlike him—she questioned him further. 'Where are you going?'

'Over to the Cartwrights—they asked me in for a nightcap.'

Betrayal gleamed in Brenna's eyes. He could leave her on such a night to go to his friends for a drink? Despairingly she turned, to go inside, allowing Dumas to help her.

Chapter Seven

The park was set in darkness, unbroken save for the first glimmers of dawn on the eastern sky and a flurry of activity as the sun rose upon the new day.

Michael De Lancey stood to one end, seconded by his friend Thomas Cartwright, and at the other stood the Squire Redmund Osborne, still dressed in his clothes from the ball, as indeed was Michael, and in the company of a man completely unknown to either of his opponents.

'Are you ready?' Thomas asked unsteadily. 'By God, man, it's been years since you shot with a pistol, hasn't it?'

'Indeed. I was always a lot better with swords.' The coldness of steel beneath his fingers reminded Michael of another time. Brian Cray. Yorkshire. The day he had finally found his lost niece after hearing Daphne De Lancey's overdue and tearful confession as to how she had exchanged her true daughter for a male heir to Farnley. Gold for a child. Daphne had always been mad. His hand tightened on the gun he held and he willed his temper to abeyance. He had killed Brian Cray for the harm he had done to Brenna. And now here again stood another dishonourable man from her past. Redmund Osborne. Dissolute. Overweight. And dangerous to everything they had always kept hidden.

The referee now came between both sets of adversaries and waved his scarf high in accordance with the rules, starting the men from a central position whilst counting out twenty paces.

Michael turned on the last one and aimed, his bullet whistling not even close to the one he had challenged; a look of pure glee crossed Osborne's eyes as he brought his gun up and fired at De Lancey's heart. The bullet ran straight through Michael's right arm, sending him to the ground. Then all the rules changed, for amazingly, Osborne raised his gun a second time and began to advance upon his fallen rival with a deadly intent. Just as he raised the pistol another shot rang out loud through the morning air and Osborne fell, shot through the back by an angrily advancing Duke of Westbourne.

'Damn it, De Lancey,' Nicholas swore darkly as he joined them. 'Julia Cartwright sent a note to tell me that you were here. Don't you know that duelling is illegal?'

Michael pulled himself to his feet and allowed himself to be tended by the surgeon the Duke had brought with him, no words coming forth in the shock of what had happened. Nicholas, seeing the uselessness of questioning him further, took charge of the whole situation.

'Get him into my carriage, Thompson, and we'll take him to my place and clean him up before delivering him home. Cartwright, see that the body of Osborne has gone before anyone comes by and sees it.' He turned towards Osborne's second. 'And you—if I ever hear even a whisper of this anywhere it'll be you I'm after next, understand!'

The other nodded before scampering across the park in the direction of home, wanting no more to be a part of this travesty than the Duke of Westbourne wanted him to be.

Satisfied with this response, Nicholas called Robertson, his driver, across to Thomas Cartwright. 'Help him here and join us when you have disposed of the corpse. But do it so there will be no queries.'

Robertson nodded, bending down to bring the fallen man's body across his own and striking out quickly to the Cartwright conveyance some fifty or so yards away and Nicholas scuffed at the blood marks across the grass before he too turned towards his carriage, parked high upon a verge in the opposite road.

Michael looked pale and sick when he joined him, the surgeon having finished the interim bandaging. Clive Weston-Tyler shrugged his shoulders and regarded Nick. 'It's the best I can do given the circumstances. I'll follow you home to Pencarrow House and finish the job there.'

Nicholas nodded absently, his own attention now on Michael seated opposite. The death of a man, even one as amoral as Osborne, suddenly bore down heavily on his conscience and, unflasking his silver whisky canteen, he took a long drink himself before handing it over to Michael.

'Have a drink. You look as if you need one as much as I do.'

Bending in wordless thanks, Michael took a deep draught.

'Do you want to tell me why?' Nick's words cut across the silence.

'I can tell you little of the reasons for the duel, your Grace, for to do so would be to betray a trust I hold more dearly than life itself, but I wonder if I might ask you a favour.' He halted, giving Nick the impression of a man fighting for his words. 'Could you take my niece to Airelies this weekend, chaperoned of course, to help her oversee the final details of packing? I realise this is an odd request coming from one you hardly know, but after all that has happened I would prefer for her to have a gentlemen around in case of trouble and with my arm like this…'

A light danced in Nick's eyes. Michael's supplication was an answer to the problem of the bargain made void by his behaviour at the ball, for it gave him a way, legitimately and at leisure, to see Brenna again. Chaperoned admittedly, but surely he could get her away by herself for a moment just to explain how things stood between them. The importance of the answer to Brenna's lost years was lessened in the face of such a prospect and, after all, it *was* her story to tell him. He would need to make her comfortable and secure again in his presence, try to re-establish the friendship he had been building before his own damned lust had got in the way.

Brenna came awake with a start, salt tears burning down her face, panic subsiding slowly as her eyes flicked about her own room in Greerton, emptying all corners of the ghosts of memories, her heartbeat stilling to a more natural rhythm as she registered her safety, her breathing quieter and less shallow.

She hadn't had a nightmare for years now, though the feeling of dread clung close with the memory of the man at the ball. She glanced at the clock on the

mantel. Five thirty, the house quiet with sleep and yet
strangely light. Curious, she rose, donning slippers and
a nightgown, and went to investigate, surprising Dumas in the kitchen, his face turning away from hers in
a decidedly guilty way.

'What's wrong?' Brenna's words came quick, her
glance uneasily flicking across his jacket and rain-
spattered boots. 'You've been out? Where's Michael?'

Dumas shifted uncomfortably. 'He said he will be
back after seven.'

Deep furrows creased Brenna's forehead. 'After
seven?' She gasped in disbelief. 'This morning? My
God, Dumas, you left him at the Cartwrights' house
all night? Was he drinking?' It was the only explanation to such an uncharacteristic diversion and the
thought, coupled with their seeing Osborne the previous evening, left her considerably disquietened.

A strange relief visibly crossed into Dumas's eyes
as he nodded his head. 'On instructions I was to return
for him at seven.'

Brenna grimaced, pulling the dressing gown she
wore more tightly about her neck and dragging the
wing chair across towards the fire. 'Then I will wait
here for him to return, Dumas,' she said curtly. Sense
told her that he had deliberately missed out the important details and she dismissed him with less familiarity than she usually employed.

'Oh God, Michael, where are you?' she whispered
into the quietness. The grandfather clock in the hallway chimed six and outside a pale and watery sun
crept into the sky. At least it was dawn. Surely he
would be coming home soon.

She was still pacing up and down the front drawing
room two hours later, eyes peeled to the road outside,

going over and over the last words Michael had left her with the evening before, when a carriage pulled up outside their house and the door opened to reveal just the one she had been frantic for, a black sling in place of his jacket and the Duke of Westbourne at his side.

Rushing to the front door, she flung it open to see what had happened, completely unmindful of her own appearance.

'Good morning, your Grace,' she said primly to Nicholas, barely able to meet his eyes before re-addressing her query to Michael. 'How has this happened?'

She was silenced by Michael's answering look and, taking his good arm instead, brought him inside and made him sit on a chair beside the fire, leaving Nicholas to shut the outside door and follow them in.

'He may need some brandy. It's a gunshot wound.'

'Oh my God, you have been in a fight, Michael, with the Duke?' The words were out before she could stop them, low and horrified, her eyes coming quickly up to Nicholas Pencarrow's as if searching for an answer.

Nicholas was still. 'With me,' he parried, 'but not against me. We were both on the same side.'

Brenna took a breath of relief. 'And who was it, might I ask, you were against?'

'Redmund Osborne,' Michael responded. 'Nicholas shot him dead.'

The room whirled for Brenna as she groped her way to a chair. 'Dead?' she said in a whisper. 'You're sure?'

It was not said in the spirit any other lady of his acquaintance might have phrased it, thought Nicholas suddenly, but rather in a tone of unmitigated relief, and his eyes were dark as he watched her. More secrets, more fears, and the whispered name of a man she had promised she had no memory of. The world of Miss Stanhope came peopled with the ghosts of many troubles, and Brenna, catching his wordless enquiry, turned away from him, willing herself to stamp out the exhilaration she suddenly felt. A second chance, another beginning, where before only an ending had been, and it was the Duke of Westbourne she had to thank again for such an action.

Michael spoke across a widening silence. 'I want you and the Duke to go together to Airelies this weekend to supervise the packing, for I cannot travel like this, Brenna, and Nicholas has said he will go in my stead. You will be chaperoned naturally. Your aunt Elsie will go with you.'

Brenna's mouth fell open at such a preposterous suggestion and she began sternly, 'Of course I would not go—'

Michael interrupted before she managed to get any further. 'Yes Brenna, you will go. I have arranged it and it is what I want and as such I will hear no argument.' The words were so unlike her uncle's that Brenna's anger subsided and she merely sat there, her eyes downcast.

Nicholas turned towards Michael, wanting to be gone from the discussion before the arrangements could be changed, angered at Michael's heavy-handed approach, yet unable to release Brenna himself from a commitment he badly wanted. 'I will see you on Friday, sir,' he said quickly. 'Miss Stanhope…' He turned to Brenna, but she did not raise her head, merely muttering an inaudible goodbye.

At the sound of the carriage departing Brenna leapt up, compliancy replaced instead by renewed anger. 'I won't go with him, Michael, and nothing you can say or do could make me. The whole idea is totally and utterly preposterous and I can't think for the life of me what game it is you are playing. I'm twenty-four now and no longer biddable, not by you, not by Nicholas Pencarrow, not by anyone.' She was shaking as she finished and daring him to reply in any way other than that which she wanted.

'He saved my life, Brenna.' The sentence came bare and soft across her anger and stilled her completely. 'He shot Osborne dead when he turned his gun on me a second time and when the Duke asked for a reason why, I could give him nothing. No, don't turn away...' He caught her with his one good arm. 'Your fears are my own fault. I should not have hidden you away so much. We cannot live in perpetual fear of the Red-mund Osbornes of this world. There are good men out there too. Nicholas Pencarrow is one such good man, Brenna, and I think, as such, he deserves at least a hearing.'

Brenna could not even begin to contemplate his logic. 'A hearing?' she scoffed, her eyes scanning his face just to check he was serious. 'And what of the kiss, Michael? He dragged me into a room at the ball and kissed me.'

'And that is all?' he asked, her answer seemingly important. 'He let you go when you wanted?'

Unsure, she nodded, and he relaxed. 'It's the way of men, Brenna. A kiss can be a shared thing, both given and taken.' But she was listening no more, strid-ing out of the room, disappointment and anger written clearly all over her face with her uncle's uncharacter-istic refusal to listen to such obvious reason.

Chapter Eight

Brenna packed up the last pieces of bread and cheese into a wicker hamper and, adding some oranges and a bottle of wine, pulled the cane handles shut. The knocker sounded just as she finished, and she tensed as Michael opened the door. Today the Duke was dressed in browns, his short tweed jacket thrown casually across breeches and fitted into long well-polished boots, the cravat at his neck soft and barely folded. At least he'd come looking as though he might help her with some of the jobs that would need to be done and she smiled unexpectedly at the thought of him shifting and sorting pieces of furniture.

'Miss Stanhope.' His greeting was wary and Brenna's frown deepened as she sighted the Pencarrow coach, the insignia emblazoned in gold for all to see. Climbing in, she felt as if she had passed some invisible threshold of safety, the feeling jumping to new heights as he made to join her.

She sat across from him, hands clenched at her sides, angrier than she could ever remember at being forced into such a journey. Swallowing, she shifted her position in an effort to distract herself.

Nick watched her. 'You would like a blanket?' he questioned politely, but she merely shook her head and continued to look away from him.

He was not daunted, his own uncertainty diminished with each passing mile as anticipation replaced apprehension. No matter what happened in the next few hours, there would be no way that she could escape his company. No Letitia anxious to have his attention, no duties to see any other soul greeted or farewelled, no strictures, no formalities.

Tentatively he broke the silence. 'My home of Pencarris is roughly an hour and a half away on the Southern Road. Would you be averse to calling in to collect some papers? Your aunt is not due to set out for another three hours so we should still arrive at your home before her.' He looked at his timepiece. 'We could have luncheon at Pencarris as it is past noon.'

Brenna nodded, her spirits sinking. His home. His country house. Would there be other members of the family present to misconstrue their togetherness? His grandmother? His brother? She sighed, for short of rudeness there was little she could do to avoid this proposed detour.

Pencarris came into view after nearly seventy minutes of awkward conversation and before she had expected it. They turned a corner and from her side of the carriage a castle seemed to rise from the trees as if lifted into place by some unseen hand. Shades of Arthur and his sword set in stone and she could almost imagine the banners of an ancient joust flying from the battlements. As they came closer, even the leadlighted windows adorning the many towers glistened in welcome.

'It's beautiful.' Her eyes met his in an honest appraisal of a home she suddenly comprehended to be very important to him. 'Do you come here often?'

'As much as I am able. It's where I grew up.'

The place where Nicholas had been a child! Her eyes wandered to the view of Pencarris and across the gardens, greenly luxuriant; it was all of fifteen minutes after passing through the gates before they finally drew to a halt in front of the house.

As the carriage door opened, Brenna mentally prepared herself for the barrage of servants she expected to materialise at any moment, frowning in bewilderment when they did not. Nicholas himself helped her out and sent the driver back with the horses to the stables behind.

'This is the least peopled of all my houses. It's for the quietness I come here,' he added, watching her.

Her eyes lit up at his confidence. 'In the carriage I thought it looked like a castle straight from Camelot.'

He laughed. 'I used to dream of just that. Guinevere, Lancelot, King Arthur, the fables of valour and battles all have peopled this place in their day and run across the lawn in the shape of two small boys with their father's sword taken from the armoury and without permission. See that belvedere—' he pointed towards the lake; tucked to one side and almost smothered with a large leafless wisteria was a latticed garden house '—Charles and I used to make that Pencarris and we'd defend it forever against the foes of evil and iniquity. Did you do the same at Airelies?' Surprise touched his tawny eyes for, as he looked directly at Brenna, a raw and unguarded sadness spread across her face.

He wanted to catch her to him then and demand what it was that hurt her so, but he could not. Pencarris shimmered behind them as if in a dream and today he wanted all the visions whole and unbroken, for he knew now, no matter what was to come, that he would never desire another woman as he did Brenna Stanhope. The thought made him falter, for he knew too well that love came only at a cost. Yet as Brenna stood before him in her simple navy dress, threadbare almost at the elbows, dark hair blown into long unkempt ringlets, it was as if she and Pencarris were wrapped into the very fabric of all his dreams.

Brenna bit back the retort that had formed at his question. Pencarris made her unwise, she decided, a living fairy tale that had no position in her world; it reminded her with a crushing regretfulness of all the things her own childhood had not been, a birthright gone before she was even one day old.

'I never played such games,' she said, volunteering more to him than she ever had to another person before. 'My battles were more real.'

Nicholas grimaced at the hurt in her words. 'Would it help to talk? I'd be a willing listener.'

Darkness crossed into Brenna's eyes and, without meaning to, and very unexpectedly, she burst into tears, turning from him and walking quickly towards the lake, finding in the belvedere a seat out of eyesight to any who may be looking from the house.

Nicholas, following, leaned against the latticed wall and Brenna caught his gaze and held it firmly, her expression far from the uncertainty he imagined to find there.

The sight of her defiance brought a smile tugging at Nicholas's lips as he forced himself to stay where he was. 'Brenna Stanhope, if I could put an image to Guinevere she would stand full in the shape of you.'

'Oh, no,' Brenna retorted, feeling the potency of what he told her buoy up her spirits. 'Heroines like Guinevere never cried, for they got exactly what they wanted.'

'And what is it you want?'

'Independence!' It was so far from what he'd hoped he remained momentarily speechless as she continued. 'And the right to a freedom that beholds me to no other person as the means to fund my orphanage.'

Crossing his arms, Nicholas's brow arched in speculation. 'As a single woman that may be hard to find.'

Violet eyes brushed over him as if she fought some inner battle, for suddenly she stood so breathless with an idea she hardly knew how to form it.

'I have heard it said that money can be made with wise investments and also that you seem privy to the very wisest of them all.' She stopped, wondering if what she were about to say next would offend him in some way. 'If I was to invest say, one thousand pounds into some scheme you recommended, I'd pay you a dividend, of course.' She continued hurriedly, noticing how he shifted uncomfortably, 'What sort of earnings could I expect to make from such an investment?'

'High risk or low?' he countered implacably, as she scanned his face, trying to decipher his feelings.

'High,' she answered without hesitation, amazed at the sum he forwarded, for, even with a percentage taken, it still made for a very tidy profit.

'Though you do realise the greater the risk, the greater the likelihood of loss, don't you?' Nicholas asked quietly, barely able to contain his amusement at Brenna's calculation of a fortune.

She nodded. 'But I'd have a say in what I wanted to invest in, wouldn't I? You'd give me an idea of likely success?'

'It's the normal practise for an investor to talk over such things.'

'And there'd be no need for any others to know, would there?' The money that she spoke of had been gifted to her by Michael years ago, and as the last of their independent money, she did not want the creditors to know of its existence. 'And no shady deals either?'

He turned away, unable now to keep the mirth from his eyes. Brenna, thinking that she had offended him, jumped to her feet.

'I didn't mean it how it sounded,' she said from behind him. 'I know you to be a gentleman, it's just that making money so easily poses a moral problem for me.'

'It does?' he smiled, glad she could not see his face.

'One person's profit indicates another's loss,' she clarified in all seriousness.

Laughter rang out and tinged his next words as he faced her. 'Brenna, my dear, my money lies in shipping mostly. It's the cargo of the East come to England. Spices, silks, tea, that sort of thing, and I pay their makers handsomely.'

She reddened, both at her mistake and his endearment. 'Of course,' she muttered, the talk of high or low profit ventures having the effect of throwing her right off balance, for all of her experience with gambling had come with misery and degradation, and even in the face of her own desperation she wanted to know that she was not inadvertently furthering any such enterprise. She shuffled uneasily, prickly in defence. 'It's just this is a field new to me, that is all.'

'Women aren't normally interested in finance,' he countered.

'Women aren't normally forced to be,' she returned.

'Some find other means to buoy an empty coffer.' His eyes ran across her in such a way she was left in little doubt as to his meaning and she frowned unsure at the propriety of his suggestion.

'Marriage,' he enlightened her. 'They find a rich man and solve all their problems.'

'Oh!' she spluttered, turning away, his own marriage proposal hanging between them awkwardly, though common sense told her that he could hardly be referring to that! Still, she had to make him understand her own position and she began in an earnest discourse. 'I am a spinster by choice, your Grace, and the title sits easily with me now for it allows a freedom I could never as a young girl have hoped for. I did my season, for God's sake, in a society where the highest accolades go to those who are also the most beautiful, little acknowledgement to the underneath person or to any inherent goodness and honesty there lies concealed beneath a plain exterior. I spent four months in London shifted between rooms like some piece of furniture, lost amongst the charms of other more well-endowed girls and ones far more ready to play the game than I. I never understood their desires, you see, or aspired to their dreams, the lofty heights of the *haut ton* and a group of people I didn't even know about until the night of your ball. I didn't measure people by the amount they made, the beauty of their houses, the grandness of their titles or the suitability of their acquaintances. I didn't then and I still don't now, so the idea of exchanging my financial problems for some well-endowed purse would only be repugnant to say the very least.' She stopped, uncertain that she should say any more and certain she had already said too much. Nicholas listened in amazement.

Did she truly not realise the extent of her own beauty or the forcefulness of her wit? 'Not all people measure others by the criteria you mention, Brenna. There are some who would scoff at the world of the débutante just as you do. Myself, for instance.'

Brenna broke quickly across his words. 'No, that can't be, for are you not the very ones who profit from its existence?'

'Profit?' he returned implacably. 'How so profit?'

'You all find suitable wives amongst their ranks, do you not?'

'I never found one,' Nicholas replied.

'Well, I am almost certain you will, for they are like flowers. Every year there is a new bunch for you to pick from.'

Nicholas, intrigued by her lack of guile in seeing her own self as a candidate, said carefully, 'I'd be interested to know, as you are a graduate of the débutante system, what it is you think I should be on the lookout for?'

Brenna coloured, certain he was jesting with her until she looked at his face. There was an air of such seriousness apparent she tethered in her own cynicism and tried to answer him in kind.

'As a failed member of the corps I may not be the best person to give advice, but I think, your Grace, you should watch for those whose mothers seem to control their every move, and I also think the truly beautiful ones to be equally as dangerous.' Dark eyebrows raised in puzzlement and Brenna continued with renewed intent. 'They need only cultivate their outward appearance, you see, and in doing so they forget about the inward one.'

'You think, then, it is impossible to be both beautiful and clever?'

Brenna thought about his question for a moment before answering. 'From my experience one definitely seems to preclude the other.'

Shaking his head, Nicholas extended his arms, turned her towards him and Brenna felt again that pure bolt of recognition. 'I know of one who has both and in abundance.'

Me. He is talking about me. Her blood beat loud in her ears from such an admission. *Beautiful and clever* and as far from teasing as she had ever seen him. And in that moment, framed in the beauty of all that was Pencarris, Nicholas was to Brenna the embodiment of a prince from the world of fairy tales, his words perilously real and wonderfully sweet. He had proclaimed to her what he would not to all the hopeful young girls of the season and in doing so he gave her a position, if just for a moment, far from the one she had always held in society. She felt exhilarated and triumphant, the careful control that swathed her normally like a blanket, like a talisman, like a memory, washed away under his sensuous dark-green gaze.

'Nicholas.' The name tripped from her tongue in a silent whisper. 'I cannot understand what it is that is happening between us, but it must stop.'

'I would always protect you, Brenna,' he said quietly, unprepared for the hurt that crossed into her eyes.

'From what?' she challenged, tipping her face up to his and surprised as his finger brushed her cheek.

'From whatever it is you fear.'

She felt the warmth with a jagged longing and stopped herself from leaning into him. Strength, certainty and power. And the promise of protection. A heady pledge indeed. She could smell the scent of his man's body and sense the fire inside. *If only she were Louisa... If only she were braver... But if he ever found out...*

Her eyes came up to his in confusion and fear, but also in a softer desperation. And it was this more than anything that made Nicholas rein in his charm and sheath the pressure he longed to exert in order to break through her reserve. He stepped back and gestured to the coach.

'We'd better be off, Brenna, for the road becomes dangerous after dark and I would be loath to be caught on it.'

Especially with a woman as tempting as you, he wanted to add, but wisely didn't.

Airelies came into sight before evening, and Brenna was both sad and pleased to see it, for this would be the last time she came here as mistress of the place, with the sale deeds going through before the end of the month and the new owners taking possession.

Looking around as they swept through the front gates, she could see the age of Airelies in a way she never had before, the driveway bumpy with the roots of trees and the building itself sporting many broken tiles and a rusty guttering.

'It looks a bit sad after Pencarris,' she found herself saying apologetically. 'Though I used to think it was the most beautiful house in all of England when I was growing up.'

Nick's eyes took in the more obvious problems. 'If you were the new owner and could do just as you wished, what would you do to change it?'

She smiled, his question one she had often wistfully asked herself of late. 'Not much. A few tiles and the garden. Mostly I like it just as it is, but Michael says the new owners will refurbish it completely. They'll probably knock that piece off for a start.' She gestured towards a low outbuilding on one end of the double-storeyed manor house. 'But that would be a great mistake for that's the lightest part of the whole place and even in winter the sunshine slants on an angle almost to the back wall. We used it as a conservatory and I had my piano there.' She stopped, amazed she had offered him so much.

'And where is your piano now?' Nicholas asked softly.

'Oh, we sold it. I have the orphanage one now and it's every bit as good,' she continued quickly, not wanting him to see how much the sale had hurt at the time.

She lied with a straight face and Nicholas, watching her, felt his chest tighten in a way he could never remember feeling before meeting her. Out of sheer self-preservation he tried to change the mood.

'And the gardens, what would you like to see done out here?'

Laughing, a spark of pure joy came to her eyes. 'I'd fill them with roses and lavender and foxgloves and delphiniums, and down there...' she gestured to the river '...I'd build a gazebo just like yours and I'd have a bridge to cross the stream to a field filled with daffodils.'

'Quite a scheme,' Nicholas commented, intrigued by

her lilting speech and by the dimples that played near her mouth. 'Did you think to ever turn your hand to garden design?'

'No, but perhaps I should…' She tailed off, humour tingeing her words.

'Why?' He couldn't help but ask.

'I could offer my services to the new owner and use the wages to invest in your schemes.'

She was teasing, though he took her words at face value. 'I would lend you and Michael money, Brenna. You know you only need ask.'

Firmly she shook her head, embarrassed by his suggestion. 'No, we're fine really. We got a good price for Airelies and the rest of Michael's property is very safe.' It was untrue, of course, but for now she could proffer nothing else. All these questions. Did he know more than he was letting on? Had Michael even talked with him, perhaps? God forbid, if that was the case he would know everything she said to be lies! Her eyes flicked up to his, trying to read his mood and, taking comfort from the warmth evident in his answering smile, she changed the subject, ushering him into the hall of Airelies with pride.

Mrs Fenton met them as they turned into the conservatory, smiling when she spied Nicholas, her eyes awash with unhidden curiosity. 'Oh, it's you again, sir. The one with the gun Miss Brenna rescued down in the copse.'

Nicholas inclined his head to her slightly and answered without rancour, 'The very same, only this time I managed to get an invitation inside.'

Both women looked uncomfortable as Brenna made the introductions. 'Mrs Fenton, this is Nicholas Pencarrow.' She gave him no title, knowing that to do so would be to throw the housekeeper completely into a panic. 'Michael felt that with all the trouble around here lately that it might be wise to be accompanied by a…' she hesitated, trying to find the right word '…protector.' Her words left him with a resounding impression of laughter and challenge. Here at Airelies she seemed to find a footing that was missing in London, the seriousness of living and running an orphanage buried, a little, by the child who had grown up here. Another piece to the puzzle, he thought, though, in the presence of Mrs Fenton, he deemed it wiser to turn his mind to other things.

The last few hours before supper were spent looking through the house, Nicholas interested in both its layout and the many memories of Brenna's youth.

One of the rooms on the darker side of the building was filled with drawings encased in golden frames. Brenna with her dogs, Brenna on the swing, Brenna and Michael in the garden, Brenna rowing her boat. The lack of the presence of any others intrigued Nicholas.

'Were there any others your age in the neighbourhood for you to make friends with?' he felt prompted to ask.

Brenna hesitated, her glance skimming across the wall, noticing her aloneness in a way she never had before, seen as it was from an outsider's point of view. She shook her head slowly, taking time to answer. 'I liked being with Michael and I had Dumas as well as Mrs Fenton. She'd make me picnics and we'd eat out on the lawn in the summer when it was hot, and Albert the gardener would give me rides in his wheelbarrow right down to the lake and threaten to push me in.'

She'd warmed up to it now and without meaning to kept going, each word telling Nicholas more and more of the solitary girl she'd been, ensconced at Airelies with only the servants and an elderly unmarried uncle.

'I remember once seeing a whole lot of children together in Marbank, another village a few miles from here. It must have been a school outing, I suppose.' She frowned and tilted her head as if trying to remember. 'I felt frightened by all of their energy and noise. Michael at first wanted me to go to a private school for young ladies in Wickham and he insisted so forcibly we actually went…' She stopped and turned uncomfortably towards him, the memory of the retelling nearly every bit as painful as the reality.

'And what happened?' Nick's voice came softly across her confusion.

'I was so sick that the teacher brought me home even before the day had finished and I didn't move from my bed for two months.' Dark eyes ran over his surprise. 'I was nervous, you see,' she continued as if by way of explanation, 'and much more inclined to the peace and harmony here.' She gestured to the house around them. 'You had Pencarris and dreams, I had Airelies.'

And nightmares, she almost added, stopping herself even as she thought it.

'Then it must be hard to see it sold.'

Turning away, she answered with practised nonchalance, 'Home is where you make it and Michael is getting older. He needs a cosier, smaller place nearer to London and his businesses.' She suddenly hated lying to Nicholas, who looked faintly curious at her reasoning, causing her to wonder again if he knew more of Michael's financial position than she gave him credit for. Wanting no further introspection, she turned on her heel, leading him away from the inside memories and out instead to the gardens, which lay at the back of the house.

'My grandmother planted those,' Brenna said, pointing to azaleas and rhododendrons that framed the far hills, vivid colour when in blossom amongst the unending English green. 'She was a wonderful woman, according to all that was written of her. She lived alone here for nearly sixty years. Her husband was killed, you see, before he was thirty, and she lived to be ninety-seven. Sixty-seven years of vigilance remembering a man who, finally, was younger than her own grandsons grew to become. Michael said he'd watch her observing his father's portrait each morning before breakfast and talking to him in the end as she had done right in the beginning. An old lady asking for help from the likeness of a lover forever young.' She smiled. 'I used to think it was the saddest story I ever knew of until I realised she had the vision of a man who would never escape her and never let her down.' Challenging eyes met Nicholas's who answered in kind.

'And never warm her bed or hold her through a thousand lonely nights?' He'd expected shock, but dimples showed instead.

'Oh, no, you have it all wrong for she liked the local minister and he her. On Sundays they'd celebrate the week's passing with roast dinner and it was rumoured that he never went home until the dawn.'

Laughter echoed across the glade as Nicholas contemplated all that she had told him. 'I like this woman more and more,' he said when he had finally caught his breath. 'What was her name?'

'Charity De Lancey.' Her own reply matched his in delight, and fresh laughter erupted as they went to view the gardens planted at the end of another century.

It was almost midnight and Brenna rolled around fitfully in her bed, pulling up the feather eiderdown to cover her coldness and willing herself into a sleep that seemed far from coming. Her mind rolled over the events of the day. Pencarris. Airelies.
Nicholas.

Everything had been lovely! Lunch by the lake, dinner by a roaring fire that had been built in the small dining room. Even Aunt Elsie joined in the card games the Duke had set up to amuse them both, laughter ringing through the night as they each tried their hands fruitlessly to beat him. Brenna smiled as she remembered it all. How fitting her love of Airelies should end so happily. Today her world had been readjusted. Changed. Altered forever. New emotions scorched her body and they all centred on just one person.

Nicholas.

Her heart thudded loudly as she conjured up his face, eyes alight with the promise of laughter and protection. And that something else that she could still give no name to. Warmth covered her cheeks, though a movement outside her room alerted her to someone's presence. There was a creaking of the floorboard she knew to avoid and the handle in her room turned in a stealthy silence. The breath froze in her mouth as she sat up, ready to leap from the bed should the visitor proceed any further. Who could it be? Why would anyone come here unless…?

'Oh my God.' The words were torn from her as she

jumped from the bed, a black-masked stranger bursting in and striding towards her.

'You're to come with me, lovie. Led us a dance you have, but someone wants a word with you.' Dark eyes gleamed through the slits in the mask as he brought one hand across her breast, squeezing the fullness hard, the other hand gripping the back of her nightgown. The scream, which had died in her throat to a mere gurgle, resurfaced as she regained her sense of self-defence, and she lashed out with such force and so unexpectedly that the intruder dropped away, tearing her gown before he let go, allowing her to run straight through her door and into Nicholas's room in search of shelter. In her panic she pushed the door full against its hinges, which had the effect of sending Nicholas bolt upright in his bed and out of it before she realised he was naked, the moonlight slanting against his golden body. Even in the midst of her own fears she could not fail to register his sheer masculine beauty and the long lines of muscle and bone caught in the half-light. Strength, power and safeness. She shivered as he drew her into his warmth.

'What is it, Princess?' His voice was husky.

'There's a man…he tried to grab me.'

Nicholas was gone from the room in a second, gathering his dressing gown as he went. He strode out of sight, and she heard him shouting orders to his men before he returned five minutes later, a grim look on his face.

'He's gone,' he began slowly, retracing his steps to stand before her. Looking down, his whole body stiffened at what he saw. Where her nightgown, high-necked and long-sleeved, had been ripped across her back it now hung down limply to her waist, revealing two unmistakable scars of a whiplash raised in the beam of the mantelpiece lamp.

'My God,' he groaned, pulling her towards the light and turning her around so that he could get a better look at what he scarcely believed to be there. 'Who did this to you, Brenna? Who hurt you in such a way?'

Brenna threw his hands away and shrank from him. Unshed tears of hot shame shone brightly in her eyes now that he had seen the badges of that which she had tried so hard to hide forever.

'I shouldn't have come in here,' she began uncertainly, heading for her own room and cursing herself for not realising earlier the state of her night attire. But she was not to be so lightly let off, for Nicholas Pencarrow had had enough and he was at the door before she was, slamming the portal shut and ramming the bolt home.

'Now, Brenna,' he said softly and with deadly intent as he rounded on her, grabbing her wrists and holding her still. 'Now you are going to tell me how a girl well cosseted in a family of unquestionable name came by such abuse, and,' he added in a voice even lower, 'it had better dammed well be the truth.'

'I won't tell you!' she shouted, trying to loosen his fingers and pushing at the hands that held her, tears of frustration pouring down across her cheeks as he turned her into his own body, pinning her from behind into stillness, hard-thewed arms closing like steel bands across her movements.

He would hate her now. Hate her and despise her and expose her. Everything was finished, over. Black despair spiralled inwards as shaking tore through her whole body in violent spasms of shock, her breath coming harsh and desperate. Her eyes flitted across to the window. No escape there. She knew also the door to be impossible to unbolt in the time she would need to prise it free. Wide eyes, dark with supplication, met his.

'Please, Nicholas, let me go.' Her voice was an aching whisper.

'I can't,' he returned. 'Damn it, I can't.'

The words tumbled into her mind like a death knell. The final turning of a key in a lock between now and then; a sentiment pronounced in the very vortex of choicelessness, for it left her suddenly with the knowledge that, without the truth, she would hurt Nicholas in a way he would never understand, and with it, she would hurt him in a way he would not want to.

He had killed a man to salvage her name and helped her in ways that left her mind awhirl with gratitude. And finally, in that moment, just before he would be snatched away forever, she realised his friendship had meant more than she had ever been prepared to admit. Green eyes flinted dangerously as the firelight slanted across his face, darkening his tan and lightening his hair. The tick of a muscle in his cheek was all that broke his stillness. Everything about him was masculine, and strong and right. And he deserved at least an explanation.

'I was born Brenna De Lancey and became Brenna Cray all in the space of the first day of my life. Daphne and Fenton De Lancey had six daughters, you see, and I was their seventh...' She stopped and swallowed, unable to go on. Her voice felt shaky and shallow. She was amazed when Nicholas's words came to fill in the silence.

'George De Lancey, tow-haired and large and very different from his sisters, took your rightful place until his death, your father following his only son in a matter of months, so great was his sorrow, and your mother tripped from reason into insanity, overcome finally with the guilt at having swapped her youngest daughter.'

Eyes raw with grief lifted to his. 'You found out this about me?' she questioned.

He nodded. 'I went up to York two weeks ago and met your mother and sister Charlotte. The portrait on the wall let me see both your absence from and your likeness to a family that should have been yours.' He stopped. 'I also know that Redmund Osborne threatened you in a way I could never fathom. Was it he who did this to you?'

Pain crossed her face and also surrender and, dropping her forehead to his chest, she took refuge in the contact…for the first time and for the last time. She felt the sharp pang of loss as his warmth burnt into her skin. With a swallow she began, her voice sounding strange even to her own ears. 'He came to the brothel my foster parents owned. The place I was brought up in…'

Nick felt his heart slam into his chest. 'You were brought up where?' He hadn't heard her right, surely, and he bent to listen again.

'A brothel in York,' Brenna whispered, tears gathering in her eyes as she did so.

'Lord, Brenna,' he said shakily. 'Lord,' he repeated. 'You were a…' He couldn't say *whore*, couldn't make the word come as disbelief lodged in his throat.

'No. 'Tis not as you think. I grew up in a brothel, but I was not like…' She stopped. Loyalty to Louisa and Helena and Miriam stopped her. All girls with even less choice than she had had; and years of judgement from others had made her wary of righteous truths. *Not like them? Not like that?* Swallowing, she summoned her last shreds of dignity and faced him directly. 'The blood money my mother paid the Crays played on their conscience once or twice, and Brian Cray was no novice as a whiphand. Louisa, Helena, Miriam and I could die or survive. We chose to live.'

'Louisa Greling?' He could barely splutter the name of Francis's mistress. 'To live? How?' He was shouting now and furious. 'Like this with your nightdress shredded over whiplash scars and the faces of men you once knew intimately popping up at every social function.' His eyes darkened as he let her go, one hand threading through tawny hair. 'A brothel. My God, Brenna, with your experience how you must have laughed at my paltry proclamations of want.' His tone was cutting and derogatory as he turned away towards the wall, slamming his fist into the hardness. The plaster shuddered and gave way; as he pulled back to slam it again she noticed blood on his knuckles. 'It was all an act with me, then? Right from the start? You played everything false?'

'No,' she whispered, almost voiceless, and hating the red fiery anger in his eyes. 'It was not like that.'

'Not like Redmund Osborne said it to be?' She winced at the tone of his words. 'I shot him as a liar, Brenna. I shot him because you called him so. You had me shoot a man in cold blood for a lie that was your own and still you did not tell me?'

'I could not tell—'

He cut her off. 'When would have you told me then? After I had killed a dozen more? Never?'

The fine sheen of sweat on his forehead gleamed against the light. Already anger was distancing them, leaving them as strangers. No middle ground, she thought, no pathway to another understanding. She tried to bridge the widening chasm as she began to speak, quietly at first and then with more resonance.

'I couldn't tell you, don't you see, and I warned you of that right from the start. At Worsley when you returned the gun, in London when you came with words of thanks, at the party you threw at your house and at the ball. I was just trying to protect you from me, and I told you that. I told you all the time, but you heard only what you wanted to, enjoying the mystery of my circumstances, imagining only small transgressions, little unimportant faults in a character you knew nothing of in the first place.'

Tears filled her eyes as he caught her glance and she could plainly see his loathing, and though she wished him gone she had not, as yet, finished her explanation of a past that finally she would not be blamed for. 'I wasn't quite one day old when I came to the Crays and twelve when Michael finally rescued me. Twelve years in a place which would put me outside proper society forever, no matter who might deem it different.' Her voice broke, but she made herself continue. 'You asked me once what it was I truly desired and I told you I wanted independence. Because that is all that is left to me, don't you understand. There *is* nothing else.'

Turning away, her teeth pinched at her upper lip as she willed pain to delay the collapse she knew would come.

Nicholas. Nicholas. Even his name was beautiful. But she wanted him to see her strong, purposeful, sailing well on the course she'd plotted for herself in a life that gave him no footing to accompany her. She didn't need his pity, his anger, his regrets. They were but weak counterpoints to the power of his adulation, which had, until only moments ago, been hêrs. Soon he would be gone and she knew as the Duke of Westbourne, and head of a family that could trace its lineage back a thousand years, he would never be back.

Nicholas watched her and breathed in deeply, trying to regain control, all the illusions of the girl before him so shattered he could barely think or talk as the truth sank in. No wonder she'd refused his offer of marriage, for with this knowledge she'd entrusted him with, he would never have made it. Brenna Stanhope De Lancey's past precluded a future between them. Cut off from innocence and rightness as she was, left forever in a no man's land, still peopled with those who might have known her once. Tiredness and uncertainty etched his face as anger changed into unfathomable loss. Nothing made sense any more. He could neither refute her arguments nor refuse his logic, for she had placed him as far from herself as anyone ever could. Stepping back towards the door, he gathered his clothes.

'We will talk of this again, Brenna, one day when we can both cope better. Right now I am returning to London. Robertson and Thompson can stay here to watch over the house and I will send back the carriage for you and Elsie in due course.' He stopped, unable to say more, and she didn't even turn as he left, merely closing her eyes in order to listen better to the sound of his going.

Nicholas spent the remainder of that night and the next day at his club in London, gambling away a fortune on hands of cards he cared little about. Word reached Charles by the second day. He came quickly from Hertfordshire, bounding into White's with the speed of one with the devil well set on his heels. The room smelled of wine, smoke and the stale odour of drinking. Nicholas's voice, slurred with the effects of alcohol, reached his ears even before he saw him.

'Come on, James,' he admonished. 'If you don't play there'll be someone else willing enough to step in and I'd rather lose to a friend.' Harsh laughter followed and the scraping of chairs as both stood, and Charles watched in amazement as Nicholas took a drunken swing at Lord James Weatherby, a friend for nigh on twenty years. Missing, he fell in a heap to the ground, too befuddled even to rise.

James spied Charles and came across to him. 'Thank God you're here,' he said in obvious relief. 'I can't get him to quit and I daren't leave him to play with the others who'd be bound to take the advantage.' He fished into his pockets for what seemed to be close to fifty chits for IOUs. 'Here's his losings, though I doubt if he honoured all his promises he'd actually have much left to play with.'

Charles looked at the papers placed in his hands. Yachts, houses, horses and gold. A warmth spread unbidden to his eyes.

'Thank you, James,' he said quietly. 'If you could just help me get him into my carriage, I'll take him home. Do you know what happened?'

James shook his head. 'He talked of a betrayal. At first I thought it was a woman he meant, but later I wondered if it was not something of his own making of which he spoke, and a name was mentioned: Brenna.'

Charles nodded. He'd never seen Nick like this before. In the face of all calamities, no matter how serious, his brother had always managed a calm and reasonable stance. Looking at him now, his hair tousled and cravat askew, the growth of a few days' stubble shadowing his jaw, he seemed totally unlike the brother Charles had always known so well.

'Come on, Nick,' James said quietly as they carried the Duke's half-conscious form between them and out into the night, observed keenly by the rest of London's society men, interested in this latest scandal from the Duke of Westbourne.

They reached Hertfordshire in a matter of hours, Nicholas sitting quietly and unwilling to volunteer anything to Charles's gentle prodding.

'It's Brenna Stanhope, isn't it? James said you had mentioned her name.'

Tawny eyes filled with pain rounded on his brother, the strong slur of spirits still in his voice. 'Do you have your flask, Charlie? I need a drink.'

His brother shook his head. 'I think you've had enough tonight.'

'No, damnation, I haven't had anywhere near enough. I need to forget and all I do is remember.' He flung an arm across his eyes, willing his visions of Brenna away. Brenna at the piano, Brenna at his ball in a remarkable gown, Brenna at Airelies her back crossed with the lashes of a brothel. 'I wanted her.' His voice came broken and low. 'I wanted her so damned much and now I can never have her.'

Charles swallowed back his concern and spoke in earnest. 'I don't understand the problem.'

'No, neither do I, and that's the worst of it.' He was talking cryptically now and Charles, understanding not a word, merely sat and listened to his brother's ramblings. 'Don't you see, Charles…she needed me as much as anyone ever will and I walked out.' His knuckles ached, the physical pain seeping through his mind to dull the mental one. 'I walked out on her like all the rest, as bad as them, her parents, her foster parents, her sisters, and the brother who never was. No one except for Michael has ever given a fig for her and now he's fighting bankruptcy, and I can't do a thing to help her. I can't.'

Charles sifted through the monologue, trying to piece the parts together and make some sense of the whole. 'Does she love you?' he asked.

Nicholas shook his head and closed his eyes against the pain of the question. 'No, she never did,' he whispered so quietly that Charles had to strain to hear. 'And now she never will.' The curse of his father was coming true, the reality as damning to him as it had been to Gerald.

Anguish engulfed him, the final certainty of the loss crowding in on him and sending his thoughts racing over other alternatives. He'd go to India aboard *The Kristina* next month. She was long overdue to sail and the trip promised to be an extended one. Twelve weeks in the tropics right now would suit him admirably, away from violet eyes and fears with which he could no longer cope.

Brenna Stanhope was no more a dream for him to consider his own. Her past was too full to ever warrant another proposal. She was dead to him now, just as certainly as anyone could be. He'd keep on with his payments to the orphanage for the sake of the children, but that would be the end of it. He never wanted to see or hear of her again. She'd tricked him in a way, she and Michael privy to a secret so terrible it should never have got to the point of being told. And he had been a fool to let himself believe they could have had a life together.

The air from the opened door rushed in on his face and interrupted him from his thoughts.

'We're here.' Charles's voice came as if from far away. 'Do you need a hand?'

Nicholas shook his head and tried to rise, his legs buckling beneath him and Charles's arms acting as a crutch under his own. The night sky above them was bleak and endless, not even a small moon anywhere in sight to break the dark. Nick, for a moment, pressed his brother close, holding him tightly against the reality of what it was he had just discovered.

The dreams of the son of Camelot had faded noticeably in the last thirty-six hours.

Chapter Nine

London—April 1862

The day was lovely as Brenna checked again the address on the small embossed card in her hand, which had arrived four days prior. She knew the brief letter attached from Lady Brentwood almost off by heart: *Perhaps you could come to a small luncheon party I am holding on Friday and speak about Beaumont Street. While I cannot promise the patronage of the others present, I do commit myself to the expenditure of some moneys and would very much like to be included on your list of benefactors.*

Such a sentiment needed following up and as Brenna alighted from the horse-drawn omnibus and proceeded to Clarence Street, dressed in her customary navy-blue velvets, she was amazed to find none of her nervousness or apprehension anywhere left on show.

The past four months had robbed her of a fear of discovery that she had found, after Nicholas's departure, to be much less daunting than she had always anticipated. No bailiff had arrived at her doorstep, no outraged group of society ladies and gentlemen had withdrawn their funds from Beaumont Street, no telling gossip had reached her ears. Indeed, the very opposite was true, for suddenly her orphanage had become rather a fashionable thing, and every day now another invitation arrived to ask her to speak about her children.

Smiling, she looked up at the sky and felt the thin warm sun of April upon her face. Her exposure at Worsley had forced her to grow up in a way she'd never before been made to and she refused to let her mind wander on different possibilities, for just thinking about Nicholas made everything ache. She was a woman in charge of who she was and what she believed in, no longer looking back across her shoulder watching for the past to pounce. It had pounced at Airelies and she had survived, just as she had survived her childhood in Yorkshire with the Crays. She smiled and forced herself to breathe. Still surviving. Still here. Still partly alive even without Nicholas Pencarrow in her life, though goodness, how she missed him.

Stopping before an ornate and beautiful town house in one of the prettiest streets of London, Brenna bustled forth and strode up the path. The doorknocker sounded quietly across the daytime noises and she smiled at the butler who escorted her into a salon filled with twenty or so well-dressed and older women. As she looked more carefully, she noted some men in an adjoining room who appeared engrossed in something in a glass case on the far side of the wall.

Lady Brentwood, the Countess of Hammond, rose from her place on the sofa as she caught sight of the young Miss Stanhope and, raising her hand, signalled for quiet in the room, which was filled with chatter. Brenna glanced at those closest to her, lost in the sea of names the Countess was reciting, though fazed suddenly by the only one that she had feared ever to hear again.

'The Duke of Westbourne and his grandmother, the Dowager Duchess.'

His face came around from the other side of the room at the mention of his name and she caught his eyes across a sea of shoulders, greener than she remembered but every bit as cold. She felt the beat of her heart waver palpably. If Nicholas had meant to unmask her he'd have done so before now, though she knew by the gossip he'd been away in India. Brenna weighed her odds quickly and recognised safety. If her secret were out she'd hardly be here and the occasion was too important to waste on mere conjecture. She'd need to trust in her instincts and all of them told her of the Duke of Westbourne's continuing confidentiality.

With disquiet she cleared her throat, waiting for the Countess to find her seat and, mindful now of a silence that had settled across the room, she looked directly at Nicholas Pencarrow and began, 'A person told me once that no one's future is hopeless or changeless or barren despite what has come before, and I like to believe in that.'

Nicholas smiled, recognising his own words from almost half a year before, and as she noted his slight response her eyes shifted to the others present. She spent the next quarter of an hour giving a basic outline of her hopes for Beaumont Street, ending by giving thanks to all present for their time and patience, though deliberately not looking towards the back. The room filled with appreciative comments, all inspired by the beauty and humbleness of the orphanage's young founder and caught in a vision of a world set right in its wrongness, and also much interested in the personal magnetism of Miss Brenna Stanhope herself.

Lady Brentwood read the moment perfectly as she led Brenna across to a large piano at the end of the room and enquired as to whether her young guest would deem to favour the assembly with just one simple tune, for it was rumoured the girl was wonderfully good at playing.

Nick straightened at the prospect, his attention now firmly caught, and Brenna coloured. Uncertainly she looked around, catching Nicholas's eyes the first second she did so. The unspoken challenge in them was enough to make her sit on the piano stool and run her fingers across the keys.

An odd feeling of animation swept over her as she played 'An Die Musik' by Schubert, her fingers working the ivory keys in complete harmony with the tune, eyes closed as she breathed in the loveliness of the sounds, and the room was silent when she finished. As Brenna looked around in confusion the quietness turned into enthusiastic applause and Brenna was embarrassed by the Countess's subsequent outpouring of superlatives. 'Miss Stanhope, you are both an angel and an artist, and I am certain the patrons here today will be more than generous in their remunerations for already I see offers of help.'

Elizabeth, the Dowager Duchess, approached her at the end of the queue, extending her hand and holding Brenna's warmly. 'You play far better than Nick does,' she said simply, 'and we all thought him to be good.'

Dimples left Brenna's cheeks as the subject of their conversation came to join his grandmother. 'I didn't know you played, your Grace,' she said with difficulty, noticing both the tan on his face, which suited him so well, and the grimace in his eyes as he caught the words.

'Compared to you I don't,' he answered shortly, before turning to his grandmother. 'Grandmama, would you excuse us for just one moment. I have a business matter to discuss with Miss Stanhope.'

'Of course, dear,' Elizabeth answered immediately, intrigued by the defences Nicholas seemed to have built instantaneously about himself. She knew him too well to know it as offhandedness, for a beautiful woman had never elicited that response before.

Looking around, Nicholas noticed the back room to be empty of people, all now grouped in the front salon about a table laden with a well-appointed luncheon, and Brenna allowed him to guide her across to an alcove where she stood framed against the window, her eyes raised to his in enquiry.

Nicholas ran his hands through his hair. He'd forgotten how amazing the colour of her eyes were so close up.

'You look well.' His voice was guarded.

'You do too,' she countered, a flicker of unsureness on her face. Surely he hadn't sought out her company merely to tell her this? That game was long over and they both knew it.

'I got home from the east to find your name everywhere. They call you the Nun of Beaumont Street in my circle now. Did you know that, Brenna?'

She coloured, sure now that he was making fun of her, and turned to leave, but he caught at her wrist, and she felt a shock akin to pain run through her at the contact.

'No. We need to talk.' His voice dropped into a

husky whisper and her wide eyes turned again to his, lost in the familiarity of him and sensing again that thinly concealed power that lay barely below the surface of Nicholas Pencarrow's personality.

'I think we long ago said all there is to say, your Grace,' she enunciated quietly, noticing already the looks directed towards them by the others present. Her glance lowered tellingly to his hand, which still circled her wrist. Instantly he let her go.

She took some steps towards the others before re-thinking her plan and turning slightly. 'I've built a world around myself that you may laugh at and others misinterpret, but 'tis all I have to work with, a fragile barrier against a past I try now not to think too deeply about.' The words came hard but she had to say them, had to make him know what it was she had become, a true believer in the possibilities he used to understand.

He nodded briefly and watched her leave, making no move to follow, instead turning to one of the servants, asking him to bring a straight and liberal brandy.

Elizabeth joined him as he sipped the last of the drink.

'You knew Brenna Stanhope would be here today when you asked me, didn't you?' His voice came barely civil.

Elizabeth swallowed and raised her eyes to squarely look at him. 'I do not normally interfere in your life, Nicholas, but in this case I have made an exception, for I know just how you are feeling—'

'What the hell is that supposed to mean?' He cut off her words before she could explain. 'You could have no idea of my feelings, Grandmama, and I would have your spoken promise that in the future you will not interfere as you have today.' He was as angry as he had ever been with her, a situation exacerbated by Brenna's effect on him and by the unresolved tensions that seeing her again had forced him into confronting. His gaze rested on the other guests crowded around the table, hemming in his explanations.

God, how he longed suddenly for the country, for the wide open spaces, away from the intrigues of society and his position in it. He swallowed and softened his tone, seeing his grandmother's worry and her love shining through the hurt of his anger, her familiarity dear, suddenly, amidst all that was strange.

'Come, let us join the others,' he said in a quieter tone, liking it as she curled her arm through his.

Brenna sat in the carriage she had hailed, barely able to take enough breath. She felt sick. She felt exhilarated. She felt desperately lonely.

Nicholas. Nicholas. Nicholas.

Nothing could have prepared her for the sight of seeing him again, touching him, hearing his voice... A shaking hand came up to her mouth. Today he had seemed distant and reserved, all of the 'Peer of the Realm' on show and none of the man. Wealth, manners, tradition and expectations covered him like a cloak. Gone was the man she had joked with at Airelies and danced with at Pencarrow House. Gone was the teasing Duke on the lawns of Pencarris when he had offered her more than simple respect. In his place stood a harder, more detached man who might have once admired her but now...

She felt his loss like a blow. What was it he had said they called her in society...the Nun of Beaumont Street? With his acquired knowledge of her background, how he must have laughed at such a description. And yet he had never betrayed her. Extracting a handkerchief from her reticule, she blew her nose and wiped her eyes. This hopeful introspection would never do. Nicholas Pencarrow's world was at the opposite end of the scale to hers, the superficiality of society juxtaposed against the real need of her starving East End orphans.

'Forget him.' The words were torn from her throat and echoed grimly around the little carriage. Nicholas Pencarrow was dangerous to everything she had become and everything she had worked for and if these baser untried feelings that blossomed within her at the mere sight of him were allowed to flourish, then everything would be put at risk.

Taking a deep breath, she sat up and tidied herself. Nothing and nobody would destroy the independence she had worked so hard for. She was old enough to be over all these girlish feelings and hopeless dreams. Folding up her handkerchief, she stuffed it in her purse and rapped her hand against the door of the conveyance. At least a mile in distance from home, she calculated happily. A brisk walk through the streets should dissipate the feeling of restless energy that swirled through her.

Nicholas saw Brenna again before the week was out, and he realised as he stepped into the foyer of the Royal Children's Hospital that, as much as he may wish it to be different, the two worlds they inhabited would at times collide.

Letitia at his side laughed loudly. ''Tis the Stanhope girl, is it not, Nicholas? My God, what is she dressed in?'

Amanda Wharton beside them seemed happy to explain. 'A puce sack, I think. Belinda Turner was saying just the other day what dreadful taste Brenna Stanhope seems to have.'

Letitia smothered a giggle and Nicholas turned away. He wished not to be confronted again by his memories, his anger and frustration of the other day still sorely testing him, and a hardness crept into his face as he struggled to control his annoyance.

Brenna, looking up at just that moment, caught his irritation and swallowed nervously, smoothing down the skirt of her dress as she perused this afternoon's programme. Her own spirit of confidence, however, reasserted itself, given Nicholas Pencarrow's lack of want to come any closer, and she turned to Frederick Castleton to give him back the paper he had so kindly lent her.

'Does it look too boring?' he asked, surprising her with a bawdy wink.

'Oh, no,' she faltered and moved towards Kate. 'Not at all.' Given he was one of the patrons of the place, she could scarcely say different, though the addresses looked to be long and numerous and the Duke of Westbourne's name, she noticed, was almost at the top. He was a board member too! She had not known that, but of course, why should he not be? She swallowed carefully and tried to concentrate on what was going on around her.

Letitia watched Frederick Castleton's solicitousness, and that of half a dozen other young men about Brenna Stanhope, with a mounting scorn.

'You would think she'd realise what a reprobate

Freddy is, wouldn't you?' she said with feeling to
Amanda Wharton and loud enough for Nicholas to
overhear.

'Oh, they say he's the essence of a gentleman
around Brenna Stanhope, Letty. All the men are, actually, when I give it thought. It seems she brings out
the protectiveness in them. Can't for the life of me see
the reason, but there it is. Why, Catherine Sloane heard
that Freddy fills the flask he always carries about with
him with tea when he calls on the Beaumont Street
Orphanage, and Bramwell Carstairs is rumoured to
have written a poem especially for her, and lewd and
common it is not. And the other day at Lady Brentwood's she is said to have delivered a rendition of
Schubert on the piano so awe-inspiring that all present
dropped to their knees and kissed her hem.'

Letty pulled a face and turned to Nicholas. 'You
were at Lady Brentwood's the other day, Nicholas. Did
you partake in such adulation?'

Hard eyes came slowly up to hers as he drew deeply
on the newly lighted cigar and his answer was flat and
cold.

'Miss Stanhope played the piano and received the
customary praise, nothing as vulgar as Amanda retells
it, but if society needs to embroider the merely dull to
make it more palatable, then so be it.'

Amanda frowned at the slight and began retaliating.
'They put your name amongst her list of conquests,
Nicholas, though, looking at the Nun of Beaumont
Street, I cannot quite see the combination of puce and
violet sitting at the head of your ancient family seat.'

Nick shrugged, not willing to be part of Amanda's

sarcasm for a moment longer and not trusting himself
enough to stay silent.

With annoyance he excused himself and went to
find a drink.

An hour later Brenna, standing momentarily alone,
was aware of someone joining her at the window, and
she knew without looking up that it was Nicholas Pencarrow.

'Miss Stanhope.' His words were accented in the
way she remembered so well.

'Good afternoon.' Her own voice was low and nervous. She was far from feeling up to sparring with him
and wished with all her heart that he might just walk
on. Everything about him made her vulnerable.

'I enjoyed your piano recital the other day. You've
been the talk of the town ever since.' He spoke softly,
though threatening golden lights danced in his eyes.

'That sounds daunting,' she replied.

'Do you play often in company?' he continued, as
if he had not heard her answer.

'Only if the hostess is as insistent as Lady Brentwood was.' She lightened her tone to match his. 'And
only if the piano is a Schimmel.'

'Where did you learn?'

'My education may have started late, your Grace,
but my uncle was determined to make up for my earlier lack.' For the first time she looked at him directly,
eyes sparking. 'I can also read the constellations in the
night sky by heart, or discuss with you in three different languages the philosophies of Plato or the merits
of the collective works of William Shakespeare.' Noticing Nicholas's puzzlement, she explained in Latin,
'My mind was always free, you understand.'

Unexpectedly he laughed. 'I had forgotten your abil-
ity to always surprise me.'

Hearing the hard-edged humour, Brenna licked her lips to try to still an escalating feeling of panic. 'And you me, your Grace.'

'How so?' The query was laconic, but she pressed on.

'Your confidence regarding my childhood, Nicholas. I have appreciated your discretion and I thank you for it.'

His eyes blazed at her use of his first name and carefully he reached for her hand. 'You thought I might betray you, Brenna De Lancey Stanhope?' he countered.

He spoke her name like a caress, in a whisper, like a lover might, like the Nicholas she used to know before her secret had also become his, and try as she might she could not bring it on herself to snatch her hand away. Rather in the midst of this crowd she felt a certain safety and power, and a recklessness that she recognised as a feeling only he seemed to be able to bring out in her.

'Other men would have.'

The golden lights in his eyes turned to fire and she felt the pressure on her fingers deepen. For a moment everything seemed displaced and, as the room narrowed down to the two of them, she felt his heat as an aching physical need.

'Other men would have what?' Letitia Carruthers's voice burst across the stillness, pulling them apart and away from each other. Her frown was thunderous. The way she threaded her arm through Nicholas's was also telling.

'Good afternoon, Miss Stanhope. Still soliciting funds? No wonder the men you canvass do not have the heart to refuse you anything…'

'Letitia.' Nicholas's warning was explicit.

'I am sorry, my love,' she replied, her voice honeyed and husky. ''Tis just that the Beaumont Street Orphanage does after all need its founder to have a spotless reputation and you know how easy it is for gossip to begin…'

The room darkened and spun around Brenna, her eyes meeting Nicholas's in silent entreaty and widening as he bent to place a kiss in the soft skin of Letitia's neck. 'Come, Letty. I think you have had enough to drink. Let me take you home.'

The sheer sensuality of the gesture distracted Letitia, who threaded her fingers through his, her face creasing in a smile. Only Brenna had seen Nicholas's glance of warning as he had stepped back and allowed her room to pass and she felt an instant bolt of anger. He was warning her of what exactly? Of the precariousness of the path she travelled or of his attachment to Lady Carruthers? They deserve each other, she thought as she excused herself summarily, her mood blackening further when she saw the Duke of Westbourne did not even have the manners to glance up and say goodbye.

Nicholas watched Brenna as she walked through the crowd and away from him and cursed Letitia at his side, even as he bent to listen to her with a practised interest. Brenna was as vulnerable as he had ever seen her and Letitia's jealous utterings had warned him of the need for care. His kiss may have distracted her venom for now, but Brenna Stanhope De Lancey's safety balanced on brittle ground. Biting down on his rising irritation as Amanda Wharton rejoined them, Nicholas grimaced. Brenna's presence today had brought back all the feelings he would rather not acknowledge. She was beautiful and she was penniless, she was the celebrated Nun of Beaumont Street who was born into a brothel, a fallen angel who cared for London's poverty-stricken orphans even while telling him that the thing she wanted most out of life was independence. She was an anomaly. Soft and hard, weak and strong, a woman who flouted all that other women wanted most and stood alone because of it. It was his duty to forget her, his responsibility to dismiss a woman who could only do his status harm. And yet he could not.

One touch of her skin, one whisper of her name, one look again at the amazing directness of those violet eyes and unexpected dimples and nothing was certain. He remembered everything familiar about her with an ache and chastised himself as he did so.

Chapter Ten

Brenna dreamed that night of Pencarris, and of Nicholas, and of possibilities between them that she had never ever considered, before waking up in a film of drenching sweat and the knowledge that she wanted him in the way of which other girls spoke, with a fairy-tale ending and the first real awakenings of herself as a woman.

The wafts of smoke came as she sat against her headboard, too bewildered to even try to get back to sleep, her heart beating strangely in a motion all of its own, her body wanting something she knew of only in its bestial form, yet yearning for a passion she understood should be different. Distractedly her eyes noted the mist that seeped beneath her door, registering the danger as if in a trance, tentacles pulling her into its dewiness, down into the very haze of consciousness and up again into the white-hot heat that burst loudly against her door.

She screamed as the last of the shuttered veils fell away.

'Michael. Michael. My God.' She was out of her bed and in her uncle's room in a flash. Her uncle lay in bed fast asleep and she ran across to him, pulling off the covers and shaking him into wakefulness. 'Wake up, our house is on fire!'

Michael rose from the bed and assimilated their danger in a trice. 'Get out of here, Brenna, and I'll follow you—' But he got no further.

'No I won't leave you. We'll get out together.' She pulled at him, bringing him fully against her and, shuffling towards the window, ignored his protests completely, her mind all on the task of getting her uncle through the opening and into safety. The door behind them blew open as she pushed Michael through and she leapt across the sash herself, landing almost on top of him, the flames now licking at the outside walls, though higher up than where they crawled.

Two hours later while they were sitting in the small living room of the next-door neighbour's house, dressed in all they owned and covered in thick rough blankets, Nicholas Pencarrow burst in through the door and into a space that scarcely seemed to contain him. The other occupants pressed back against the walls, appreciative of the fact that they were in the presence of someone important.

His eyes went immediately across to Brenna, noting the red patches on her face, one arm swathed in bandages and her feet blackened with the ash of a narrow escape.

'I would speak with Miss Stanhope and Sir Michael alone for a moment.' His order was obeyed immediately, the door shutting behind those who owned this little house.

Nick met Michael's glance with directness. Visibly, across these past few months, De Lancey had aged immeasurably, his face fatigued, his eyes drawn tight across baggy cheeks, his bearing stooped by circumstance. Within a moment Nicholas's mind was made up. All the prevarication of reason was gone at one sight of Brenna's bruised face, the blankets about them attesting to the meagerness of what they had escaped with.

'I have talked with the fire brigade and they are of the opinion that an intruder knocked over a lamp that set the flames. As the house has been rendered uninhabitable I'll take you down to Pencarris and we'll look at options in the morning.'

Brenna took a breath to speak, to effect a denial, closing it again when she realised the precariousness of their situation. There lay nothing between them and poverty now save the charity of those able to afford it, and Nicholas's offer was not to be turned down merely because of pride. Her eyes washed over with tears that she fought against shedding, her fingers brushing the moisture from her cheeks where it caught in the thickness of a bandage. His eyes registered each action and a blush crept into Brenna's cheeks as she remembered her dreams. She stood then slowly, wincing at the blisters on the pads of her feet and Nicholas, finally able to bear it no longer, walked straight across and lifted her into his arms.

Nicholas tensed for the inevitable anger, but Brenna merely curled into him and laid her head against his shoulder. She felt safe and protected and tonight, after all that had happened, she could find no reason at all to pull away.

With care he placed her into the plushness of his carriage's velvet seat, pulling a blanket across her knees and lighting the lamp that hung, caught in iron filigree, by the window.

Michael came behind them, and Brenna watched as Nicholas made sure of her uncle's comfort before he hoisted up the small steps and positioned himself inside the conveyance opposite her.

Within a minute they were gone, having nothing to bring with them from their own house save the nightclothes they were in, and Nicholas, seeing the lights of London receding, reeled with the relief of having got them this far without an argument.

Michael watched the Duke of Westbourne intently, and uncertainty punctuated his next sentence. 'This offer of help is much appreciated, your Grace, but it will only be for a short stay. Tomorrow we will go to…' He stopped, finding it difficult to go on given their lack of alternatives, and Brenna leant forward protectively to take his hand in hers.

'Tomorrow we will go to Beaumont Street. The orphanage has a source of clothes and some spare beds. Everything will be all right, you'll see.' She felt stronger now, away from the burning house, the prying eyes, the indecision. Of course they could always go back to Beaumont Street. Why had she not thought of it before? She shivered as she observed Nicholas, silent and smothered in the shade of night time just as he had been in her dreams. Had he seen? Could he know? She cursed her imagination with a vengeance.

Nick listened to their plans without saying a word, every fibre in his body vibrating with an anger only Brenna Stanhope had ever managed to incite in him. Slapping his wet gloves against his thigh, he looked out the window. *Nothing* would be all right as far as he and Brenna were concerned. He wanted her like he

had never wanted any other woman in his life before
and he knew he could never have her. The night lamps
blurred in the distance as they travelled through the
blackness and the air inside the carriage was heavy
with question. In the half-light he could see that the
blanket had slipped down across her shoulder, the
shadow of one breast outlined through flimsy lawn.
With care he changed position.

'You are comfortable?'

'Yes. Thank you.'

'And warm?'

'Yes.' She coloured as she saw where he looked and
tucked the fallen blanket more firmly in around her
neck, and their eyes caught across the small space,
both distrustful of the reactions they invoked in one
another. Michael's dozing snores echoed softly in the
background.

'I spoke with the constable. The police don't think
the fire was an accident.' When he saw she would not
answer, he rephrased his next words as a question.
'Why would anyone want you dead?'

'I am not sure. Perhaps they have a gripe against
the orphanage.'

She was clutching at straws, and he knew it, for
amazement swept into his face.

'You believe that?'

Overcome by honesty she shook her head, barely
able to give word to the other alternative. 'I think it's
Michael and I they are after.'

A silence lay between them, Nick trying to think of
some way to fashion a protection around her and
Brenna trying to understand why he should be both-
ering.

'We'll be more careful in the future now that we

recognise the threat,' she said flatly, cowed not at all by his frown when he looked up.

'You would be no match for people who kill others, Brenna, even given a warning. Can you shoot a gun with accuracy? Parry with a rapier?' He waited as she shook her head. 'Could Michael?'

She dropped her glance and was still, fists clenched tightly at her sides in vexation at his patronising tone. 'No.'

Breathing out, Nick began with more gentleness, 'I'll place a man at Beaumont Street, a guard. It's my fault this has happened, after all, and you and Michael make an easy target.'

Brenna's eyes flicked up to his. So this is why he had come? Because of Worsley? Part of her felt relieved and part, disappointed. 'There's no need—'

He interrupted her before she went further. 'Yes, by God, there is. Look at you. Look at Michael. Next time you may not be so lucky, and there will be a next time, Brenna.' He swore beneath his breath as he saw her shake her head again. 'When Michael wakes up I will talk with him then.'

She faltered, not certain what it was he alluded to now. 'Why?'

'To see if his attitude is more reasonable than yours.'

She laughed at that and sat forward. He could see she was angry. 'I'd forgotten about your masculine bias, your Grace. In my world such a stance seems ludicrous, but then in yours the men of the *haut ton* never could stand a woman who reasoned things out for herself.'

'Perhaps it's just as well, then, the position of the aristocracy is tenuous enough as it is.'

Dimples quivered in response. 'Humility sits ill on you. I'm more at home with the arrogance.'

Laughing out loud, he leaned back and watched her, perplexity and admiration battling with sheer damned want.

Nicholas spent the whole of the next five days in London, two of his big ships having come in from the East and needing his attention and, whether or not he admitted it to himself, to have a break from the increasingly difficult presence in his life of Brenna Stanhope.

He sat in his office at Pencarrow House and thought of her, angry for doing so for, despite all his intentions to maintain a distance, his wants and needs of her as a woman kept resurfacing. He needed only to look at her now to feel a growing hardness in his loins and a corresponding desperation in his head. Frowning, he stood and shifted the papers he was working on into a briefcase. He'd go up to White's and have a drink. Charlie or James might be there. And afterwards there was always Deborah Hutton to quench the restless thirst that drummed through his veins at the mere thought of challenging violet eyes.

The club was almost full when he arrived, the hour later than he imagined when he looked at his timepiece. As soon as he entered, he felt an undercurrent that seemed somehow to be directed at him. Nicholas was used to gossip and speculation. As the Duke of Westbourne it had seemed to go with the title, but tonight was different. Tonight he felt both baffled and tense, for as he walked he heard his name linked with

the only one in the whole world with whom he would
not have expected it to have been.

Charles met him in the middle lounge by the bar,
raising his eyebrows in greeting. 'You seem to have
very publicly added another feather to your cap, Nicholas, and one I presume from your reaction, which
comes totally without foundation.'

Nick gritted his teeth, waiting in silence, waiting for
the confirmation of what he knew was about to come
next.

'Letitia Carruthers has told London that the Nun of
Beaumont Street has fallen, that she has been dis-
avowed. She has told the *ton* the truth as she sees it:
that of Miss Brenna Stanhope's affair with Nicholas
Pencarrow.'

The glass shook in Nick's hand, so hard did he
squeeze it. 'And on what grounds does the honourable
Lady Carruthers base such information?'

'From all accounts, a visit that she paid the other
day to Pencarris. You see, Brenna answered the door
dressed in your night attire.'

Nick clenched his teeth and asked acerbically, 'And
she could not imagine any other reason for such an
outfit. A fire, for instance?'

'I tried to tell her when I saw her last night at the
Carltons' ball, but the damage had already been done
and you know how it is, people believe what suits
them. Miss Stanhope's disgrace suited Letitia. And as
for the *ton*, it was desperate for any tasty morsel. With
Queen Victoria's penchant for morality, a good scandal lies so thin on the ground these days.'

Charles said each word in undisguised anger and
Nick felt his brother's loyalty with relief, though he
stayed silent as Charles went on.

'Perhaps it would have been less of a story had Brenna encouraged others to court her, but she didn't, and those with their toes trodden on because of it can be spiteful. The women too. She conquered London with her cleverness and beauty and it doesn't pay to have both. Those with little of either only hate her all the more because of it.' He stopped and took a drink before continuing far more softly, 'It is the way of life and of London, brother, and I can't think how you're going to clear her name.'

'That's enough, Charles.' Nick's voice hissed through his teeth as he looked around the room at eyes hastily turned away from his and finished his drink.

'Let's get out of here.' Charles nodded and followed his brother, James Weatherby joining them as he came down the stairs from dinner, all three of them pointedly refusing to look at all concerned by what had happened, though as they neared the door a party of the younger set turned to observe them, one particularly loud-mouthed man questioning just loudly enough for Nick to hear him.

'How do you explain your nun's attire, your Grace?'

Nick changed direction in an instant and headed straight for the youth who now looked far less self-assured than he had been a minute earlier. 'If you must speak of something of which you have no knowledge, nor are ever likely to, then kindly do so more quietly and with some effort to learn the truth.' And with that he shoved him roughly backwards, squaring his shoulders as he looked around the group. 'Miss Stanhope's name deserves none of this gossip attached to it and is tarnished only because she has the misfortune to be the target of a rumour that is based on a complete and utter falsity.'

'If she's half as good in bed as she is on the piano, I wouldn't mind a go myself.' The comment came unexpectedly from a lad heavily slumped across a stool at the bar, and Nick's temper, sorely strained all night, broke without warning. He grabbed the slovenly offender and punched him senseless to the ground, all hell breaking loose as he did so, for Charles and James rushed forward to drag him away and the others, fearing more retaliation, made to stop them. The whole of one end of the club was suddenly awash with fighting bodies.

Twenty minutes later and decidedly the worse for wear, Nick, Charles and James stalked through the main doors of White's and out into the darkness, Charles's eyes alight with a mirth the others seemed far from sharing.

'Well, Nick,' he said slowly, 'if they didn't believe the rumours before I'm sure they will now. Your reactions hardly lie within the tepid bounds of mere friendship.'

Nick, holding his hand tightly within the silk lining of his jacket to dull the pain and swelling, looked around guardedly, unable to refute the truth of what it was his brother said. It was James who spoke into the silence.

'Brenna Stanhope makes you foolish, Nick. At least between friends acknowledge the fact as truth.'

The muscles in Nick's cheeks showed his tension plainly as he spoke more honestly than he meant to. 'I can't stand by and see her ruined. She has never deserved that and would be the last person in the world that it should happen to...' *Again*, he almost added, his mind reeling across her possible reaction to this newest turn of events.

'Then what's the alternative?' James's eyes flickered to Charles, an unspoken question passing between them before returning to Nick.

'I've yet to think of one,' Nick said savagely, his arm shooting out to hail his coach, which was stopped a few yards up the road. 'Right now I'm going home.'

Nick arrived at Pencarris well after three o'clock in the morning. He hadn't meant to even come, but he found himself ordering Robertson to take the London Road instead of the one back to Pencarrow House. Climbing the steps up to his room after dismissing newly arisen servants back to their beds, Nicholas had a wild and urgent need to check that Brenna was safe; that the harm done to her reputation in London had not physically manifested itself in any form at Pencarris.

Her quarters lay a good distance from his, though upon the same floor. Quietly he tested the portal, relieved when it admitted him an entrance, though the darkness inside confounded him anew, coming as he had from the lighted hall. He stopped still, caught in the blackness, and listened to her breathing for a minute whilst his eyes accustomed themselves to the light, and then he moved forward.

She lay tousled against the bedclothes, her gown pushed up slightly around shapely ankles, her hair spread across her pillow and catching her in its silken mass. His eyes roamed lower to her face, eyelashes dark and still against her cheeks, which in the light of this moon seemed unnaturally white.

Panic gripped reason and without meaning to he

bent to touch her, pulling away the moment warmth
suffused his hand and watching as she moved on to
her back, stroking the pillow and murmuring something unintelligible into the night.

Lord, what was he to do? Nick brought his fingers
up to his forehead to stroke away the pressure he could
feel building there. How could he tell her of the gossip
that raged across London, linking their names together
as lovers and tearing down all the restraints and con-
trols she had laid down so carefully and over so many
years? Already the support in society for her orphanage would be withering, as the Nun of Beaumont
Street was parodied as the Duke of Westbourne's newest scarlet woman. Damn, he wanted her warm and
willing in his bed, not cold and angry. Not bowed
down under the label of fallen or wanton or promis-
cuous. Not hating him for a lack of protection and a
litany of lies. Unless…

He searched in his pocket for a pen and paper and
quickly scrawled a note, placing it carefully to one
side, caught beneath her pillow lest she knock it to the
floor with her restlessness.

Brenna awoke later that morning to find a note
placed next to her. Sitting up, she read her name upon
the paper and knew it at once to be from Nicholas.
How it had come there she had no idea, though common sense told her he must have put it there after she
had fallen asleep. The thought disturbed her as did the
contents of the missive: *Please join me in my office as
soon as you are able. N.*

Sense told her it was urgent and thus she dressed
for the part, donning a plain blue-velvet gown and tying her hair back simply, leaving all the accoutrements

of a far finer lady alone in her newly expanded wardrobe, which had been provided courtesy of the Duke of Westbourne despite her protestations.

Nicholas's office lay to the back of the house, a large and welcoming room that she had been in only once before, and she knocked with growing agitation upon the heavy mahogany door.

'Come in.' Gingerly she turned the wrought-iron handle and let herself inside.

His glance met hers as she took the first step towards him and she was amazed to find him in his evening clothes, his eyes red rimmed and tired looking, a twelve-hour stubble dark upon his chin and, most surprising of all, a large bandage artlessly wrapped about his right hand, beneath which she could see the telltale signs of the dark crustiness of blood.

'You've had an accident!' The words flew from her in a horrified tone as she thought he might now be the target of what had been previously meant for her and Michael. My God, not again.

But he shook his head and placed his hand firmly into his pocket. 'Nay, 'tis my own fault and of no import.'

Brenna stood still, trying and failing to make sense of Nicholas's dress and manner. She reverted instead to silence and waited for his cue.

He motioned to a chair before his desk. 'Please sit down, for I have something to discuss with you.' Her fears escalated to new heights—his voice was as serious as she had ever heard it.

'You did not tell me that you had had a visit at Pencarris three days ago from Letitia Carruthers,' he said, slowly waiting for her answer as if it was important.

'I didn't realise you would need to know.' She could feel her heart beating faster.

'People like Letitia love to gossip, Brenna, and my nightshirt with you inside it provided her with much to say.' His eyebrows raised slightly. 'I presume that part of her story was true?'

Colouring, she gritted out an affirmative, icy tentacles of apprehension wrapping themselves about her composure.

'Would it be too much to ask why, then, you were at the front door dressed like that in the first place?' The sentence came with little humour and much urgency.

'I'd seen one of your servants in the front gardens with an armful of flowers not two minutes earlier and so, when no one answered, I supposed it to be her and went to it myself.'

'I see,' Nick said, sitting forward, his hands balanced across his knees and looking down at the ground. 'Did you try to explain the matter to Lady Carruthers?'

'I did, but she wouldn't listen.'

'And you didn't think to explain it at all to me?'

She shook her head as Nick stood, leaning against the sill behind him in an unconscious gesture of weariness.

'The thing is, you see…' he tilted his head to look her straight in the eyes '…Letitia Carruthers has misinterpreted your stay here as something far more intimate.'

She frowned, for his words could mean anything, and seeing her incomprehension he interpreted it all for her.

'Putting it much more bluntly, she thinks, as indeed half of London now does, that you are my mistress.'

Brenna paled and stood, scarcely able to take in the gravity of his announcement.

'They think I…we…' She couldn't finish as pain slashed across her face.

'The orphanage's funds will be hit badly,' Nick continued, trying to bring the subject to the less personal and give her some time to recover. 'And though I will top up the deficit to keep the place running, it seems nothing can resurrect your name.'

Blank eyes surveyed him as her tongue ran across dry lips, trying to fashion some sort of solution and failing in her quest.

'There is one way that I can see to still the critics,' he said carefully. 'We could leave for Italy. Today,' he added as he saw the storm clouds brewing in her eyes. 'Go on an extended holiday until this whole thing blows over, until the memory of it is distant and another scandal takes its place. No one need know anything.' He said the words casually and hated the way they sounded, but there was little else he could offer. Quietly he pushed himself forward and came to stand before her. 'I would protect you!'

She listened in stupor at his suggestion and her heart began to thump in her ears. Digesting the implications of just what it was he was offering, she realised he would ruin her completely. Her answer came as definite as she could make it. 'It's out of the question to leave England like that and with you. I've weathered worse storms before and I can do the same with this one, based as it is on lies.'

Nick shook his head. 'Perhaps you do not understand the might of the *ton*, Brenna, as I do. Even I could not weather the storm, as you put it, for long, were I a woman caught in such a compromising position. You will never be accepted into any house of repute again as things now stand, and you place yourself in a position of extreme jeopardy and in danger from compromise from every quarter.'

'Because I am a woman. Because your name stands above even such a slander as this, and whilst my reputation is in tatters, yours can only be shining all the brighter. It's the man's perspective, don't you see; all her fault and all his right. Letitia Carruthers in her stupidity just fails to register the cause.' She stopped, barely able to continue, the gravity of the whole situation hitting her anew and seeping slowly home. Angry eyes met darkened ones and she struggled for breath. 'After all these years of hiding the truth, is it not ironic that a lie should be the very thing to catch me out. And from *your* Lady, my Lord!'

Grace, dignity and honour. Suddenly Nicholas knew what he liked so much about Brenna Stanhope.

'She was never *my Lady*, Brenna.'

'Never your paramour? Never your lover?' The words were torn out of her in mounting anger and she waited until she saw he would not answer. 'Never the previous occupant of the position you now offer me?' Tears filled her eyes and she willed them not to fall.

We could leave for Italy...until this whole thing blows over... No one need know anything.

The back of her throat ached with sadness, but still she pressed on. 'Do you love me?'

'Pardon?'

'Would you love me?'

'I would protect you.' He said the words carefully, playing for time. She noticed he did not look at her as he poured himself a brandy. Fresh blood blossomed against the whiteness of his bandage.

'Why would you do this, then? Protect me?'

Putting down his glass, he crossed the room and stood at the window, looking out.

'Because I want you, damn it. Because ever since the first day we met I have wanted you.' He turned and she could not negate what he had said, the lust plain in his eyes.

''Tis a high price, then, that *I* must pay for *your* want, your Grace.' Her words were neither kind nor gentle, so angry was she at his detachment.

He swore at that and leaned heavily against the wall behind him. A gilded picture of some ancient ancestor shivered with the movement.

'Ladies usually decline a proposition with more tact, Brenna.' The words reverberated with a sizzling rage as he moved forward.

'And gentlemen usually mention the word love.'

His eyes flared, the pupils black against gold, and he caught her wrist and raised her fingers to his lips. 'Love me then, Princess.'

For a second she saw hope etch his face and was confused, until she realised it was the physical expression of which he spoke and not the other. Her fingers burned in his and she looked up.

'Do you feel this too?' His thumb stroked the soft tissue of her palm and molten heat pierced her.

'No.'

'Liar.'

Letting go of her, he stepped back. With darkness bruising his jaw and one hand bloody, he unexpectedly smiled. 'James was right, Miss Stanhope. You do make me foolish. But you saved my life and the very least that I can do for you now is to try to save yours.'

Later she was to think that this was the exact moment when her heart broke. With the early morning sun slanting down across his hair, giving it burnished lights and firing his eyes to velvet, Nicholas Pencarrow, the Duke of Westbourne, was achingly handsome. And absolutely unattainable. And she knew at that second that he would never ever be hers.

'I thank you for your offer of *protection*, your Grace. But I shall not be needing it.' She did not look at him as she left the room to gather her belongings.

Everybody in London hated her. Everybody from the wealthiest ex-patron of Beaumont Street to the lowest-paid tradesperson who serviced the kitchens. She was a scarlet woman without morals, a courtesan without a protector, a person scorned for her lack of virtue and absence of remorse.

She had become the ill-fated and imprudent Miss Stanhope.

She had heard it from Julia Cartwright when she had come to call at Beaumont Street this very morning.

Poor unmarriageable Miss Stanhope. All words she had heard bandied in her first coming out and now repeated. God, what had happened to the woman she had fostered so carefully in between? The self-determining, self-governing woman of independent means and integrity? Banging her fists against her thighs, she resumed pacing around the back garden. Everything had fallen to pieces just as Nicholas had intimated it would, the money from his generosity the only funds now holding up the orphanage coffers. Blood money. Guilt money. For Julia Cartwright had intimated that the Duke of Westbourne continued with his round of social events as if she had never even existed.

Why had she let Nicholas take her to Pencarris in the first place, damn it, when she could have so easily come here to Beaumont Street? *Be honest*, she chastised herself. *Why?* Because she had hoped for something more from him. Something fine and good. A sob escaped her lips and she wiped the tears from her eyes. And instead…instead he had asked her to become his mistress. Like Louisa. Like Miriam. Like the past she had sworn to leave behind. Anger at her own stupidity surfaced and she leaned back against the wall, feeling faintly dizzy, though a commotion at the end of the garden had her looking up. She blanched as Nicholas Pencarrow strode towards her, tall and darkly urgent, Betsy and Kate at his heels.

'He insisted on coming through.' Betsy's face was bright red. 'We could not stop him.'

'I need five minutes alone.' Nicholas ignored the women completely and spoke directly to Brenna, who in answer pulled out her uncle's fob watch from a pocket and set the minute hands.

Waiting until the two women had gained the steps, Nicholas began to speak. 'Your name is damaged, Miss Stanhope. Your prospects are nil and the principles upon which you have founded your orphanage stand dissolved with your refusal to let me protect you.'

She could hardly believe his words. 'You have come here to tell me this?'

'No. I have come here to tell you that there is no possible way that you can stay on in London without protection. At this moment the doyennes of virtue are merely outraged. Soon men of questionable morals, knowing your reputation, will begin to call on you. Uninvited. Do I make myself clear?'

'Men like you?' Her own anger flinted against his.

'Not quite like me, Brenna.' He ran his hand through his hair and took a deep breath. He wanted to wring her neck and he wanted to kiss her both at the same moment. Lord, she confused him like no woman he had ever met before. And he was the only one in the world who could save her. 'I have come here to ask you to be my wife.'

She stepped back, astonishment blanketing anger. 'Because you feel sorry for me?'

'No. Because I am a gentleman, and because I have ruined you. The rules of good manners now suggest matrimony.'

His words were ground out. He was as angry as she was. As trapped as she was. The tone and formality of his address made her answer in kind. 'I am certain, your Grace, that any tome on proper conduct would absolve you from responsibility, given the details of my past.'

He smiled at that and turned the timepiece into the light. 'You have three minutes left, Brenna, in which to say yes.'

It was the softness in his voice that disarmed her, and the chips of gold in his eyes. Looking away, she began to shake. Any other time she would have been stronger, would have refused his proposal outright, would have demanded love or admiration or at the very least respect. But not today.

After two long weeks of being vilified by every person she had come into contact with, she had no defences left. Even an unwilling and pitying proposal of marriage had its appeal.

'You do realise how much you risk? With me?' she managed to say finally when she had her emotions under control.

'Yes.' At least he did not fake pretence.

'Anyone could expose me.'

'They won't.' Again she felt the pull of his body against hers. His strength. His power. The way he moulded his world to get exactly what he wanted. And right now she could see that he wanted her. Desire stamped his eyes. Not all pity, then. She smiled, surprisingly empowered by his lust.

'There will be no intimacy until…' She could not go on. His proposal had been nothing like those in her dreams, and the nightmares from her childhood were suddenly real.

'Until you feel comfortable with me.' He filled in the sentence with such an implacable politeness she felt duty-bound to qualify it.

'It won't be soon.'

'Later, then…'

She could have sworn she heard amusement in his voice, though when she looked up there was none.

'And you do not have to give me things. Just the orphanage money. That is all I will be asking for.'

'Very well.'

'And if my past should resurface in any form or shape, I will leave.' The frown across her forehead deepened. She did not want to be kind. She did not want to be generous. She wanted to hurt him as much as he had hurt her. He did not love her and he never could. And, after all, it was *his* mistress who had ruined her.

'Very well.' His words were quiet and she caught his glance, surprisingly languid and carefully devoid of feeling.

'I accept all the terms you have set out on the condition that I may add one more of my own.' Leaning forward, he met her gaze directly. 'Whilst in public I would expect you to behave towards me in the way of a wife. Outside of our bedroom I want to give none the power of the truth, for it can hurt us as easily as this gossip has.'

She nodded and tried to still the shaking that had overtaken calmness. Marriage to Nicholas Pencarrow. She could barely envisage what it might be like. Looking at him now, bounded between conditions and contracts, everything seemed unreal and dreamlike.

He loves me.

He loves me not.

She felt like a dandelion whose thin strands of reality were blown hard into a gathering wind.

'I will have my lawyers contact yours and we could be married as early as a week from today. Would that be suitable to you?'

He was speaking and she tried to listen.

'Yes.'

He did not touch or offer her his hand. He did not kiss her cheek or tender any reassurance. Just a slight bow and he was gone.

As he left, she glanced at Michael's watch. In four minutes and forty-seven seconds her life had been changed forever.

Chapter Eleven

The lilting notes of the wedding march seared across the silence and, when Nicholas lifted his gaze to face Brenna, he held his breath, for, dressed in his mother Johanna's own wedding gown of ivory silk, the girl he had left in the garden one week prior was transformed. Wild dark ringlets escaped from the laciness of a diamond tiara, the errant curls framing wide eyes and high cheeks, and he smiled as he noticed the wildflowers of Pencarris in her bouquet. With unmistakable hesitancy she came forward to stand beside him, tipping her head to his as she reached him, fear as clearly visible as resignation. His heart twisted and for a moment his own resentment at the whole situation waned. They were caught together in this charade and she liked it as little as he did. Less, perhaps, for despite all her conditions she must also know the Church ordered obedience in the role of a wife.

Her fingers clutched his own unexpectedly. Looking down, he saw her nails were short and the bare skin on the back of her hand was so white and clear he could see the thin veins of blue beneath. A surge of protectiveness rushed through him and he squeezed her hand tightly. Not love, then, but something damn near close. Something tenable and workable. The action caused her to look up.

'Have faith, Brenna, to know that I would never hurt you,' he whispered, readjusting her fingers so that they were interlaced with his own.

The words were just what she wanted, a quiet reassurance of his promise to remain the gentleman and, despite herself, she tightened her grip on his hand and nodded at the waiting clergyman.

'I am ready!'

The service began with a lilting reminder of all it was that the couple would be entering into, not lightly, not irreverently, not with infidelity or untruth but with a wholehearted commitment, and Brenna was amazed to find Nicholas smiling when she steeled herself up to glance his way, her own mind certain that if the man's soliloquy continued in such a fashion the very roof of Pencarris might well cave in upon them.

The exchange of the vows was short and to the point, said firmly on his behalf and whispered on hers, the twenty or so people in the room having to strain to hear from Brenna the affirmations they knew by the nod of the priest's head to have just taken place, a slight buzzing emanating from those who followed the opinion of the society rumours and who felt that this marriage was not by a long shot a wise one for the Pencarrow name.

And then Nicholas confounded them all, for he raised his bride's hand in his and turned towards her. His words began softly, though well articulated, vibrating with an honesty none could question and far from the logical and calculating Duke of Westbourne that they were all so much more used to.

'I promise to you, Brenna, and in front of these our witnesses, to observe all the needs and wants you bring into our marriage and to honour your sovereignty of choice.' A light smile flickered across green eyes as he leant towards her and whispered, 'Short of reading our agreement out in front of everyone and plighting my troth to that, this is the very best I can do to try and banish the fears that I see so plainly in your eyes.'

A reluctant smile tugged at the corners of her lips, and the minister, relaxing for the first time, spoke firmly across the hushed silence.

'Then I pronounce you man and wife.'

From the few weddings Brenna had ever attended, she knew the next expectation was for the groom to kiss the bride and nervously she looked around at Nicholas, but he shook away the words poised on the clergyman's lips. Reddening, she reverted to silence.

Amusement at her reaction made Nicholas observe her more carefully. He liked to see her flummoxed. It told him more about her own emotions than ever she would have admitted to him. It also made him damn weary of the whole rigmarole of this wedding, for without intention he felt an arousing interest in what the final outcome of this night might bring. Given that they still had much time before they could with decorum retire upstairs, he clamped down on his imagination and, as they walked into the drawing rooms, grabbed a glass from a tray on a table filled with champagne.

'Here's to you, my lady, and to a marriage made in heaven.' The words came flat as he lifted his glass, knocking back far more of the liquid than a normal toast might demand. Wiping his hand across his mouth, he wisely tipped his passion into a smile and

helped his wife to her seat before taking his own and
turning to speak to his brother who had just joined
them.

Brenna could hardly credit the words he had just
said. A marriage made in heaven? Did he joke already,
this farce reducing their friendship merely to ridicule,
so absurd were the premises of its existence in the first
place? Did the strictures of her as his wife already
wear thin set against the visible sum of all that she
was? She shifted uncomfortably in her seat, trying to
keep her fears from being too plainly aired, and her
arm came into contact with her husband's. Normally
she would have pulled away, but tonight at the wedding table she found that she did not want to; the
warmth of his skin even through the jacket he wore
was strangely comforting and tangible, an anchor to
an increasing unreality, a prop against a growing hys-
teria. Marriage. The wedding night. Here at the top
table she was submerged by the Pencarrows, by their
traditions, by their expectations. Even her name was
lost in the process.

Brenna Pencarrow.

Her heart raced in a storm of foreboding and she
leant against Nicholas for shelter.

He tensed at the contact and waited for her to pull
away, amazed when after a minute she still leant
against him, his whole body centring itself on the feel
of her even as he talked with Charles. Finally, when
he could stand it no longer, he turned questioningly,
their eyes meeting across the small distance and dash-
ing together like two sharpened swords, raw and open
against a world that could easily disclaim them.

Brenna shielded her dread and nervously pulled
away from his nearness.

'Your grandmother has done a lovely job with the table, the flowers, the candles. Even the plates are lovely.' She stopped, biting her tongue against further inanities, and observed him as his eyes flickered briefly to the patterns on a crockery set neither of them had the slightest interest in.

'After dinner would you dance with me?' His question came out of the blue and without preamble and against her will she found herself nodding. He turned away from her then, without even an answer, all the discrepancies in this conversation highlighted as neither observed any true show of manners, whirled as they were by another current hidden beneath every word they had uttered, dual screaming denials of a feeling that threatened to explode both their worlds with an intensity that neither could weather alone and an overriding knowledge that because of it each would need to be wary.

The speeches were performed as if in a void for Brenna as she took solace in the wine, consuming in unaccustomed abandon the draught that gave a numbness to unthinkable fears, though all the glow of sparkling champagne settled to lead in her stomach as strong fingers encircled her wrist.

'You promised me this dance.' His voice was husky.

'I've promised much today that makes nonsense of good intentions.' Her reply was brittle and Nick gentled his tone.

'It's been that bad?'

'Worse,' she stammered, more uncertain now that they were on the dance floor and his arms were around her fully, the rhythm of the waltz pressing them together.

'I thought you might flee when I first saw you. What stopped you?'

Dimples flared despite her circumstances. 'Cowardice!'

It was the last thing he'd expected to hear her admit. 'You're afraid? Of our wedding night?'

She blanched white and he could feel her pulse quicken. 'You can't possibly expect that we should have one given the circumstances of our marriage in the first place.'

'The two don't have to cancel each other out, Brenna.' His eyes roved across her.

'No!' She cried and went to pull away, frightened by what it was he was saying and where it was the words were leading. 'You promised to obey the agreements of our marriage and once again today before the priest. I don't want it different.'

He smiled. 'And you always get what it is you want?'

'I don't understand.'

'Neither do I and that's the truth of it.' A wry look came into his eyes. Was it in jest he teased?

Drawing in a breath she tried to keep her answer as light as his. 'Pray you have not discovered too late, Nicholas Pencarrow, that it's the wrong woman you have married.'

'Nay, love.' He laughed as he tightened his grip upon her body. 'It's you I want, Brenna Pencarrow.' The name made his heart miss a beat. 'And the sooner you understand that, the better it will become for us both.'

He was careless now, her proximity sending reason awry, for her body felt warm in his and soft. He was surprised when she flung herself free from his grasp and stalked off through the gaping crowd, oblivious to their whispered mutterings.

Michael tried to stop her as she passed him, but she stormed by and hurried up the stairs to her room, bolting the door behind her and crossing to the window. She would not cry. She would not fling herself on the bed and sob out all the tenseness that had been building across this terrible day, leading towards a wedding night made all the more threatening by Nicholas's barely concealed sexuality. She was not ready for this, though footsteps outside warned her of another's presence.

'Brenna!' It was Nicholas and he was angry. 'Open up.'

'No!' she shouted back, facing the door and trying to work out new alternatives should the portal he was straining against actually give way.

'Damn it, Brenna, unlock this door now. This behaviour of yours comes within no agreements.'

'And neither does yours,' she hissed, jumping in fright as the whole door caved inwards, swaying drunkenly on hinges pulled almost from their place within the wall, plaster and mortar falling in a pile upon the floor below.

'My God.' Brenna's hands clutched at her throat as she surveyed Nicholas's anger. She'd never seen him like this before, and will herself as she might, her feet would not fly even a step in any direction.

Four strides had him beside her and he pulled her through the dividing door now thrown open and into his own bedroom, slamming the door shut as he did so and ramming a bolt of steel home into the door jamb.

'Now,' he said, turning to where she stood, 'this day

has played hard on us both, the promises of eternal love straying far from where it is we place the limits, but still I thought we had agreed on manners! 'Tis our wedding day, after all, and, though you may not have given it any consequence, people do expect a certain code of behaviour from any newly married couple. You gave me a promise after all, the one condition I attached to a proposal far from what I had imagined my own nuptials to be, and tonight you have broken your word completely.' He advanced on her, speaking slowly and with a deadly intent. 'Unless I see a dramatic improvement in the spirit in which you enjoy this evening, then I shall be able to break my own word with impunity.'

'And just what is that supposed to mean?' she shouted as his wrist flew out to capture hers.

'Take it as you will, Brenna, but remember, your position is far more tenuous than mine. A kiss? My husbandly rights? Who can tell what anger will let me enjoy?'

The fight left her immediately and, sensing it, he let her go.

'I will give you two minutes to be downstairs and joining me. If that is not the case, then I will be upstairs and joining you.'

Nick's heartbeat thudded with relief in his throat as he saw her nod. God, how he hated all this and, Lord, how he wanted her. Why could she not take his protection in the way it was given? He knew the answer even as he coined the thought. Because protection in Brenna's childhood had been synonymous with something far more sinister.

Still he stayed on tack. A shaky start to a union whispered already as unsuitable was just what they did not need. Soft words said now would only break her down further and he wanted her strength of purpose intact to face whatever else that this night might throw at them.

She came behind him, not even tarrying for the time he'd accorded her, wanting to make the entrance together rather than alone and knowing that what he had said he had also meant.

The doorway to the drawing room loomed and Nicholas, waiting for her at its opening, was amazed at the change he saw. Gone in an instant was the angry reluctant woman he knew her to have just been, replaced instead by Brenna Pencarrow, newly radiant bride, an expression on her face that told others she was more than a little repentant for a silly lovers' tiff now forgotten and kissed away, for to his utter disbelief she even crossed to take his arm in hers and together they went in to meet their guests.

The evening slipped by hour upon hour until the midnight tolled and Nick, sensing the lateness, whispered down to Brenna, 'It's time for us to go upstairs.'

She tensed, knowing the protocol. Would the others follow? Did the old custom of bridal bedding still hold sway amongst the Pencarrow family, weighed down in many respects by the fetters of tradition? She blanched as she gathered up the courage to look around the room, her gaze dropping as Nicholas came to join her. Had he not warned her to be compliant? Had he not insisted on the condition of pretence and manners no matter what else transpired, and had he not threatened her with the consequences otherwise? Husbandly rights. Indeed, they were his to use should he be intent on taking them. Docility and compliancy! Those were the terms. Her own rage calmed in self-preservation even as she felt Nicholas's arm about her waist.

Wordlessly they threaded their way through the group that gathered about them and, as their intention to retire was noted, Nicholas stayed for a moment to stop and converse with Charles. As Brenna looked back from the next landing, she saw the family spreading across the bottom step to deflect any persons who might have wished to follow.

The door to her room still lay at a strange angle, though with none of the mortar in sight, attesting to the presence of Nicholas's London servants. Stepping around its bulk, she crossed to her bed, throwing the tiny batiste nightdress laid out there hastily beneath it and turning as Nicholas entered into the room behind her, trying to determine whether or not he had seen her actions. His attention, however, seemed more fixed upon the state of the door, his fingers prodding the bent-over hinges where the weight of the portal had pulled them from ancient sockets.

'This can't be mended tonight, Brenna,' he said without looking up. 'You'll have to sleep in my room.'

'I will do no such thing.'

His eyes met hers, creasing at the corners with her horrified reaction. 'You would rather chance it out here with me?'

'You wouldn't be in there too?' Her voice came tiny and hopeful.

'No. I'll be standing sentry in this room.' He leant with a casual grace against the wall behind him and parried with a direct sensuality, 'That is, unless you would like it otherwise?'

'No,' she answered quickly; this evening was shaping up far more to her liking than she had otherwise imagined it. He'd stick to the bargain? She'd sleep alone? The thought brought a rising optimism and a reprieve she could barely contemplate and she hurried on to consolidate her position. 'The arrangements you speak of will suit me fine.'

He watched her relief without comment, smiling as he crossed into his own room, and content to have her company if not her consent. Tossing a log in the smouldering fire, he drew up two chairs.

'Come and join me for a moment. It's the first time I have had the pleasure of a midnight chat with a beautiful wife.'

She tensed, seeing in him the man who was more dangerous when he was charming than ever he could be when angry.

'There is no need for flattery, your Grace, for the agreements call for nothing but honesty when we lack company.' She looked about pointedly. 'Which at the moment we certainly do.'

'And I cannot, then, hope for friendship?'

A redness flushed her face. Her spite at his manners seemed belittled by his honour.

'Of course you may. You wish to talk?' Without waiting for his reply, she crossed to the chair opposite and settled herself into it, tucking her feet beneath her and smoothing down the folds of the voluminous skirt. This done, she raised her eyes to his, forcing a quietness where before had lain panic. 'What is it you would wish to speak about?'

'You.' The reply came back without hesitation, eroding away all her carefully laid calm like a wave might a sandcastle, and she shifted away from his gaze, unfastening the tiara that lay heavy on her head with shaking fingers.

'You know as much about me as ever I have let another know, your Grace. Quite simply, there's not much more to say.'

'What I see is what I get, you mean?' he laughed and handed her a glass of amber liquid. 'As it has always been the opposite, Princess, forgive me if I believe otherwise. But tonight let's bury the hatchet and toast a victory.' He lifted his glass and clinked its crystal lightly against hers. 'Here's to the death of malice and the birth of truth—Letitia's lies against our conditions. Does the balance please you as little as it does me?' Green eyes glinted with an implacable politeness, confounding her anew at the way he could turn around their conversations.

'I don't understand.'

'And neither you shall for a time, Brenna,' he replied darkly and struggled to lighten his mood, watching as the headdress she had been fiddling with sailed gently on to the rug, wild black curls released from confinement, tangling with abandon about her shoulders.

'The trappings of the Pencarrows can be quite daunting. You are the first woman in all my life who has not wanted to be engulfed by what I can give them.' He rubbed his neck and leant backwards.

Brenna sighed and finished the drink, letting Nicholas pour her another one, liking the way it relaxed her memories and dulled her anticipations. It made her feel sleepy and floating, banishing dread to a place far off and distant. Dimples came easily to her cheeks as she watched him, caught in the light of the fire. 'If you are not careful, you may find I take more meaning from your words than you had bargained for. I am a flawed and ageing spinster and sometimes it is nice to

believe for a time even such nonsense as you speak.'
She downed the new glass, sense bringing her hand
across the rim as he offered her more.

'Flawed and ageing?' His tone came without humour. 'Have you not looked at yourself in a mirror?
How could you have missed what it is I can see every
time I glance your way? You are a beautiful woman
who drives men to distraction even before they understand how much more it is they never see.'

She shook her head, holding up her hands to him as
if to fend off the sentiments and unable to stop the
building laughter. 'Many have warned me of your
charm, your Grace, and should I be of lesser resolve I
may even come to believe you and regret tomorrow
what I could not interpret tonight as the wants and
needs of any man faced with the prospect of an empty
marriage bed, no matter who be the bride.' A frown
creased her forehead as her glance fell to the drained
glass before her. 'What did you say this drink was
anyway?' Accusing eyes raised with doubt to his, her
own lack of control escalating into a whirling vortex
of unreality.

He lifted the bottle and read the label. 'Bourbon.
One of Kentucky's finest. Even weathered sailors find
it a strong brew. Do I dare to hope that it may loosen
your restraints as well, my love?'

Brenna giggled. 'And lay the battleground between
us bare of soldiers?' She shook her head, tilting it to
one side and observing him with a growing seriousness. 'In truth, Nicholas, you fared poorly today in
your choice of wife and though I could never repay
you completely for your protection, I will try.'

Nick was silent, surprised by her admission. Should
he push his advantage further and reap with bourbon

what he never could without it? Integrity won over barely as he walked across to the window, watching the departing barouches without interest as he clamped down on stronger desires. Even knowing that it was the wine that spoke dulled none of his ecstasy. His ice maiden was melting slowly by varying degrees, and beneath the signed marriage agreements he glimpsed a possibility of something far more real. Smiling, he caught his reflection in the window.

His wedding day.

His bride.

Brenna Pencarrow.

A surprising jab of delight rushed through him and he stiffened. He was becoming as fanciful as his father and look at the pass that love had led him to. If he should lose Brenna as Gerald had lost Johanna… Cold fear coursed across reason and, turning to press matters further, the smile quickly died from his lips.

She was asleep, pressed against the chair like a fallen angel in her crumpled ivory silk dress, unmindful of the material as few other women of his acquaintance would have been, dark eyelashes arced against the smoothness of her cheeks, her breasts rising and falling in a slumber he knew would last till the morn.

'Damn,' he cursed softly, crossing towards her, entertaining the thought even then of shaking her awake, but the peace and quiet on her face seemed so far from the turmoil and uncertainty he'd seen etched there all day and night that he could not quite bring himself to do it.

With care he placed his arms beneath her back and under her legs, lifting her easily up against his body as he strode to his bed and turned down the covers. Slowly he lowered her to it, sitting her in his arms whilst he freed the row of tiny buttons from the loops that lay full down her back, marvelling at the intricate delicacy of such feminine attire and marvelling anew when the gown fell away to reveal the soft folds of thin lawn and lace underclothes.

'Brenna, love,' he whispered, bringing her close to him as he lifted the wedding dress across her head, his eyes going unbidden to her breasts where the material strained across well-formed and rounded mounds. ''Tis not quite what I had wanted for our first night as a married couple, but it will do.' He tucked the eider-down up around her chin and blew out the candles beside his bed and a smile came wide across his lips. Ah, yes for now it would do.

She woke with the sunshine pouring in across an unfamiliar bedroom through curtains left unpulled from the previous evening and the breath left her body as she realised the dress she had worn was gone, and that somebody, presumably Nicholas, had put her into his bed.

She had fallen asleep! She smiled as she remembered the circumstances. Nick had been plying her with a nonsense she could barely recognise through the haziness of bourbon, but it was her body that had come to the rescue. She wondered how he'd coped with the insult of such an unwilling listener and her cheeks flushed. Had she not flirted with him whilst complimenting him on his charm? My God, two glasses of bourbon and she forgot all her promises? All their agreements? All of her past?

With a growing hesitation she stood, looking about his room for any signs of the early return of its owner, though all she saw was her marriage gown left untidily across a jacquard chair, and Nicholas's dressing gown draped across the wardrobe door. 'Remember that he does not love you,' she whispered to herself, pulling away from the coverlet and walking to the window, bathing in the sunshine as if it would re-energise her flagging spirit. Suddenly the future looked more uncertain than she had ever felt it. Nicholas Pencarrow was a man she knew could not merely be played with and any repeat of last night's performance would leave her next time far more vulnerable. He was a gentleman, but not a saint; many were the rumours she'd heard of his feminine conquests.

Heavy footsteps down the hall alerted her to the presence of another and, fearing it was Nicholas, she ran for the gown a few feet away. Too late! A short knock at the connecting door brought her around face to face with her husband, a smile planted firmly on his face as he caught her quandary.

'I'd keep going for the gown if I were you,' he quipped and waited as she reached for it, pulling it roughly from its hanger and shrugging it on. It was so long even her feet were covered in folds of material and Brenna felt immeasurably safer and stronger.

'It was you who put me into bed last night?' she questioned.

He grimaced slightly. 'My ardently executed prose of love does not usually have the effect of sending the prey to sleep.'

Against her will she reddened, their exchange from last night still very much in her mind. 'Given the conditions we each set upon this marriage, I am surprised that you should bother with the flowery rhetoric in the first place.'

He ignored her, green eyes sweeping across her state

of undress. 'Bourbon softens you, Brenna. Let me bring you a glass before breakfast.'

She reined in a smile and turned away from him. 'I think that I shall never drink the brew again.'

'That dangerous?' He came forward, at her back now, almost touching, and without realising she was doing it, she held her breath, her body centred on the man not six inches away.

'It's too early for a sparring match, my sweet. Let me take you for a carriage ride and show you Pencarris instead.' His voice was so soft and sensual that she turned, colliding with his chest as she did so. His fingers came up to brush away the curls that had fallen across her forehead and she saw for the first time that he was indeed kitted out in his riding gear.

Brenna brightened considerably. 'That would be lovely,' she said, and harmless, she thought, stepping away as one of the servants bustled in with a bucket of hot water, followed closely by a woman behind him who wheeled in a breakfast trolley laden with the treats she was fast getting used to in Nicholas's houses. He'd organised all this well in advance, she thought, confused again by his lightning-quick mood changes. Why, even now he stood and joined his retiring band of servants, departing without further conversation at all.

Three hours later after touring the lands and roads of the Pencarrow estate, they came down into a tavern in the village of East Winton and all eyes turned towards them as they entered, a low murmur of surprise buzzing around the room.

'Your Grace, you did not let us know that you were coming.' The tavern proprietor motioned to his staff for the alcove table to be set, a screen pulled into place to give the impression of privacy. Half a dozen serving girls swung into motion, dressing a table hitherto undressed with flowers and silverware.

Brenna smiled as they were escorted to the table, for in Nicholas's company everything seemed easier, less of a struggle. Sitting opposite him, she saw him suddenly as others did, the sun from a nearby window highlighting the planes of his handsome face. Nothing about him was ordinary. Even the clothes he wore added to the virile masculinity that seemed unpractised and without guile, the cravat at his neck tied only loosely and with none of the foppish detail she had seen the dandies wear in London.

And his eyes mesmerised her, golden green and sweeping across the whole room before him without any hint of surprise. He didn't expect people to run as they were now to do his bidding. He didn't even notice. The whole scene of deference had probably been played out before him so many times that he truly did not recognise the effect his name and presence had on people. Accolades, whispers and homage came without remark, without comment, without reflection. And without a trace of arrogance.

Brenna could not help but admire a man who stood so alone and so completely separate from a world that exalted him.

'Do you always cause such a furore, your Grace?' she asked with amusement.

He shrugged and answered slowly, 'I seldom eat out at places at which I am not familiar.'

'And I can see why.'

His eyes flickered at the tone she had used and he caught her glance and held it. 'It's well the crowd here is jovial, Duchess. Were it times of old I may well have had to fight for my right to be at your side.'

Brenna's glance came up to his in enquiry and Nick, catching the drift of her doubt, began to smile.

'It is you they look at, Brenna, not me. You confound them all with your beauty.'

She shifted in her seat, more pleased with his admission than she would ever let him know, but honest too in her denial. 'Even a plain woman can look beautiful when viewed in conjunction with strong wine.' Her glance took in the empty tankard before him and Nick smiled.

'If I didn't know you better, I would be sure you fished for a compliment.'

Without meaning to she laughed. 'Take care, your Grace, for after the difficulties of the past few weeks I accept any commendations with heartfelt thanks.'

'Then give me leave to tell you it's not only wine that turns men's heads, but beauty, and yours lies well within the bounds of heaven-sent nectar and is one hundred per cent proof.'

Brenna held up her left hand in protest, the light catching the ring on her fourth finger and making her bold. 'No wonder your name is well heralded around London by its feminine gender, Nicholas Pencarrow. Did you need to go to school to learn such sweet talk or is every Lord doled out a liberal dose of such flattery at birth?'

'Well, now,' he answered slowly, his amusement apparent, 'any man of lesser stock may well take your words as a rebuff, though my praise lies bereft of the practise you so glibly accuse me of. I stand guilty only of relating a truth as all but you do see it.'

'It seems I must remind you, Nicholas, that 'tis your

power that reflects my standing here. They see a Duke so they admire his Duchess. Nothing more.'

'And are you *mine*, Brenna?'

His voice was husky and her world stood still, any noise receding into a background of nothingness. Just Nicholas. Just her. For a second she was tempted to risk it all, to acquiesce to his naked want and hope that love might follow, but the memories of childhood stopped her. She had spent twelve years growing up in a place where lust was all that was important and twelve years of seeing how it never was enough. With an effort she reined in her confusion and strove for a lighter tone. 'Indeed, here in this tavern I am *yours*, Nicholas. For were you not by my side I'd still be waiting for my meal.' She smiled at him and felt a thrill of energy.

'Dukedoms have their uses, then,' he replied and leant back in his chair, stretching as if to dispense tension. A lock of hair fell down across his forehead at the movement and he pushed it back with his right hand. The gold of his ring glinted and in this light she could see a row of tiny emeralds encrusted in the swords. Beauty and danger—two words that described him exactly. Desire sliced through reserve.

'Is the crest on your ring the insignia of the Pencarrows?'

He shook his head. 'This is from the ancient line of the Dalraidan royalty, my father's heritage.'

'When did he die?'

'Twelve years ago. In India.'

'So you have been the Duke since you were…?' She tried to calculate his age.

'Since I was twenty-one.'

'It must have been hard at first.'

He looked up and she detected puzzlement.

'To be the head of the House of Pencarrow, I mean. So much responsibility.'

'I've always looked after people. My brother, my grandmother, my tenants—'

'And now me,' she broke in quietly.

He put back his head and laughed loudly. 'No, Brenna. You have seldom let me.'

'This marriage of ours…?' she qualified, letting the question hang in the air.

Unexpectedly he leant over and took her hand in his. 'This marriage of ours is not a responsibility. Believe that.'

The chips in his eyes burned brightly, reminding Brenna what it was he wanted of her. Reddening, she pulled away from him, ignoring the questions so plainly written across his face and was pleased when a passing patron known to Nicholas stopped to talk.

She was not ready for what Nicholas wanted yet. Not ready to cast aside her doubts and entertain this man's lust. He had never offered love. Never asked for it either, though sometimes his notions of responsibility and protection seemed surprisingly good imitations of what it was she desired. Taking a large sip of the table wine to calm her raging uncertainty, she ignored the way Nicholas watched her across the shoulder of the other man and was pleased to see the publican and his wife approach the table with their luncheon.

Chapter Twelve

Nicholas was called away to London early the next morning, and Brenna decided to accompany him and spend the day at the orphanage.

Beaumont Street was buzzing with excited children as she joined in the day's routine, though not without a few initial hitches. The cream head-dress and coiffure were changed for the more known and familiar loosely worn locks, and her intricately beaded over-jacket was discarded for an older, thin lawn blouse of Kate's. Worn on top of the billowing fullness of the original skirt, but with the crinoline's petticoats removed, the effect of her apparel was both theatrical and unusual, and Brenna was glad that no visitors were expected at all that day to see her garb.

Towards mid-afternoon, however, Frederick Castleton, the Earl of Lamont, arrived, being ushered into the little office just as she was finishing the last of the entries into the big ledger they kept for delivered goods. Crossing the small space between them, he took both of her hands in his. 'You look happy as a married woman.'

'I am,' she replied as he kissed her on the cheek,

and at that moment Nicholas Pencarrow also appeared in the doorway behind them, his eyes taking in the scene and darkening with anger as his gaze fell on the intimacy of their gestures, his wife's fingers still clasped by Castleton's and her own dress wildly inappropriate for receiving any company at all.

Brenna snatched her hand away, a blush of crimson covering her face at the intrusion adding to the illusion of being caught out illicitly.

'Your Grace,' she stammered, 'I did not expect you so early.'

'Obviously,' he replied, nodding briefly to Castleton and falling back on silence once manners had at least been observed.

Brenna jumped nervously into the gap. 'I am sure you know Frederick Castleton.' She stopped before weakly adding, 'He is here on business.'

Nick's eyebrows raised up slightly as he fixed the younger man with a steely gaze. 'Business looks good,' he joked without humour and was perfectly still.

Pencarris softened Nicholas, Brenna decided at that unlikely moment, and London hardened the edges of an already hard man. His next words worried her more.

'She's my wife, Lamont. Touch her again and I will enjoy tearing your arms from your body.'

'But, your Grace, I was not—'

'Get out.'

Danger glinted in his eyes as he dismissed Castleton with merely a look and Brenna could only bow her head as he left. Today Nicholas Pencarrow was feudal in his anger and totally out of place in his assumptions about her compliancy.

The door shut to absolute silence and it was a moment before Nicholas broke it.

'I think it may be wiser to acquaint Lamont with the news of our marriage. I get the impression that he thinks you are as much on the market as the commodities he deals in.'

'Oh, you do, do you?' She had had all she could take and anger surfaced where uncertainty and hesitation had earlier lingered. Boldly she strode up to him. 'Freddy Castleton was here as a patron of Beaumont Street; if you must imagine it to be otherwise, then at least afford me the honour of airing your grievances in private next time. You embarrassed Freddy with your accusations and high-handedness, and he is too nice a person to deserve any of it.' She stopped and turned to her desk, shuffling the papers into order and tying them with a piece of string before depositing the lot into a satchel he recognised as his own. 'And if you do not trust me…'

His hand shot out, hard as steel and matching perfectly his voice. 'I do not trust the reaction you inspire in men like the Earl of Lamont.'

'He is a boy, Nicholas.'

'He's older than you are, Brenna.'

'He was here to offer his congratulations.'

'He was here because he wants to bed you.'

'Then that makes him little different from you.' Her eyes met his and she felt the familiar pull of awareness. In the light thrown from the window she could make out the darker circle of green above threads of pure gold.

'I am your husband,' he ground out the words stonily.

'In name only.'

'Because you demand it such.'

'No, because you offer nothing else.' She was angered by her breathlessness.

'You're saying you would like it different?'

A knock on the door brought them both around to stare into the face of an astounded Betsy Plummer, and Brenna pulled away.

'Your Grace,' Betsy uttered, registering the presence of Nicholas. 'I didn't realise that you were here.' Immediately she withdrew, and without another word shut the door behind her.

'Wise woman.' Nick smiled without humour and turned back to finish his conversation with Brenna, who still stared at the closed portal.

'You scare them all,' she whispered, seeing again the effect he had on others.

Nicholas shrugged, less than interested. 'It's what you think that counts.' He was angry now and empty. The image of Castleton's hands clasped with joy by his wife, as far from her own reaction to him as he could ever imagine. Damn, she was his wife after all, and even given their agreements he could not watch himself be cuckolded, no matter how innocently. Brenna had no right to be welcoming another man's advances when every crumb he had thus far managed to extract from her was won with so much strain. Just as she had no right to look so damned sensual with her hair loose and mussed up and wearing a blouse and skirt so thin he could see the lace of her underclothes beneath them. Without warning he felt tired by the battle as he never had been before, all the progress he'd been making laid to waste. Reaching out, he took her chin in his hand and brought downcast eyes up to his.

'You will come home with me now, Brenna.'

He did not say the words gently and, scared by a new glint of the old game, Brenna slapped her open palm hard against his face before she could stop it, making him step backwards, hands at his side, a muscle ticking in his cheek as he garnered his emotions into check.

'Given the circumstances of our being thrown together into this marriage, I'd find it preferable not to have you wince every time I touch you. It bodes ill for our fourth condition, would you not say, even regardless of transgressing the truce of friendship, which I thought we had in place.'

His voice was as flinty as she had ever heard it and Brenna paled as puzzlement crossed her countenance. She had slapped him and insulted him and still he stepped back from hitting her? He would not retaliate even given such direct provocation? All the old reasonings built up from her childhood crumbled in an instant, and she could only stare as he retreated further, pulling the door shut behind him and leaving without another word. Did he mean to return for her? Would he come back later in the evening to ferry her home to Pencarris, knowing she had no conveyance readied here?

Home.

The word burnt in her mind like a beacon and she brought her hand to her mouth, covering the sobs wrenched forth by the admission. Home. And she had lost it before she had found it. He had left her, carrying the red welted mark of her fingers upon his cheek, and he would not be back.

Nicholas bounded from his coach and up the stairs to Pencarrow House, ignoring Robertson's query as to whether or not he would need the coach again that night, and ignoring every single servant who approached him on one pretext or another until he reached his own suite where two chambermaids worked diligently, tidying up the last of the embers in a cold and fireless grate.

'Get out!' His words came without manners and they scurried past, all the rumours of a Duke made softer by the new Duchess of Westbourne put to flight as the door behind them shut with such a force that it sent them running faster.

Nick squeezed his fists with rage, calming slightly under the scrutiny of silence. Lord, his wife was turning him into a man he could not recognise and he had no idea why.

He would leave Brenna at the orphanage tonight, he wouldn't go back and he wouldn't send Robertson to escort her here either. Let her see her choice and know its limits. Let her bed down in Beaumont Street after Pencarris and try to see her way clear to fashion a future that, after all, she'd signed as willingly as he.

He'd be dammed if he'd grovel.

A card on the mantel behind him caught his attention as he paced the room. Deborah Hutton had invited him to partake in a supper at the Theatre Royale. A smile flickered at the corner of his lips. And if half of London was there to see the newly married Duke of Westbourne up to his old tricks, then who was to mind? Certainly not his wife, she'd made that eminently clear. Quickly he bathed and dressed. The show would begin in two hours and tonight he didn't want to miss the opening.

* * *

Brenna tidied up the bed as quietly as she could, mindful of the sleeping children who still slumbered nearby, and absently rubbed at a headache that had built through the night into a throbbing pain.

She'd hardly slept, Nicholas's anger whirling in her mind each time she closed her eyes. Her own reaction was every bit as reprehensible as she saw again the red welt standing out bright across his cheek and the hurt in his darkened eyes.

It just couldn't get any worse.

Twenty minutes later it did, as Julia Cartwright, on an early morning outing, regaled both Brenna and Betsy with an account of the Duke's whereabouts from the night before.

'I did not like to tell you, of course, but how could I not?'

'Tell us what, Julia?' Even the normally unflappable Betsy was hard pressed for patience.

'Your husband, dear.' She looked directly at Brenna, lips puckered in obvious criticism. 'He dined with Deborah Hutton last evening. The opera singer, you realise. Not at all the thing.'

Brenna paled and tried to pass off the gossip with as little reaction as she could possibly manage, rising with a smile as the woman finally announced her intention to take her leave, and sitting the instant she was alone.

Nicholas hadn't been regretting his actions, he hadn't been sleepless from worry, he hadn't even thought of her again, rushing instead into the arms of another woman he'd known previously and a singer at that. Betsy's quiet reappearance galvanised her into action.

'Would you send Arnold with this message to the Dowager Duchess at Milford House, Betsy? Tell him it's urgent and that I'd need to know of the answer straight away.' Her eyes went to the clock at the mantel, thankful for the earliness of the hour. 'I've asked for a coach to take me back to Pencarris. Michael is there and my things. Obviously I'm not sure of my position right now and London is the last place I should like the newspapers to find me.' She hesitated. 'When I am gone, I want you to send a note to Nicholas at his town house. Only when I am gone, not before and just as a precaution. For I need him to know how things stand between us.' She swallowed and faced Betsy, appreciative of the warm arm draped around her.

'Don't do anything rash, Brenna. The first argument always seems worse than it is and busybodies like Julia Cartwright are notorious for making much more of things than they ought.'

Brenna nodded, knowing the situation to be quite different than where Betsy placed it, yet not wanting to worry her, and she hurried from the room before the older woman could question her further.

Brenna's gaze took in the empty fields of greenness and she closed her eyes and concentrated, listening to the sound of the horses' hooves muffled against the mud on the road and the fall of light rain on the roof overhead. She hadn't stopped since leaving London, hadn't even alighted when the servants, all unknown to her, had rested the horses at an inn, their gazes brought enquiringly to a woman they had not seen before, the new Duchess of Westbourne. She'd used the time instead to formulate a plan, a direction, a new

beginning for both Michael and her. They would have
to live in London, of course, but not anywhere where
she and Nicholas might possibly cross paths again, and
not where the society folk, once acquainted with the
knowledge of her divorce, could ever scorn her. Shaking fingers caressed the silk of her skirt, bunching the
fabric into her fist to try to quell her growing apprehension, when she heard a shout outside and felt the
carriage slow. Brenna, turning in her seat, could see
an unmarked barouche travelling fast behind, the
horses' mouths foaming in their hurry, the driver signalling at her coach to slow down.

A frown came into her eyes as she tried to determine
the message. Not highwaymen, she hoped, though the
size of the conveyance and the demeanour of the driver
seemed far from hostile. A voice from above alerted
her to the intentions.

'We're stopping, your Grace. Brace yourself.'

The horses almost skidded to a halt, leaving Brenna
clutching at the seat with her hands and pushing
against the opposite seat with her feet. As the motion
settled, and without warning, the door beside her was
wrenched open, Nicholas appearing from without, the
hat he wore shielding his eyes from the rain that had
begun now to fall in earnest and his cloak pulled high
on his neck to stop the moisture.

'Can I get in?' he asked softly.

Brenna nodded, for short of pushing him out forcibly, which she was sure she could not do, she had no
choice. These were his servants, his horses, his coach
and she was still his wife. No one would help her here.

Nicholas pulled the door closed behind him and
rapped his cane upon the roof to set the conveyance

into motion again. The creaking of the road noise covered from interested ears anything that was said inside.

The expression on his face was firmly schooled and totally unreadable.

'I received *this* this morning. Would you care to explain it?'

Her eyes dropped to the note she had sent, which he now held in his hand, cursing herself for ever having done so.

Haughtily she answered, 'It's fairly self-explanatory, your Grace. Our marriage is over.'

'Because of the gossip imparted to you this morning?' His voice was filled with censure.

'Exactly!' she spat out, having no reason to be kind. 'A midnight tête-à-tête with one of London's foremost sirens does not exactly go hand in hand with the sort of union I had in mind for myself.'

Nick frowned, seeing her hurt, and began in earnest, 'Listen, Brenna—'

The last straw of Brenna's patience broke. 'No, your Grace, you listen. I married you in good faith and I never would have knowingly done the name of Pencarrow harm. Freddy's handshake was just that, and your imaginings, while both lurid and unacceptable, make more sense to me today in the light of one who knows no moral boundaries. A whore, Nicholas, and a self-made one—if you meant to bring me pain you could not have chosen better. A handshake for a public bedding, the crime befits not the punishment, I think, but therein lies my foolishness, for after all you are the Duke.'

She was silent now, panting in her wrath, shaking both with the bareness of his betrayal and her reaction in seeing him again.

'I did not bed her, as you put it.' Nicholas's denial came quickly. More slowly he added, 'I meant to, but I could not. I came home at midnight and drank until dawn. Your note arrived soon after.'

Brenna tensed, unsure of what he meant or of what he wanted from her. 'You mean the intentions were there, but the reality lay otherwise. Your Grace, what am I to say to that when all of London thinks differently? Where now do I fit into the scheme of things? A wife without ears and eyes. Without feelings. No.' Her anger had resurfaced at the comprehension of the uncomfortable place he had relegated her to. 'I won't be that person.' Her voice broke at the last word as she slapped away his offered hand. 'I won't be the laughing stock of a society with little to recommend it save large amounts of money, and enough spare time on their hands to slate anyone who tries to act with honour. Your nightcap with an old mistress might well come within the bounds of decency given your licentiousness, which I might add is legendary.'

'Enough, Brenna.' The words came with a cold authority, but nothing could stem her tirade now.

'Stop! Why? Because you don't wish to hear the facts or know the truth. What's right for one person of title is wrong for another without? Social importance precludes manners and does away with common decency? Do you never take responsibility for your actions?'

'Yes, indeed. It's why I am here and not in a warm bed with an old mistress as I had intended, for it is you I have need of.'

Cold admiration crossed his face as he leaned back against the seat in thought, gleaning in her rampage the seeds of a wit he'd seldom found in another.

And she was right.

The Pencarrow name had again been splashed in scandal and she was the one who had risen to defend it, its newest member and one whose secrets were headier than any mumbled hearsay any paper could ever print. Nick felt humbled and astounded and totally at a loss to calm her anger, and Brenna, watching him, breathed in with vigour, uncertain of a man who would not shout back, who would not hit out, and still said he had a need of her.

The seconds rolled into minutes, the silence courted now by each of them as they struggled for something else, and unexpectedly it was Brenna who placed forward a peace offering.

'I thought you would not return for me. I thought you meant to leave me forever at Beaumont Street.'

The genuine sincerity of his last statement was seeping in. *He needed her.*

Yes, indeed he did. And after last night she needed him too. It was a shaky new beginning but it would suffice.

His eyes darkened as he saw her defences down. 'I was jealous of Castleton. You never hold my hands like that.'

Her brows raised in amusement. 'I never married Freddy either.'

'*Touché*, sweetheart.' He leant forward and took her hand in his, glad when she did not pull away, for it felt warm and real, and though he longed to bury his face in her palm and beg her forgiveness, he didn't.

Instead he turned the ring she wore, his ring, feeling the weight upon her littleness, understanding in that circle something that could never be broken and willing her to know it too.

Wordlessly and sensuously.

Looking out of the window, he suddenly had an idea. 'Would you ride home with me? 'Tis less than a half an hour and I would like to show you Pencarris from the high hills.'

She hesitated before nodding, her mind imagining the adventure of which he spoke and conjuring up a freedom she had never before experienced. But to sit so close to Nicholas...

The horse he had brought around was a chestnut stallion, and Brenna, looking up into its dark brown eyes, was pleased to see an intelligence and gentleness there. She was afraid of horses and Nicholas knew it. She put her hand up nervously to stroke the muzzle. 'He's beautiful.'

'He's yours!'

'No! I told you I would not accept such gifts.' She was amazed when he merely shrugged.

'Suit yourself, Brenna, though under the proper spirit of the union of this marriage all that I have is yours.' More softly he added, 'I would never dispute that, you know.'

Brenna smiled, glad that the tension from the past two days seemed gone.

'We call him Pegasus.'

Her eyes lit up in delight. 'The winged horse of Bellerophon?'

'Exactly.' He watched her, liking her knowledge of the ancient Greek classics. 'He came to me as a foal from Charles's favourite, Xanthus.'

'And you are sure that he is gentle?'

'I will show you.' He offered her his arm as a step to mount, intrigued by her hand, which stayed clinging to his as he got her up there. The horse danced his protest and Brenna's heart raced anew as Nicholas came up behind her.

'Now,' he said so close she could feel his breath on her ear, 'take hold of these reins like this and twist them about your fingers. That way, even if you are distracted, you will not lose them.'

Brenna leant back into him, her whole being riveted by the speed they travelled at, the wind in her face knocking the breath from her laughter as on they went across the fields and towards the forest some miles off. Finally she sensed Nicholas drawing in the horse, slowing him again to an easy canter, and with reluctance she sat up straighter, pulling away even further as he clucked the horse to a stop, though for a second he made no move at all to dismount or take away his arms, which rested now on her hips.

She turned to check on what it was he was thinking, her face only inches from his and it was if she could not turn away, so forcibly was she reminded of the dream she had had the night of the fire at Argyll Street. Only then Nicholas had been as far away as ever and now he was her husband.

'You ride well,' she said, dropping her gaze from his.

'I've practised much,' he returned shortly and stood in the stirrup, dismounting with ease and standing directly below her. 'Give me your hand.' She jumped and pulled back.

'Why?'

Ribald laughter split the quiet afternoon air. 'Because, my dear, I would help you down.'

'Oh.' Her heartbeat thudded in her ears as she leant into his embrace, surprised when he took not her hands but her waist, his fingers spanning the smallness and

lifting her into him without strain. She felt his body
with shock, hard and rigid against her softness and his
eyes came down to hers, tipping down towards her lips
before he stepped back to see to the horse.

Brenna stood and watched him, amazed at her own
disappointment. Had he not seen her reaction? Did he
not know of her acquiescence? The places still burned
on her body where he had touched her, his hard thewed
frame searing away the coldness she had held in tow
forever. He wanted her and did not take her? She
wanted him and could make no move. Nicholas turned
all the agreements upside down with his unexpected-
ness.

'We will stop here?' she managed, walking away
towards the vista the place so obviously afforded and
conscious of the fact that he was not joining her. 'You
do not like the view?'

'Very much so.' The reply came so warm that she
turned in surprise, blushing when she realised it was
not the vista to which he alluded as he raked her form
without apology. 'Are you always so shameless in
your pursuit of women, sir?' A musical lilt took away
the sting of the censure and Nicholas smiled as he
straightened.

'My shamelessness, as you so succinctly put it, is
aired only for my wife. In public I shall be all the
doting husband.'

'And here?' The breath held in her throat.

'Here you are as safe as you want to be.'

She frowned, watching to see if he jested, and reasoning by his seriousness that he did not. The sentiment left her somewhat shipwrecked. How safe did she
want to be?

Accordingly she turned and made much of the view,

using the silence to formulate her answer. Could she ever hope to pull off a relationship based on truth?

Part of her screamed 'yes,' but the sensible part answered quietly, 'How wise do you think it is to hope that my past will never ever again resurface in the shape of another Redmond Osborne? How many more men are you prepared to kill simply because they know of my secrets?'

The question did not disconcert him in the least. 'I would shoot every man in London just to see you safe.'

Brenna shook her head. 'No, Nicholas, you do not understand. I would not let you kill another just to clear my name, for soon in place of bumblers there would be one who you may not so easily dispose of.'

'You would worry about me?' Surprise laced humour as he smiled softly. 'Come to London, Brenna, and I shall show you.'

She held his glance, feeling herself drawn into the safety he so easily promised, feeling out here on the hills overlooking the Pencarrow lands an impermeable strength and invincibility. Perhaps it was time to redefine herself. Nicholas had already done so, to an extent, by giving her his name. And this time in the world of the doyennes of righteousness she really would have an ally.

Still, she could not so easily let go of old premonitions. 'Would we stay long?'

'There's a ball I would like to attend on Friday. Otherwise it would be left completely up to you.'

'And you think that it is wise?'

'Definitely.'

Brenna, liking his confidence, allowed herself to be drawn into the excitement.

London as the Duchess of Westbourne.

She shook her head at his nonsense. 'Your self-assurance always astounds me, your Grace. I remember at Airelies once, just a few months after I had met you, thinking how easily you stalk your world getting what it is you want and how little I seem to be able to fashion mine.'

'You credit me with too much. There are things that seem as far from my grasp now as they ever were.'

Smiling, he came forward, catching Brenna by the hand and pulling her into his arms. He leant forward, one hand bundling her hair into his fist whilst the other cradled her back, edging her closer into his ardour. His kiss was soft at first, but deepened when he felt no resistance, his tongue slanting into her mouth to taste the sweetness and his fingers running across the arches of her chin to try to bring her closer.

Then he pulled away, tracing the shape of her nose with one finger before placing it against her bottom lip.

'Give me leave to ask you now, Duchess, just how easy it will be to ignore the thing that has built between us. Could you encircle this moment within the marriage conditions? I think, Brenna, even you will find the task beyond your capabilities.' With care he moved his fingers to the pulse at her throat. 'One simple kiss and your heart races with all the fire of a woman wanting more. Just imagine the possibilities if you decided to kiss me back.'

He turned then towards the horse, biting his teeth together in an effort to quell a raging torrent of lust that had built in reaction to this one simple kiss. He was floored by the intensity, by the sweetness, by the forbidden ripeness of his wife and the promises she held of distant maybes, and he could barely trust himself to turn and face her as he went to mount for fear some expression he found in her face would unleash a control he had never before lost hold of.

Brenna, for her part, took his offhandedness as anger, a slap in the face against a kiss that for her had changed her perception of the act forever. With awe she raised her hand to her lips, feeling his wetness and his strength as if he still was held there.

Spiralling images of the drunken men she had seen as a child slammed against the beauty of Nicholas's kiss. Gentle, careful and demanding. She stood as naked as she ever had in emotion and he chose not to see it? Tears welled bright in darkened eyes as she met Nicholas's glance.

'I would like for you to take me back now.'

He held out his hand to her and watched as she gathered in her skirts and came up behind him, and this time they raced for Pencarris at a breakneck speed, Nicholas making no attempt at all to give her another lesson in the skills of horsemanship.

Nicholas had gone into London before she had woken the next day, leaving Charles to bring Brenna with him when he came later in the morning, and thus, resplendent with two cases of clothes tied on to the back boot of the landau, they got away just as the clock in the main hallway of Pencarris was chiming twelve.

Charles sat on the seat across from Brenna and watched her. Today his sister-in-law was back in the dark blue velvets she'd favoured in London and the colour engulfed her like a shroud, dim and dingy against the blackness of her hair now that he had grown used to seeing her in the lighter shades. The hat she had chosen also howled of a fashion far from the mode of the day and he wondered aloud at its source.

'Nicholas had the hat made for you with the other things, Brenna?'

She coloured. 'No, this one was all my own choice. I got it in the markets on a walk with Betsy the last time I was in London.' Her hands flew to the hat, checking to see if the angle was correct as she noticed Charles's frown. 'You do not like it?'

The words came like a child might entreat an adult to give favour to an old and treasured toy, and Charles, for the life of him, could not disappoint her, retreating instead to silence as he could not give her an outright lie.

Brenna observed him and began quietly, 'I've never gone in for fashion much, you see. At Beaumont Street the whole thing was a moot point and now…' she gestured with a smile '…now Nicholas has solved the problem completely by doing all the choosing himself.' She stopped, hoping the words did not sound like a criticism.

Charles chuckled, liking her uncertainty. 'I wouldn't worry too much about all that if I were you, Brenna. Nicholas did not take you as his wife just because of the clothes you wear, as many other men are apt to do, and give thanks for that. Fashion, you see, is as fickle as the heart under such circumstances and most brides thus inclined find themselves with an empty bed after the first season.'

Despite herself, Brenna smiled, seeing a glaring fault in his argument. 'And a woman of substance never does?' she countered.

'Not if she's clever enough to let her husband do the choosing.'

Charles's rejoinder reminded her so forcibly of Nicholas's teasing that she retreated into silence, not wanting his flattery to go further and Charles was instantly contrite. He leaned forward on his knees and said quietly, 'Is there some problem between you and Nick, Brenna? He went off this morning looking like hell.'

Brenna sighed and decided to trust him, for she could see in his face an honest concern for both her and his brother.

She started quietly. 'If you knew one thing for certain and another thing just barely, and each given time could cancel out the other, would there be any point do you think in pursuing the second?'

Charles grinned, his mind hurrying to determine the meaning of such an obscure and difficult question. 'The thing you know barely, is it a knowledge from the heart or from the mind?'

'The heart.' Brenna did not hesitate in her answer as she remembered her own reaction to Nicholas's kiss.

'And the other?'

''Tis a fact.' She squirmed in her seat as she thought of her childhood.

'Love versus fact,' Charles paraphrased without padding. 'There are some who would say love can conquer all.' A wicked smile came into his face. 'Take Chariclea, for example. Her Theagenes managed to overcome the hurdles and live happily ever after. And Daphnis and Chloe, and Rosalind and Orlando from the intrigue of Shakespeare's pen, or even Victoria and Albert, whose political alliance transpired into a love match—'

'But what of Romeo and Juliet, Isolde and Tristram,

Othello and Desdemona?' Brenna interrupted his dia-
tribe, the heroes in her examples far less lucky in their
quests.

'Well done,' Charles said quietly. 'And Nicholas
and Brenna? On which side would you place their
story?'

She stiffened, pushing back against her seat for distance from Charles's observation and now, not caring
to mask her reticence, she admitted bravely, ''Tis the
question I am asking you, for I don't seem to have any
others to confide in.' The dam had broken and Brenna
found she could not contain her fears for one moment
longer. 'I don't have a sister or a mother, and Michael
is not up to any such confidences.'

'And Nicholas?' Charles's query brought her for-
wards. 'You do not feel you could talk it out with
him?'

Dark black curls shook with a vengeance. 'He's the
problem, don't you see. I can't love him and I can't
not love him, and he won't let me stand up any place
in between.'

'I should hope not.' Charles's eyes twinkled, enjoying his sister-in-law's disclosures with an unforeseen
relish. More seriously he added, 'Nicholas told me
once that he would be like our father and fall in love
once and for ever. He told me that just after he had
met you. I didn't believe him then, but I do now.
Would that help you in your quest?'

Once and for ever. The words reverberated in
Brenna's mind. And yet he had signed the conditions
of their marriage with as much relief as she had. She
looked up doubtfully as Charles continued.

'As the Duke of Westbourne, he also could never
have been pressed into marriage if he genuinely did

not want it, no matter what the repercussions. Don't you see, Brenna, 'tis not the risk you make it out to be, this loving business. All you need to be is honest.'

Her eyes fell before his candour. It was all a risk and she could not tell Charles the true reason why. She could ruin Nicholas with an ease that left her gasping and the Pencarrow name with it. If Charles knew the full facts as Nicholas himself was privy to, would he be so careless, so free in his advice? Would he have risked everything in the way Nicholas had, and was still?

Of a sudden she wanted to see her husband with an indescribable yearning, her eyes darting to the scene outside, trying to determine how far they had gone and yet had to go, searching for the lights of London.

Once and for ever—the words were sweet with their rhythm. For ever and ever and all she had to do was to chance loving Nicholas.

Pencarrow House glowed like a Christmas tree as they finally pulled into the drive, the servants warned of the incoming coach and waiting for its arrival.

Nicholas himself appeared at the doorway even as it opened and, encouraged by her smile, took her hand helping her to alight.

'I am sorry I was not able to accompany you here, Brenna. One of my ships has run into problems and I needed to sort them out before she sailed on the afternoon tide.' His words came softly through the gathering spring wind that blew about them, reminding them of winter's recent passing. Nicholas reached down to take a blanket from the seat of the coach behind, wrapping it about Brenna as she stood there.

Tears came into her eyes as he completed the action,

surprising Nicholas as he noticed them in the moon-light. 'Does all go well with you?' he asked with a genuine concern.

Nodding, she pulled away, overcome by his famil-iarity and her need for him and relieved when he turned to Charles, still seated in the coach.

'Thanks for bringing Brenna down, Charlie. Are you coming in?'

'No, not tonight, brother.' His tone was sure and accompanied by a lurid wink, though Nick frowned, uncertain as to his meaning.

'I'll see you tomorrow night then, at the Lascelleses. Come in for a drink afterwards.'

Charles nodded. 'For certain,' he replied, watching thoughtfully as his brother and Brenna walked together up the stairs.

Pencarrow House was just as Brenna remembered it, the whole of the bottom floor a series of intercon-necting drawing rooms hung with paintings and velvet curtains and lit by chandeliers which sparkled in the ceilings.

The sumptuousness after Pencarris floored her anew and she wondered at the comparison. This house was the sum of generations of Pencarrows, but Pencarris was purely Nicholas's.

He was watching her now, carefully. 'It's been a long time since last you were here.'

She drew in a breath. 'The first time I met you again.' Her eyes went unbidden to the ceiling to see if she could make out the moonbeams, but tonight it was only dark. 'It seems so overstocked compared with Pencarris.'

He laughed. 'My thoughts exactly, though some of the rooms are less formal.' His conversation was cut off by a number of servants who had come to stand behind him, obviously awaiting their orders concerning the comfort of the new Duchess of Westbourne, and Nicholas turned to Brenna.

'You must be tired after the journey. I will have Mrs Nixon show you to your rooms and draw a bath. Later we will dine together.'

Supper that evening was a strained affair, neither wanting to jeopardise the fragile truce that lay between them, and each wary of a new stage in their relationship.

Once and for ever. Charles's words whirled in Brenna's mind, though looking at Nicholas now, he seemed as far away and formal as he ever had been, careful not to touch her when he helped her to her seat, careful in his choice of conversation, light and general and as far from the personal as he could have made it.

Keep it calm, Nicholas chided himself as he crossed the room to pour himself a straight brandy that he drank immediately while watching his wife as she came from the dining room. The kiss from yesterday burned across all his thoughts, sending his eyes to her lips, so desperately did he long for a repeat. Irritably his teeth ground together as he struggled to think of something to say.

'Your journey up was enjoyable?'

'Oh, indeed. Charles made it more so with his conversation.'

Without meaning to she blushed profusely, leaving Nicholas to enquire with feeling, 'What exactly was it you were speaking of?'

'Clothes!' The word came snatched from memory and Nick's frown deepened.

'The whole way to London? I did not realise that
either you or Charles found the subject so riveting.'

Without meaning to Brenna laughed, his assumption
so ridiculous. 'Well, perhaps not the whole way. Part
of the conversation was about you.'

'And my clothes?' he quipped, beginning to smile,
and reluctantly Brenna did so too, her eyes dancing
across his white linen shirt matched with a loosely tied
cravat of the same colour. Dressed in the mode of a
man not expecting other company, she was desperately
and suddenly aware of his virile masculinity and of his
innate sense of style.

With a firm shake of her head she brought herself
back to the subject in hand. 'Not so much the clothes,
your Grace.'

'But the man inside them, your Grace?'

He used the title as she did and again his humour
brought confusion. With an effort she made herself
explain further. 'This marriage of ours seems beleaguered with inconsistencies. I just wanted to confide
in someone who knew at least the rudiments of our
agreements.'

'And you could not think to confide in one who
knew more than that?'

'Charles asked the same question.'

Her mouth tightened and Nicholas knew he would
hear no more. Mentally he stored it in his memory to
ask his brother the details when next he saw him, and
with an effort he drew the conversation away to the
more general. 'The Lascelleses' ball will begin around
ten, Brenna. I have had the House of Gilles fashion a
suitable gown over the past few days and Mrs Nixon
will show it to you in the morning. If there is anything
amiss you need just to let me know as one of the

couturiers will be here at eleven to help you dress.
Would you wear your hair down for me tomorrow? I
know it is not the fashion, but I like it long.'

Brenna blushed and nodded, her husband's intimacy
sending all her wits awry for she wanted to please him,
wanted to feel his arms on her shoulders and his lips
on her mouth. She dared not look up at him lest he
read in her eyes these thoughts, this *frisson* of sensual
awareness so unfamiliar that it set her body pulsating
with a new and dangerous energy.

She was stunned and desperately outside her depth
as to the expected outcome of such an onslaught,
though, watching her husband casually draped across
the opposite sofa, the realisation hit her of an unde-
niable sense of belonging. And of possession.

The thought brought a smile to her lips and her own
complacency to an end. If she stayed here much longer
she would hardly merely be kissed. No, Nicholas was
not a man to be trifled with and fobbed off with such
a paltry offering. Already she could see his rising manhood beneath close-fitting trousers, and a twinkle in
his golden eyes that told her he might have some clue
as to where it was her eyes had just strayed. Thus,
without further hesitation, she rose and turned towards
the door.

'Goodnight, Nicholas.' The words were wooden and
strained and his answering reply was barely audible as
she slipped from the room to begin her hasty ascent
up the staircase.

Behind her, Nick took a deep draught of brandy and
leant his back against the soft leather of the couch.
Damn, but his wife would make him a eunuch before
the week was out if tonight's episode was anything to
go by, for his loins ached with the want of her. He

smiled as he remembered her covert glance at his hardening manhood. This caper they cut would have to soon be over, for the rules across the past few days had changed distinctly from what they once had been.

And tomorrow he would play his trump card.

Chapter Thirteen

Nick was standing with a drink in one hand and a cheroot in the other, watching the flames in the grate lick the back of the fireplace, when the slight rustle of silk made him turn, the politely placed smile he'd pinned there changing to complete and utter awe as his wife came before him.

'My God.' The words came torn from his throat in one single sound and then there was silence. Brenna advanced nervously.

'I am sorry if I am late…' She patted at the ruched golden silk in her skirt as her eyes fell with appreciation to his apparel of unbroken black, the copper in his hair highlighted by ebony. He looked different tonight, different and dangerous, all the power of a Duke on show with little of the tameness of the *ton*. And this dress she wore complemented his exactly. Gold and black, light and dark, fire and water. It was the mix of alchemy come to life, the attraction of opposites long in conflict and suddenly in balance.

Husband and wife.

All of a sudden the titles fitted not because of conditions but in spite of them, and both knew it.

Nick made much of stubbing out the small cigar and placing his glass upon the mantel, for he needed the time to gather his scattered thoughts. It was as if he was seeing her again for the first time, knocked like a skittle in a game he had no control over and never would. She was so incredibly fair. More than that, beautiful, radiant, stunning. All the compliments he'd paid out to women in a lifetime of flirtations rolled into one and found wanting. Smouldering eyes locked into hers and his voice seemed oddly husky as he pushed away from the mantel.

'I think we should go.'

Brenna's face fell. He would not comment on all she had laboured so hard to achieve across this day? He had not noticed? With disappointment she bit her lip and followed him, heartened somewhat when he stopped her just as they reached the door, turning into her closeness and pinning her to the spot.

His hand came out softly, touching an errant curl with a reverence and a reticence before falling to her cheek and her throat, making circles as it went to her shoulders, caressing the silken rose buds that gathered at the top of full sleeves and pushing the bounteous crinolined petticoats backwards.

'Stay close to me tonight, Princess.'

'I will.'

The promise was made without recourse to argument, bringing a smile to his face. All augured well for this evening. The first harbingers of a night studded in magic?

Forty servants lined up in the hall of Pencarrow House broke the spell as they walked from the room. A salute to the Duke and Duchess on their first public engagement. Normally it would be touching, tonight it was merely annoying and Nick walked through them quickly into the darkness outside with a scowl on his face, Brenna behind taking much more time in the journey, mindful of the gasps of the younger girls, their faces drinking in the beauty of her flounced gown with an undisguised pleasure. She could remember her own self at eighteen, overawed by the Originals at court, and she wondered at her husband's uncustomary rudeness.

Outside she found Nick beside the carriage, scuffing at the gravel on the drive as if in a hurry to be gone. She joined him in puzzlement.

'Does something trouble you, your Grace?'

''Tis the thought of having five hundred people ogling at you as my servants just have that makes me uneasy.'

Brenna laughed, sure he was not serious. 'You jest, Nicholas, it's the dress that they admire.'

'No, Brenna, not the dress, but what lies inside it. You will have all the young bucks scorching a path to your side in the waltzes, and that's discounting the older ones who'll be leering at you through steamed-up monoglasses on the sidelines.'

'And where will you be, your Grace?' she asked with a beating heart, sure that the answer would be all of Nicholas at his teasing best and she was not disappointed.

'Fighting my way through the throng, I suppose.' He smiled as he continued. 'I'll be the one with the bootmarks on my face when the music starts. Perhaps if you're kind you'll choose me once. I'd prefer a waltz.'

Brenna was laughing now and trying to keep her face straight as she did so. 'Stop. You will ruin everything we have spent all afternoon putting in place.' She wiped at her eyes with a handkerchief from her reticule, looking up only when she had finished and asking softly, 'Do I still look presentable?'

His teasing ceased instantly. 'More than presentable.' His eyes flicked over to the coachman standing at attention just out of earshot. He was forever cursed by onlookers. Here. Inside. At Pencarris. When did he get to have his wife all to himself, to enjoy her at a leisure he was desperate to savour? His mood blackened as he realised 'twould not be possible till much later, and with resignation he stepped towards the carriage, holding out his arm which Brenna took with a smile.

A knock from above signalled that the driver was turning into the gates of the Lascelleses' manor house and, despite herself, Brenna stiffened, straightening the folds of material in her skirt and checking her hair to see that it was all in place.

Her first engagement as the Duchess of Westbourne.

She took a deep breath and forced the tension down, though, stepping from the carriage up into the portico of Stuart Manor, Brenna was astonished when Letitia Carruthers threw herself at Nicholas, having the effect of separating her from her husband as she was pushed upwards by the throng of people who followed behind. Alone and unsure, she came into the brightly lit hall, her golden dress aglow under the flickering candles and her form attracting the attention of many other men and women who stood waiting for the major-domo to call each name.

Anger settled coldly within Brenna's eyes as she perused the crowd behind for Nicholas, engaged now in what seemed to be an intimate conversation and making no move at all to join her. *Damn him*, she cursed beneath her breath, stilling herself to a calm composure in the face of all the attention that she was getting and clasping her hands quietly in front, watching the scene with a practised nonchalance. He finally came towards her.

'Does the fourth condition of our marriage apply only to me, your Grace?' she asked with brittleness. 'Or should I get used to having you hauled off by every beautiful woman we pass?'

Nicholas smiled and tried to make light of the annoyance he felt with Letitia's latest bid for his attention, and as their names were called, he caught her wrist in his in an attempt at making peace. 'I swear, Brenna, that I have not seen Letitia since before you came to Pencarris.'

'Then she takes rejection poorly and, given the length of time you have just allotted to comfort her, I can well see why.' She snatched her hand away angrily and it was this reaction that the *ton* first saw as the couple entered the ballroom. A buzz of censure passed slowly about the great salon, a low indignant murmur aimed towards this titleless woman whom many perceived Nicholas Pencarrow, Duke of Westbourne, to be trapped by. There seemed, after all, no reason for their hurried nuptials as it was patently obvious to those about the couple that little love was lost between them. Why Brenna Stanhope had pointedly refused to take her husband's arm even as they entered, always walking a few yards in front as if to avoid any contact, and the anger in the Duke of Pencarrow's eyes because of it glinted like hard shards across the space for all to see. An ill-fitting couple thrown together by circum-

stances none could even vaguely guess at and the *ton*
closed its ranks around Nicholas and against his odd
and contrary wife.

Nick knew all of what was transpiring and Brenna
nothing. He watched her before him tense and un-
smiling, caught in a role she'd never been comfortable
in, and with the angry whisperings now inadvertently
reaching her ears she would only trust these people
less. He'd tried to take her arm as they'd entered, but
she'd pushed away and he could see her control was
not far from breaking. Running his fingers through his
hair, he looked about, trying to determine a friend
amongst them with whom they could shelter whilst he
reassembled their scattered forces. Failing to determine
anyone who looked at Brenna with anything less than
undisguised animosity, he leant across to her and said
in a flinty cold voice, 'I think we should dance.'

She shook her head quickly, shocked by the rage
that filled his eyes and, swallowing, looked away, her
whole night shattered in the first few minutes and in a
way that she had never expected. These people hated
her, she felt their coldness and whispers almost as a
physical thing and understood her position as an outsider as she never had before. Today, with Nicholas at
her side, she was both highly visible and much de-
spised, the stories of her transgressions at Pencarrow
more and more terrible in their retelling: a scarlet
woman, a gold digger—all the epithets she had always
dreaded being attached to her name and believed, simply because of who she was, an unknown commoner
who had had the audacity to trap the hand of a Duke.
With determination she straightened her back, fixing
her gaze across the heads of those around her, not willing yet to read more closely the censure. Nicholas,

leaning across to her, felt his heart turn over as he viewed the shadows in her eyes and the tightness of the smile about her lips.

'There is no choice, Brenna. You will dance with me.' His carefully emotionless voice had her looking around for an alternative, her composure beginning to fall apart at the edges, not wanting to dance, yet unwilling to stand here either within the groups of this indignant crowd. With obvious reluctance she shrugged and let him take her hand and lead her to the dancing floor, where they were sheltered slightly by the presence of other couples wrapped up in the music.

Nicholas held her tightly, and with care, his arms coming about her waist and pulling her towards him, though she stiffened at the suggested intimacy, her preferred style of dancing far more sedate than his and she tried to pull away. Hard arms held her in place and his voice came low and dangerous across the buzz of other conversations.

'We have an agreement, Brenna,' he said slowly, 'so be wary, for these people expect at least the pretence.'

She laughed then, harshly across his words, spitting at him in the lowest of whispers. 'Why bother any more at all, your Grace, for it's certain my name lies far from unsullied even with the fact of our nuptials attached to it. Let's just call the whole thing off and go home. I have no wish to continue a charade before people whose opinion I care little about anyway.'

Nick took in a breath and sought quickly for an answer. 'And let them get away with it? Let the lies triumph? Hide away for ever just as you did before, but this time with the knowledge that with a fight you

could have changed it and no excuses save for one:
cowardice.'

'No!' Enraged eyes raised to his and the word was
far from quiet.

'Yes!' he answered beneath his breath, a smile fixedly in place as he fought to hold her to the dance, his
fingers biting into her arms with a pressure undetected
by those about them.

'You're hurting me,' she said more quietly.

'Then stop hurting yourself, and start to think. These
people win tonight and they win for ever, and damn,
I can't fight them all alone.'

Her eyes met his at that, perturbed suddenly by his
words and by a truth that hit her more blindingly than
all the other lies. He was fighting for her in this room
as surely as if he'd drawn a sword or a pistol, his
actions negating all their reactions by the simple fact
that in the face of all the gossip he stuck firmly at her
side, daring them to accuse him personally, challenging all their precepts of a loveless marriage by a show
and a strength all his own. He defied the criticism by
his demeanour, he caught the hooded glances with a
directness few could withstand.

And he had smiled through his anger even at her
refusal to help him.

Brenna's arms tightened around his body, holding
him as she never had another person and whispering
in a quiet tone even as she avoided his glance, 'You
are right. Tell me what I should do to help you?'

Nick splayed his hand across her back, bringing her
closer into his body and whispered with relief, 'Keep
doing just what you are, Princess, and we may beat
them yet. The object of the exercise is to confound
them, you see, make them think this marriage of ours

truly is the love match they are certain it isn't.' Brenna
nodded and closed her eyes just for a second, hearing
the slow thud of his heartbeat across the softly beautiful music and all the fight left her to be replaced only
by a calm decisiveness. The evening so far had been
a disaster and it was plain to see these people truly
believed that she could never fit into Nicholas's world.
But his very presence here with her in the face of such
opposition negated every single argument. To be sure,
he'd felt responsible for her name being bandied
around London in the first place, but logic told Brenna
that there had to be more to it than that. He wanted
her friendship and he valued her company, and he had
kissed her twice now with far more feeling than the
narrow confines of their marriage agreement would
ever have predicted.

A warmth began to spread through the tenseness she
had felt ever since leaving the carriage and she lifted
her gaze to his. 'Do you always make a habit of fighting for lost causes, your Grace?'

Nick caught her humour, but answered without any
of his own, 'And that's what you think our marriage
is?'

Brenna nodded uncertainly. 'Surely even you can
see the problems? These people don't look exactly eager to congratulate us.'

He relaxed slightly at the plural. She understood the
situation differently from what he knew it to be and
he was comforted by the fact, for it would not isolate
her as much as the truth was bound to.

'I've been at odds with society here many times
before now, Brenna. The thing to remember, though,
is their fickleness—what's news today is not tomor-

row. Their collective memory is not so good either, and the dukedom of Westbourne can cover up much.'

She smiled, lulled for a moment by his easy confidence. 'A truly momentous scandal may be more tricky to sweep beneath the carpet, even given your illustrious titles.'

'Perhaps.' Nick was enjoying himself now. 'But a greater protection lies within the *ton* itself. Almost all the people here have skeletons in their own cupboards on at least the same scale as mine. Ours,' he amended as he saw the answer poised quickly upon her lips. His next words came quieter. 'I could ruin any of them and they know it.'

Brenna glanced up, seeing a dancing mirth in Nicholas's eyes that lay completely at odds with the danger in his voice, and she understood anew the power of his position here in society.

And just for a moment she did believe him truly to be invincible.

'Your confidence is heartening, Nicholas, given our situation, though it is said even Napoleon himself did not see he was beaten until Wellington took Waterloo.'

The music ended then, cutting off his reply, and the crowd pressed in against them once again, only this time instead of seeking the space she'd needed before she drew closer to his side, even allowing his arm to stay about her waist.

With the arrival of Charles Pencarrow and Lord and Lady Weatherby shortly after, the numbers about Nicholas and Brenna swelled to well above thirty. All the most lofty and illustrious names of the *ton* showed their support of Nicholas in a way that would defy and cut short the gossip about his wife, and those inclined at first to believe how the Duke had been entrapped and ensnared by a common money-grabber had mind to reconsider their thoughts. After all, the Pencarrows held much sway in society and it would do their own names nothing but harm should they unwisely ignite the wrath of the head of the house of Westbourne himself.

Hence the evening, begun badly, finished for Brenna, with Nicholas at her side, as one of the most memorable in all her life. She'd loved the dancing, held close by a man who'd defied all of London to uphold her honour, she'd enjoyed the conversation of his friends, clever worldly people who formed the vanguard of a group most mindful of her opinions, and she had discovered also a deference paid to Nicholas not only by the men of this London society, but also by its women. All night she'd caught covert glances towards him from beneath downcast lashes and she knew once and for all the magnetism that before she had only been partially aware of.

Watching him here amidst a group who were his peers and friends, he had no equal in her mind as he stood tall and alert, his eyes ranging across the company like a lion might its prey, watchful and dangerous even in repose, the man at Pencarris here the Duke, but uneasy in the changeover and temporarily confined by a society that could never contain him.

Husband.

The word came across the noise and the movement with a stinging clarity of joy, and a desperate knowledge of a want she had felt building across the past few weeks. Bemused, she tilted her head, trying in her mind to see just when the person she had always been had changed into this person she had become. She had softened and blossomed under the tutelage of a husband who demanded nothing intimate save conversation and two stolen kisses, and a man who had given her still the right to be herself without any form of whispered criticism. And tonight, as the lights of a thousand candles dimmed to the sound of an orchestra well tuned and manned, she stood uncertain at her change of mood, part of her shocked and part excited, the familiarity of Nicholas balanced against the power society accorded him. Why, even now her skin burned where the material of his jacket touched hers, the insignias of his ancient name emblazoned on golden cufflinks twinkling in the half-light.

With a last effort at controlling a ridiculous notion of throwing herself into his arms, she smoothed her fists across her dress and closed the fan she had been using to try to dispel her growing heat.

'Perhaps if you are ready we might depart soon, your Grace. The hour grows very late.' Desperate eyes glanced at the timepiece at his waist as she registered it to be well after two o'clock.

Nick straightened and complied immediately, eager to have his beautiful wife alone in the carriage, no matter what the price, and he turned to the Earl of Weatherby. 'Would you tell my brother we've gone on without him, James.'

James smiled, replying quickly, 'To leave the Lascelleses this early you must have much of a promise at home, Nick. It's more normally dawn before you depart.'

Brenna reddened, realising that to the *ton* two o'clock was obviously absurdly early, and, looking away, she missed the smile that spread across her husband's face and the answering wink in his friend's. It was not until they were well settled in their conveyance that she dared look directly at Nicholas, astonished at the warmth he regarded her with and the seriousness of his opening words.

'You were beautiful tonight.'

Brenna was silent, the fears in the ballroom banished now in his intimacy.

And she wanted him closer.

With an artfulness she had never used before, she ran her tongue across her lips, reason swamped by desire and by a desperate need.

Nick frowned slightly, trying to equate the gesture of sensuality with his more normally reserved wife, trying to still his imagination and his rapidly hardening loins, trying to determine in the invitation a promise of the sweetness he had sampled briefly two days ago. It had never been like this before, not across all the women and all the years and he was both awestruck and wary, understanding at that moment both the completeness in which she fastened him to her and the control he would have to take hold of to keep her apart. Desire fought sense and he lost before he had the chance to think on it further, his arms coming around her full and hard, his lips seeking hers with more ardour than he had ever displayed and she was kissing him back, pressed close against him, her fingers raking through the nape of his hair and across the tightness of the muscles on his back. Shock hit her as his hand crept beneath the silk at her bodice, demanding much more than the light flirtation she had thought to offer and, twisting away from him, she seethed with a shame she remembered only too well.

'That was wrong and I am sorry.'

Her apology amazed him, and Nick leant his head

back against the seat of the carriage, closing his eyes and willing his body back into some sense of normality before answering.

'For God's sake, Brenna, how can it be wrong when it feels so right and when I know for a fact that you must have felt it too?' His eyes held hers, his tone harsher than he meant it to be and her reaction came much more in character.

'Because I don't want what comes next,' she shouted at him blindly, 'and because I know with you a kiss would never be enough.'

He sat bolt upright. 'Damn right it won't be, but it's a good start.' Tonight not even her chagrin could touch him. He'd sampled the nectar of delight and was willing to wait with patience for the next chance, certain by her reaction that it could not be far away.

Brenna, observing him with a growing sense of alarm, sidled right up against the far door as the carriage drew into the grounds of Pencarrow House, ready to make her escape. Burton the butler hurried down the stairs and pulled open the door of the newly arrived conveyance, the smile on his face vanishing as Brenna pushed past him.

'Thank you.' The words came with a clipped politeness as she turned and began to climb the staircase to the front door. Nick sauntered behind her more casually, aware that once inside Brenna's innate sense of manners would keep her from just disappearing without any word of goodnight, and indeed, on entering the house, he found her at the base of the stairs.

'I would like to go to my room now, Nicholas. The night has been overly long, I fear, and I am awfully tired.' She put her hands to her mouth, affecting a yawn, watching his lazy smile even as she did so.

'I have something to give you before you retire. You should have had it on your wedding day, but it was here, and I thought to wait until the time when you were too.' He led her into the drawing room to the left of the landing and crossed to an intricately carved cabinet, flicking open a drawer to reveal a series of narrowly fashioned shelves. From the bottom one of these he removed a black velvet box and, turning, strode back to where she was standing.

She stared awkwardly at the present he held out to her, fearing almost to look inside, knowing the contents would reveal some priceless new bauble that she would have no compunction in rejecting. Tonight, though, she wanted no arguments, the second clause of a loveless marriage coming hard upon such a kiss as they had shared but a minute ago.

'Are you going to open it?' His words cut across her indecision and almost irreverently she snapped open the tiny brass catches. A paper rolled and sealed in navy wax lay inside, and her relief on seeing not diamonds but a parchment was so great she almost smiled at him. With care she broke open the seal and unfurled the document.

It was a deed of title to Airelies.

She saw it immediately, her name placed alone upon the rights of ownership, and her eyes raised in disbelief to his. It was the only thing he could have bought her that she would not give back, the one possession she wished to hold with such a fervency that it made all previous agreements void.

And he knew it.

'This is for me?' She uttered the words in breathless wonderment and he nodded.

'If I had to sell Pencarris, it would break my heart. I thought you loved Airelies in the same way.'

Brenna turned away from him, clutching the present to her breast and feeling hot tears scald down her cheeks. 'Airelies is mine,' she whispered, barely able to take in the truth of what Nicholas had given her. 'You have bought this just for me?' Questioning violet eyes turned to his. 'I cannot understand such a gift and as I cannot refuse it either I do not know what to say.'

He smiled. 'A simple thank you would do nicely for a start.'

She coloured and remained silent, the word ineptly inconsequential for such a present and her mind sought for another answer. 'I will pay you back. I swear it.'

He groaned and shook his head, stopping as a new thought struck him. 'How?'

Her eyebrows knitted together in astonishment at his answer, the disquiet raising to new heights as he continued unabashed, 'Wipe the slate clean of the first agreement in our marriage and I will consider myself amply compensated.'

She stared at him, trying to remember all the conditions in the clause and, seeing her difficulty, Nicholas stepped in. 'I want to be able to touch you sometimes, feel your softness and know that you will not pull away or jump back in anger.'

Doubt flitted across Brenna's face as she sought to negate the suggestion, but with the deed of Airelies firmly in her hand even this option seemed less difficult than she had imagined. She would never relinquish her home again. With caution she said with a bravado she was far from feeling, 'Define touching, your Grace.'

Nick stood still and ran a hand through his hair. 'A

kiss now and then, the sanction to hold you to me when I see you sad, and the licence to take your hand into mine.' He was careful in his demands and prudent. Too much sought now could break the *détente* completely, and Brenna, seeing he meant to press the dispensation no further, was caught in his leniency.

Watchful eyes brushed across her, touching her everywhere with a heat and suggestiveness, and Brenna wondered briefly if he meant to ravish her right there and then. Had she given the mandate or not? She held her breath, the changed position between them leaving her uncertain of everything, though when he wordlessly held out his hand as if testing her resolve she took it, his fingers caressing hers with a soft gentleness she found instantly reassuring.

'One down and two to go,' he said, his voice awash with laughter and with a glance that told her he was far more serious than he sounded.

She frowned, not understanding him at all.

'The wedding conditions,' he interpreted directly, 'I'd like them all gone! You are too beautiful never to be touched and I am too old to learn otherwise.' His hand came up to brush her cheek. 'Airelies is merely a beginning, Brenna. There must be other things you would want just as badly.'

She shook her head, amazed at his words. 'You would bargain for favours, your Grace. From me?'

He nodded. 'You may be astonished as to how far I would go and I always get what it is I want. So far you are the only woman in all my life who has not been for sale.' He smiled and let her hand go, his ears registering the sound of a supper trolley brought from without.

She flushed at the compliment, given her own background, and replied with a reluctant honesty, 'Perhaps that was the case, but in truth, Nicholas, you have bought me most dearly tonight when you deeded me Airelies.'

'Not bought, but given. It was my wedding present you did not have on the day.'

A knock on the door brought forth Mrs Nixon, pushing a wooden tray on wheels laden with a selection of desserts and coffee. 'Your supper, your Grace.'

'Thank you, Mrs Nixon. There will be no further duties tonight.'

A clock at one end of the room struck the hour of three as the servant departed, and Nicholas, seeing Brenna's glance stray to the ivory keys of his grand piano, asked with a gentleness born from a night of surprises if she would deign to play him one tune.

She played Mozart's 'Ich Denke Dien' and only for him, her eyes fixed upon him with a look he'd never seen there before. In music she spoke what her heart could not yet say to him and in a way which he could not fail to understand, and he in turn watched her boldly, watched her eyes fringed with dark silky lashes, watched her high cheekbones and reddened lips that turned up at each end, giving the impression of the beginnings of a smile.

As the music finished she dropped her own glance self-consciously, knowing for a moment a strange and intense pleasure. He was Nicholas Pencarrow, a peer of the realm, and he had gifted her Airelies tonight, eliciting only the promise of a kiss in return. Tonight she felt safe, cocooned in a world far from the one she had struggled in for so many years, the ghosts of strife buried in Nicholas's luxuries, and memories replaced by an adventure she had barely touched upon.

She had changed. She could feel it deep within herself, in the longing that welled up when she thought of his kiss, and the feel of her hands upon his body. She blushed and caught his smile.

'Penny for your thoughts,' he said and her colour deepened, though she swallowed her confusion and began bravely.

'I was thinking that if I could name an evening in all my life that I have enjoyed the most, then it must be this one.'

Her admission was unexpected and he rolled to his feet from his place deep within an armchair, capturing her wrists as he did so and drawing her up close. Brenna sucked in her breath as she felt his warmth, her own hands coming across the hard muscles on his shoulders and willing him closer.

'Nicholas?' Her whisper came unbidden as his lips came down upon hers, taking her hard against him, willing her to know the effect she had on him.

A shiver went through Brenna as his mouth opened on hers, cold dark memories being thawed by the heat of his caress. He was relentless. All the waiting months burst forth in rapturous abandon and in a ferocity that gave no heed to carefulness. How he wanted her and how little he hid it, his swollen manhood now pressed without shame against her thighs.

White heat seared through them, the reality of their coupling far more heady than even they could have imagined it, and, as Nick lost control, the door flew open, spilling forth an astonished Charles.

Brenna tore away from her husband immediately, her cheeks infused with embarrassment, and panting from the aftermath of Nicholas's kiss she brought a hand up across her mouth as if to wipe away a physical trace, wide uncertain eyes viewing her husband's brother.

Nick reacted with less surprise and far more anger. 'What the hell are you doing here?'

Charles retreated a step, though the smile never left his eyes as he replied with a mild censure, 'You did ask me in for a drink.'

Nick was man enough to admit his mistake. He *had* asked his brother back after the ball, even if on hindsight he knew it to be a mistake. Good manners overcame annoyance as he struggled to find an equilibrium he was far from feeling. 'You're right. Will you join us for a brandy?'

Brenna found her voice as she saw Nick take three glasses from the drinks cabinet. 'No, I shall not stay.' She rushed out hurriedly, her eyes carefully averted from either brother as she asked to be excused with a strained politeness. Carefully lifting up the deed to Airelies and the box it had come in, she turned and started for the stairs.

Nicholas, watching her, made to follow, calling to Charles to pour the brandy as if indicating his imminent return, catching his wife up as she rounded the first balustrade.

'There is no need to see me to my room.' Her voice was distant and uncertain.

'I know, but I want to.' His own voice sounded harsh to his ears, though he had not meant it to be. No argument or response was forthcoming, though, as she continued to climb upwards, her room reached in a silent lack of contact. She stopped at her doorway and eyed him carefully, all the intimacy of the evening dissolved in an ending that had left no time for explanation.

She felt desperately unsure and lonely suddenly for a family of her own, for a sister or a brother to confide in, for her uncle who could have taken her hand and whispered words carved from the wiseness of knowledge and experience. Tonight she felt as if her heart would break from love, all the old fears and control melted down by a man who had stood against all of London to protect her name and had gifted her Airelies only on the promise of a kiss. And yet he had not told her he loved her, not in words, and she needed the words. Uncertainty churned within her, and fear. Fear that she may have interpreted it all wrongly.

'Goodnight, Nicholas.' She frowned at the coldness in her voice.

Nick turned as the door clicked in its lock and fought for a control he'd lost hold of so badly in her company. Damn it, he wanted her so much he felt like a schoolboy again, all emotion and desperation, as his manhood became lost in the woman he coveted.

Closing his eyes in frustration, he brought his fists down hard upon his thighs. His wife was turning him into a stray dog, grateful for any thrown-out scrap or careless piece of affection, mere bones of a fulfilment he knew her not to want. And he was doing nothing to stop it, no control, no courtship. If Charles had not come in tonight when he did, God knows what would have happened. How could he have stopped? Pushing himself away from the wall, he walked downstairs towards his waiting brandy, wondering at how quickly he could get drunk.

Chapter Fourteen

Elizabeth Pencarrow arrived early the next day and invited Brenna to Milford House for lunch, though it was well after dusk when she returned, alighting from the carriage with a smile on her face. Her day out had been lovely, Nicholas's grandmother showing her a side of London she had not discovered before.

Nick was watching for her in the front room. She caught sight of him through the large windows even before she entered the house. Had he been waiting for her? His first words confirmed her suspicions.

'You're late!'

He was angry and she couldn't understand why. 'Late? Late for what?'

'Late for dinner. We always eat at seven thirty.'

A frown crossed Brenna's face. How far he seemed today from the man he'd been last night. What had changed him? The kiss? Her mind raced at the possibility that for him it may have been disappointing, or worse. Perhaps he'd felt none of the magic she herself had. Perhaps today he truly did regret her presence. Her heart sank as she regarded him. 'I'm sorry, but I have already eaten at your grandmother's house. I didn't think to send a note.'

He shrugged and walked from the room, leaving her there to watch his back as he went, dismissed like a child or a servant without even a word. A cold apprehension overtook Brenna as she made to follow him, though he had not gone into the kitchen as she had initially thought, but to the dining room, and when she turned to join him there the sight before her made her stop in surprise.

Two settings had been laid out together at the head of the table, complete with flowers and candles. A formal and intimate dinner party for two.

Nicholas, already seated, looked up, the soup given to him by a hovering servant sending plumes of steam into the air before him, and his eyes held hers with a direct challenge as dimples came quickly to Brenna's cheeks.

'You've done this for me.'

It was a statement more than a question, though when he did not answer her she drew back the chair next to him and sat down.

'I'd like some soup, please,' she said quietly, addressing the servant behind her who came forth with a plate, and Nicholas waited courteously until she had picked up her spoon before he started. Even when he was angry he did not forget his manners. She smiled, liking him for that.

'We went shopping and after that your grandmother insisted we go and have an early supper at Milford House.' A vague disquiet filtered through her as she watched him. 'I thought Elizabeth had left word here of our plans, and I am sorry if I have upset you in any way. It was not intentional and certainly not meant to cause you any worry.'

The truth as she said it was enough to jolt angry words from him.

'Damn. Of course I have been worried, and I did not enjoy the experience one bit. Next time, if you must gallivant around London without me, at least take the precaution of having one of my staff accompany you. The two accidents you have survived so far should have knocked some sense into your head, and it's damn uncomfortable sitting here for hours waiting to see whether you'll be home at all.'

Comprehension at his concern flooded into Brenna's eyes, but she was wise enough to stay quiet in the face of his displeasure, and Nicholas, observing her silence, struggled with his own emotions. My God, he'd never cared about the whereabouts of any woman before and not like this. A few extra hours with his grandmother and it was enough to send him crazy? She was doing it again, just as she had yesterday evening, all the control he'd long harnessed gone with one smile or glance. He shoved the soup spoon angrily into his plate and stood, grinding his teeth together in utter frustration, finding refuge in a complete withdrawal.

'I'm going out.'

Brenna's face fell. 'I don't understand.'

'Neither do I, and right now I don't even want to start trying.' He turned as she tried to call him back and was gone, leaving Brenna to mumble their apologies to an astonished kitchen servant before she too stood and left the table. Hurrying up the stairs to her bedroom, she felt a gnawing regret at the loss of Nicholas's company, and a sadness at the knowledge that this evening could have been infinitely different.

                    *   *   *

It was after two when movements from the room next
door told her of his return, and she laid down the book
she had been reading and brought her dressing gown
tighter about her throat, turning slightly as the door
between the rooms was pushed open and Nicholas,
shirt undone and hair awry, almost fell in, leaning
heavily against the wall as he did so, swaying noticeably with the effects, she surmised, of too much wine.

Their glances met across the space, his eyes running
over her nightgown in a mixture of appreciation and
boldness. 'Good evening, madame,' he slurred in a
good-humoured tone, though with an edge of the earlier uncertainty. 'I thought it was time to come home
and apologise for my boorish behaviour. And I think
also that we need to talk.'

Brenna stiffened, and leant further back into the
chair, rearranging her gown in place about her legs and
tighter still around her throat. Was he sober or not?
Would he push the boundaries further in drink than he
ever would without it?

She relaxed a little as he stepped back, pulling forth
a chair. Catching sight of the book she had been reading, he scooped it up from the floor. 'John Keats? You
like his work?' He opened the book to where she had
marked it, his eyes skimming the pages of 'The Eve
of St Agnes', before he began to read with practised
enunciation.

'Meantime, across the moors,
  Had come young Porphyro, with heart on fire
  For Madeline. Beside the portal doors,
  Buttress'd from moonlight, stands he, and implores
  All saints to give him sight of Madeline,
  But for one moment in the tedious hours,
  That he might gaze and worship all unseen;

Perchance speak, kneel, touch, kiss, in sooth such things have been.'

Finishing, his head lifted, green eyes searing into her for well past a minute before he began with soft question. 'What manner of man do you imagine as your Porphyro, Brenna? What lover buttress'd from moonlight could tear down your barriers held long in place by time and fear? Or will you never face your phantoms?'

A smile of uncertainty quivered across her lips, his gentleness nothing at all like the force she had conjured up when first she smelled the wine upon his breath.

'You confuse me, sir, with Madeline,' she whispered softly.

'And if by chance I do, are you so far different?' He pressed the query with a disarming charm, watching as she rose and made to set some distance between them.

'Indeed I am, your Grace. No whimful yearning maiden gazing heavenwards did I ever have a chance to be.' The last words came more quietly as she stood still to gauge his reaction, though surprise visibly crossed her face at the laugh that followed.

'You set your worth too low, Duchess.' The words came quietly as he rolled to his feet and crossed the little space to where she stood, careful not to touch her in his nearness. 'Do you honestly think every starstruck swain would measure each transgression from the perfect before bestowing their love upon the one of their affections? An in-law of questionable sanity? The taint of some past scandal? An angry word? A broken promise? Where would love be, Brenna, if it be placed upon such a pedestal? Nowhere. For it would die from a lack of humanity and honesty, a frail hot-house plant that never could survive when the winds of seasons buffeted its fragile roots. Love needs air, sweetheart, and room to grow, and be, and discover. And it needs a past and a present and a future to be a whole, as much as you may decry it otherwise.' Placing a finger beneath her chin, he raised her face to his. 'In truth, my love, the bliss of visions on St Agnes's night may well not last into the light of day, given 'tis a fiction from which they spring in the first place, the ink dried on cold parchment to sandwich even the most ardent of lovers in an eternal inanimate dullness.'

She stepped back from his intensity, the moment changed from what it had been before, and, though he watched with a warmth that surprised her, he made no move to fill the silence between them with bland words or cross the small distance with his own body.

This was another Nicholas, not the teasing swain or the reluctant bridegroom, replaced instead by a man she knew could have taken what it was he wanted from her but had chosen instead to wait, and a man tied to her in a way that would never be easy for either of them, given the knowledge of her past. Yet he had disclaimed its potency and defused the power simply by quiet reason, borne to life by the words of poetry.

Her hand went out to him then, in a movement all of its own, and she ran a finger against the rough thewed muscles of his chest, evident beneath the thin linen shirt he wore. Her warmth made him flinch though he bade himself stand still, revelling in the touch of a wife who had stood so far apart for so long.

For the first time in her life Brenna wanted to bed a man. The thought, given her lack of dress, made her redden even as Nicholas reached forward to take her hand, running his touch up from her wrist and on to her shoulder, parting the neckline of the garment so it gaped a little about her throat.

'Nicholas, I am not sure…' she whispered, as he traced a line across her shoulder blades and started downwards.

'Hush.' His voice came deep and husky as he felt the swelling of her breasts rising into his palm, pushed up in a full ripeness and searing heat. 'Look at me, sweetheart.' His words came as she turned her face away from his, not wanting him to know the exaltation, the desperation, the longing that his fingers so easily stroked into existence.

Nicholas, feeling her uncertainty, was encouraged by it, his hands untying silken bows and spreading her nakedness open to his hungry gaze.

'You are so very beautiful.' His eyes drank in her bosom, heaving now with passion, waiting for the moment when he would take his rights further, tensing as his head dropped to her shoulder, his tongue scorching a trail of wetness down on to one proud nipple teased into hardness by his foreplay. He took her into his mouth in haste, suckling hard at her sweetness, amazed that she had let him come this far.

Melting splints of pain nestled into the recesses of oblivion and Brenna moaned, her own hands gathering bunches of tawny hair and pulling him closer, pulling him down, pulling him into her, dissolving into a numbing mist and moaning with the melody of dreams. All denials fled as she arched into his heat, surprised only when his hands fell down across her stomach to stroke between silken thighs.

Danger spiralled down from ecstasy and with shock she pulled away, breathing deeply and desperately, hands retying the bands of ribbon, fastening them like armour across her vulnerability, tears of contrition spilling from bewildered eyes. Give me time, she wanted to hurl at him, and space, she wanted to scream, neither sentiment coming forth given all that she had allowed him already.

Her eyes flickered quickly across his reactions, softening a little as she noticed his own difficulty in control. He had felt it too? In earnest she began. 'This kiss… Nicholas…these feelings…where does this leave us?'

'Making good headway to being husband and wife, my love,' he replied, clamping down on the desire to finish the whole thing off right here and now. After all, was she not willing? One glance at her frightened eyes told him, not just yet. 'I am happy just to gaze, my love, and sometimes touch. Your fears need not be realised because of me. 'Tis difficult to play the gentleman, Brenna, but I can.'

His voice came deep and husky and with all the beautiful enunciation of his birthright and she smiled.

With difficulty he changed tack. 'Come with me to Airelies in the morning?'

Interest sparked in her eyes and, heartened by it, he continued. 'It would be just for one night as I need to be back in London the day after tomorrow.'

She hesitated. 'We'd be alone there?'

Nick smiled. 'We are allowed to be, Brenna,' he drawled lazily, all his good intentions to keep their conversation formal dismissed in a moment.

'There would be no proper furniture,' she hedged. 'Perhaps we should stay at the Red Rooster in Worsley. Alice Templeton is sure to have some spare rooms.'

Amusement gleamed in tawny eyes. 'By all means, Brenna Pencarrow, but be warned—'twill be one room they'll assign us to and hardly more comfortable than the spaciousness of Airelies. Though perhaps I should not try to dissuade you after all, for the thought of sharing a bed would suit me more than you could guess.'

His intimacy made her blush, her hands smoothing the heavy cotton of her nightgown in a nervous gesture that inadvertently made the material strain tightly across the curves hidden beneath.

Nicholas came closer but did not touch, one hand gesturing the warming pan plainly outlined beneath her sheets. 'It is time for sleep, sweetheart. We will need to make an early start to reach Airelies.'

His changed mood astonished her and for a second she felt only regret, before sense sent her scrambling away from him and into bed where she drew the covers up fully across her shoulders and watched as he doused the candles on the fireplace mantel before disappearing to his adjoining room, the sound of the door shutting like a death knell to a building and passionate desire.

Without intention Brenna's hands fell to her breast and she felt herself stroking at the place where his lips had just been, the hidden recesses of a thousand nights of tight control gone within one of surrender. A wild desperation brought her up to her knees as she interpreted her wants, fingers clutching at the sheets without conscious thought of any physical thing, so far did her mind wander from its more usual arc.

She loved him.

She loved Nicholas Pencarrow in every way a woman ever could love a man, with passion, with desire and with tender absoluteness. No recourse to reason or sense in this feeling, no puny contradictions or disavowals, no prissy counterpoints to decry and bewail a full turn in a circle she had never thought to circumnavigate. Nicholas had laid siege to her emotions with care and patience, and with a searing masculine honesty that had finally worn down all the conventional logic.

He had not badgered her with righteousness or beleaguered her with countless compliments—no, the opposite, in fact. All his flattery came now, she thought in hindsight, with an incredible consistency and unchanging honour. Shaking hands came to her mouth, one finger tracing the line of her lips just as he had done a few minutes earlier, and with a single movement she was out of her bed, crossing the floor to the mirror that hung above the fireplace. With hesitation she brought her eyes to the image reflected there, amazed when she saw an outline not unlike the one she had spied every other day in her life thus far. Unsure, she turned her head into the light better, searching for a sign, watching for the bursting radiance that twisted at her heart and knotted her stomach, certain that such a desperateness could not merely be hidden beneath the ordinary. Tears welled as she struggled to contain their outburst and in that moment Brenna Elspeth Pencarrow acknowledged Nicholas Rothurst Pencarrow as a husband she would have chosen above all others, the mere friendship she had professed since meeting him changed into a passion that held no boundary, no endings, no hidden restraint. Indeed, she made a step even to follow him into his room then and there, wanting again the feel of his lips on hers, his hands touching places, turning cold skin to fire, but one last piece of her past held her back. It was not here that she would begin her new beginning but Airelies. And they would be there in the morning.

With stealth Brenna settled herself back into the bed, a broad smile on her face as she savoured her power.

'Tomorrow, my love,' she whispered to the empty room quietly, lest Nicholas might pick up on the sound. 'Tomorrow I will make you understand how well you have played this game and how much I want a winning.'

Chapter Fifteen

She sat in the carriage and felt his arm beside her burning a path along the flesh of her own and, turning, found his eyes upon her in a glance that she could not meet with the directness she had always found easy.

She listened to his voice as he commanded the carriage gone and both longed for and dreaded the time that he might turn to address her to seek an opinion or an answer, needing instead the silence as a buffer against the revelation of her self-discovery of the previous night.

'Are you comfortable?' The question came without any undercurrent and still she was flustered, giving a barely incoherent reply in her haste to answer and turning back to the window in her desperation for him not to notice.

Nicholas accepted her single-worded reply with a burgeoning disappointment and fell silent himself, watching instead the English countryside passing with increasing tedium.

She was back to how it was last time they'd travelled together to Worsley, and he, in his desire to make it otherwise, had thought it would be far different.

With patience he tried again. 'Perhaps you could bring Michael down next weekend. He may enjoy it.'

She nodded but did not turn.

'He seems sadder at Pencarris. Do you think that he is happy?'

She shrugged.

'I thought he may be bored, but Harris informs me he is busy in the library each day.' When Brenna merely nodded, Nick had had enough, and he phrased the next question with more care. 'Could you tell me what it is that he has been working on?'

'Reading and writing.' Her voice was tiny. 'He's making you a gift.'

A frown filled his eyes as he surveyed his wife's back, her hair falling long from a hat perched on its top. She seemed different today, and younger. He swallowed and began with difficulty. 'It's easier having a conversation with someone when you can see that person's face, Brenna.' She stiffened. 'Are you angry with me?'

She shook her head, missing his completely baffled look, this moody reticent Brenna far from what he was more normally used to.

'Are you sick?' A further shake. 'Was it last night?' He was guessing now and getting increasingly concerned. Was she truly a woman who would never be touched? Was this to be his punishment for transgressing the boundaries of her personal privacy? Look but not touch, want but never have. A cold fear clutched at his heart, lightened by her sudden capitulation into a conversation as she shifted her position and faced him, her eyes not quite focussed on his.

'It was kind of you to make this trip to Airelies possible, your Grace. I have a great want to see it all again.' The formality made him edgy. She spoke to him as a stranger might, well mannered but unbearably distant.

'I am a kind person, Brenna.' His answer was flat as he watched her, amazed when she coloured almost scarlet and wondering how such an innocent observation could elicit so unusual a response. He was completely baffled and even more so when she proceeded to fan herself with her hand, as if the heat of the day lay already upon them when 'twas noticeable, at least to him, the nip that filled the early morning air.

A puzzled frown furrowed his forehead as he leant forward to unbuckle the window upon her side, pulling the leather strap from its place and feeling the rushing coldness of the draught upon his hand as he pulled it away.

Brenna welcomed the intrusion upon her blazing cheeks, chastening herself for her stupidity and finding no way out given his close presence and her own mounting tension.

Four hours, she calculated in an impending gloominess. She'd have an apoplexy before she arrived if she were to continue with this nonsense. Her chin went up slightly, though she still felt ill equipped to face him, her tawny knight of a thousand dreams and endings that barely bore thinking of.

One kiss and he had unstopped a genie, she decided, feeling greatly akin to the fables out of Arabia and the boy Aladdin whose life had been changed by such an action. One kiss and he had turned her to jelly. One kiss and, for all her resolve, she could make it no different, every single breath that the man beside her took searing through her consciousness with a razor-like awareness.

The wind settled about her hair, bringing forth tendrils from a quickly pinned coiffure, almost taking the breath from her throat in its strength. Her eyes shifted unwillingly to Nicholas's amusement.

'Shall I shut it now?' he drawled, an ill-hidden laughter in his words.

Brenna blushed at his observation and nodded, washed anew by his closeness. God, how she loved him and, Lord, how she trembled with the consequence.

Looking down, Nick saw how she squeezed her hands together in her lap, a pose so unlike Brenna it brought a shadow of worry to his brow. In submission she looked more remote to him than ever she was in anger and he was bemused by the change and fixedly determined to find out the cause. Why, she reminded him in her posture more of the doting and simpering misses in town, eager to catch his glance and embarrassed when they did so. His heart tripped into a stop even as he thought it, joy replacing bemusement, delight altering irritation, and his eyes ran across her in a wonderment. Could it be the same for her? Could her embarrassment come from a want every bit as great as his own and an inability to express even the smallest of feelings? Could he test his theories here and find the answer?

He stretched as if to pull at tired muscles, his arm deliberately settling afterwards on the seat behind her in a gesture of open weariness, and Brenna's eyes came around to his in a direct query of intent, foundering at his casual smile, bewildered by his carefully enacted posture of indifference.

Feeling the warmth of his arm behind her, she coughed and pulled forward slightly. Short of sitting bolt upright and admitting her discomfort, however, she could do nothing, the rigidity in her back keeping her positioned away from actually touching him. She sighed and faced towards the window, feeling his breath behind her at her neck, and blushing anew at this, the tiniest of caresses.

Nick saw the stain of red and smiled, and with infinite care he moved closer still, dropping his arm on to her shoulder and turning as she did.

Frightened eyes clashed with his, pure discomfort mixed with the harder emotion of alarm, and, unwilling to test his theory further, Nick slipped his arm back again onto the leather seat behind.

'Sorry.' His voice came quiet and singularly unrepentant, and Brenna tugged at the small bag she held before her on her lap. Closing her eyes against the brightness of the afternoon sun, she suddenly felt very tired, a fact she attributed directly to a night full of dreams. Would she ever understand Nicholas? A duke, a sailor, a man who by his own admission had never stayed in one place for very long without being bored by the routine. Did a wife not tie a man as no mistress or adventure ever would? Did the comfort of proximity compensate completely the delight of risk and novelty? Could she truly hope to keep such a one at her side, given all that he knew about her past, and never see a time when disgust would cloud familiarity? Suddenly all her plans were thrown into a disarray. How naïve she had been to plot his seduction and forget the consequences of her own. Had he ever truly admitted his love to her? Reluctantly, she shook her head. Even last night, in the heat of passion, he had not said he loved her, retreating instead to his room when surely, with all his experience, he had recognised an answering want and need in her. Her teeth tugged at her bottom lip and ground together in a lather of sudden uncertainty. Just when all had seemed to fall into place, she had thought it out again. 'Twas a fault of which Michael had oft reminded her, this introspection that denied all possibility, but right at this moment there was no way that she could let it go. With difficulty she held herself together, rigid in her stance and desperate in her want to be released from this proximity that sent all reason awry. Damn it, with space she could counter all the arguments with others. Here she was trapped into an unnatural stillness and tension. How much longer? she wondered, searching for a landmark she knew, but her efforts were unrewarded. Lord, it seemed like an eternity.

Nicholas watched her and longed to bend over and cover her hands with his own, longed to take her to him with a bold assertion, but something held him back. Fear, he reckoned, if the truth be known, fear that she might truly turn his attentions back upon him today, for after last night he had no real defences left with which to berate her. Last night she had met his passion as fully as any woman could have, more so, in her innocence and with her history, given that the gropings of any man could only dredge up the memories of a childhood she'd always longed to forget, yet still she had arched into his caresses with an abandonment that had both astonished and delighted him.

He loved her. He had always loved her, right from the first second of meeting her. Once and for ever, his father had prophesised, and he had been right. Lord, he loved her so much it scared him, for the certainty with which he'd always walked his world had fallen to pieces in a single night of loving and one that had

barely touched the surfaces of intimacy. Could someone love another in this way without the promise of
returned feeling? His heart sank as he remembered Letitia's whispered pleadings and countless other voices
from over a decade of shallow liaisons. My God, it
was his turn to see the other side of love, his turn to
feel its barbs stuck fully into the side of indifference.
Without humour he smiled—justice had its own way
of finding a mark and well he could understand its
target.

Brenna Pencarrow, love me just a bit, his mind
whispered, his eyes falling as she turned to him as if
on cue.

'You are comfortable?' The words were shallow and
stripped of any emotion. It was truly not what he
wished to say at all.

'Perfectly,' she responded, frowning as he removed
his arm from her back and searched his pockets for a
cheroot.

'Do you mind?'

*Yes. Let me feel you close again. Let me lean into
your strength as I long to. Let me make you understand
the feelings you showed me last night were not placed
solely in myth but in truth and flesh and blood.*

'No,' she said aloud to his puzzled look, as he held
the match from the small black cheroot, waiting for
her response.

The match flared and caught, smoke rising in a
plume from its fluorescence and with relief Nick drew
on the cheroot, letting it dull other thoughts. The past
few days had been an explosive mix of confusion and
comprehension, still tainted slightly by the fact that all
his hopes might yet come to nothing.

Yet she was his wife.

The phrase became an aria across the miles of countryside that they now travelled in silence, each searching for landmarks to denote an ending to a journey that had stretched out forever.

She opened her eyes in a dreamy tiredness, rubbing against the comfort and warmth of the bed in which she lay, and coming instantly to her senses when she realised her mistake.

Nicholas. She was in his arms, still in the carriage, full up against his side and tucked in beneath his chin, her hands lying across his lap in places she had never dared to touch.

With a gasp she tugged away, embarrassed a thousand times more than she needed to be.

'I must have fallen asleep,' she murmured, regretting them immediately when he answered.

'And I am glad that you did.'

Her fists clenched in her lap and her heart orbited wildly in her chest, hating this emotion anew that sent all her wits awry and any intelligence she'd once thought herself to possess completely out of the window. She had turned into a dolt and one glance, one touch, one word, was all that was needed to transform her.

Unexpectedly it was a noise from without that saved her as Nicholas's eyes lifted to the outside view and the tiny village of Worsley that now surrounded them. 'We're almost there.' She heard his words as a reprieve and a prayer and turned to position her hat back upon her head, thankful to have something to do with shaking hands.

The next moment all her own concerns were replaced by sheer and utter disbelief.

Airelies came into view as if she were in a dream, all the tired and costly errors of the place remade instead into the very idea of a perfection she'd long imagined and could never implement. The gardens lay through two huge new wrought-iron gates, each wall bedecked by stone urns hung with geraniums and falling in a profusion to row upon row of bluebells, bedded beneath newly planted camellias and standard roses.

The house had been painted a soft-hued creamy white, offset by deep timbered shutters that graced all the front-facing windows, and, along the newly smoothed drive, cherry and plane trees drooped, their roots underplanted in foxgloves, delphiniums and daisies.

With astonishment she looked directly at Nicholas.

'You have done this all as I had planned it.' Without thought she threw herself into his arms, the surprise on his face forcing a laugh from her as she soundly kissed him on both cheeks, all the reticence and embarrassment of the day forgotten beneath the joy of this surprise.

'Am I to gather from your reaction that you approve?' His voice came soft and teasing as she turned to look again at Airelies.

'How could I not when it's all just as I would have done it?' A memory stirred deep in her mind. 'I remember,' she cried in delight. 'That weekend we came down here, and you asked me what I would do if ever I was given the chance to right Airelies's wrongs. And you were the owner?' She laughed as he nodded, one hand coming to her mouth in a wonderment she could barely contain, sobering when she remembered the ending of that same weekend. And still he had not sold

it? He had never given up on her, not even then. Tears
came unbidden as she whispered in amazement, 'It
was not just a wedding gift. It was always mine?'

With care he took her hand and held it, pleased
when her fingers curled into his own.

'Yes.'

Tears stained her vision and the world stood still.

'Why?'

'Because I thought you needed some protection and
pampering and I wanted to give you a home without
a struggle.'

She was speechless as her glance flickered across
the riot of colour, which ran for as far as the eye could
see. Here at Airelies she was home and strong, and he
was her husband.

Soft fingers reached up to his cheek, eyes simmering
with a passion she'd bridled for weeks, and her lips
came to his without any attempt at the shallow quiet
kiss he might have expected, all the fires of ardour well
stirred and offered unconditionally. Even her tongue
probed into the wet warmth of his mouth as she held
his openness to him in a desperate search for what she
knew he wanted to give her.

Nick groaned and deepened their kiss, sliding his
arms across his wife's body and bringing her flat
against an arousal she could feel, the hardness of him
searing through her gown as he rode her abdomen on
strong thighs.

She was so beautiful and she did not know it. His
hands slipped downwards, cupping her buttocks to him
in a way that spoke plainly of what he wanted from
her, and though she pulled back slightly she did not
break away as he might have expected, but stood on
a halfway ground, so to speak, neither yes nor no.

Her mind whirled with a thousand refusals and she could not speak one, for the feel of his body on hers made mute her protests and void her memories. Soft eyes raised to his. 'You confuse me, Nicholas,' she confessed breathlessly, 'for it's daylight and anyone might see.'

He was stilled by this admission because it suggested that, in darkness, he might expect more and, seeing his conclusions she coloured, her own thoughts running now into the night-time hours. There was a tightness in her and a tenseness that it seemed only his body could ease. She had come full circle, she mused, as she watched him. Airelies lost, Airelies gained, Nicholas lost, Nicholas gained, her own self lost and now gained and, within that knowledge there sat a bride no longer reluctant but unsure, unsure of how to relate her newly discovered needs to a groom who had thus far been constantly thwarted.

The rest of the day passed as if in a dream, even the inside furnishings of Airelies secondary to the strategy she planned for the evening ahead, for tonight she knew there would be no more denials. Tonight she would become in truth Nicholas Pencarrow's wife.

She retired early after dinner, and prepared herself well, rubbing oil of violets into her hair as she dried it and dabbing hints of perfume in places she had never dreamed of putting it before. The maid she dismissed early, not wishing to have any witness to her ministrations and embarrassed by the gossip that she knew must fly about the house.

Tonight, as the Duchess, she was as careful as she had ever been to appear all that she was not, even at dinner her silence covered by smiles, giving the appearance of one well versed in the art of listening. If Nicholas had noticed her mind elsewhere he made no comment, repairing to the smoking salon when she excused herself early and asking only if he might stop by her room to wish her good evening. Flustered, she had stammered a definite time, for she wanted him fully surprised by tonight.

The fragility of the batiste nightgown shocked her, its curves barely covering her own, the slit from the hem finishing at her waist, leaving bare all but the tiniest fraction, and little to the fantasy of imagination. Her hair was draped long across her back, slightly damp and wildly curly from the newly taken bath, and as she bent to retrieve a towel a knock came quietly upon her door.

Nicholas… Her eyes flew to the timepiece on the mantel as she bid him entry, her voice tight and trembling in a nervous whisper.

The door came open slowly and Nicholas stepped through, the smile on his face giving way to open-mouthed surprise, his heart slamming into his ribs at the sight before him; his wife sheathed in a gown that covered little, the candles in the room behind her exposing what was left, and her eyes catching his, not in fear but in shyness, and a definite want. He leant briefly against the door, hardly daring to come further lest the apparition disappear to be replaced by a wife far more comfortable in the thick homespun nightgowns she favoured.

And he was wary. Was this to be another test that would lead to nothing, for tonight, with her dressed as she was, he knew he could not weather the charade?

His body ached for her, his manhood hard with just

one glance, the tension in him strung out as far as it could go without breaking. Tonight, if she merely played with him, he could not be certain of the ending. He trusted himself little enough without the trappings of a body naked save for a scattering of batiste and lace and he groaned her name in uncertainty.

'Ahh, Brenna love, I am a gentleman, but not a saint. Take care if the boundaries lie not where I hope them to be.'

Her eyes darkened as she straightened, her arms fallen at her side and covering nothing from his heated gaze as it travelled across her.

He came forward then, their glances caught as he walked straight into softness, pulling her hard against his body, his lips hungrily upon hers, shaking away any politeness and raining her with desperate kisses borne from want.

And she kissed him back, her hands running up his shoulders and into the nape of his neck, her mouth opening beneath his pressure and welcoming the invasion of his tongue probing into the very sweetness of her being. She would be his, there was no doubt, she loved him in a way that took away all memories and replaced fear with joy, and she rubbed her hardened nipples against his shirt, feeling the heat of his body through thin linen.

Nick groaned and twisted one hand into her hair, his lips burning hers, slanting across the soft wetness and travelling down her throat while his other hand slipped beneath one shoulder strap, his eyes questioning this unforeseen consent with a raw uncertainty. Would she refuse him now?

In a wordless answer Brenna pressed herself forward and without warning he lost himself completely, a groan sounding deep in his throat as he lowered his head, taking one nipple deep into his mouth and suckling it without gentleness. White hot shards of pleasure burst inside Brenna as he did so, and she arched against him for more, sure now that she would explode from an exquisite sensation she could never have imagined existed. He was surprising her with his finesse and he knew it, intense eyes raised to hers in challenge as he took the other nipple, feeling her hips buck from their own accord, feeling the breath quicken within her.

'Nicholas,' she whispered. 'What is this you are doing to me?'

'It's love as we make it, Brenna.' His words were husky as he trailed kisses across her cheeks and into the sensitive folds of her neck before returning to her lips. She groaned as his hands tripped paths up her inner thighs and fell just short of where it was she wanted them, waves of pleasure seeping through her, the world held at a distance, indistinct and shadowy.

'I love you,' he said simply.

Her breath stilled and her world reeled back and for a moment she believed all the whispered rumours of Nicholas Pencarrow's magic sensuality as tears of joy ran freely down her cheeks.

'You're sure you lo…love me?' Her words came stuttered and tentative and with an air of entreaty that broke his heart.

'Most sure.' Gentle fingers pushed at a stray strand of hair banishing it behind her ear. 'I love the way your hair curls.'

A hint of a smile played around swollen lips. ''Tis just the curls, then?' The query was shameless and she knew it.

'No, Brenna Pencarrow. I love the way your skin feels against mine, especially when I touch you here.' His hand fell to her nipples, hardened by the edge of sensuality she could hear in his beautiful voice. 'I love your mind, and your honour, and the colour of your eyes. I love your silence and your loyalty, and the clever quietness that hides a woman of unbelievable passion. And I love the way you blush when I say such things to you,' he added when a rose colour suffused her entire face as she pondered the ease with which he engendered the breathless anticipation she was now caught in. God, he was like some ancient sorcerer, commanding her body to an arousal she could scarcely imagine possible. Without will she shivered, and Nick frowned in response.

'You are cold?' he asked, pushing back and removing his own clothes quickly before carrying her to the bed, which lay to one side of the fire. Kneeling before her, his golden body was bathed in candlelight, the slip of material that lay askew across her body all that separated them from one another.

Without speaking she watched him, afraid to break the spell of the moment and afraid also of the thing that next he would do, for the time she had feared all her life was at hand. Darkened eyes scanned the size of him, flickering with panic as he made to join her. With a nervous start she sat bolt upright.

'I know you may think I know a lot about all this, but—'

He did not let her finish. 'I think you are beautiful. I think also that you are scared and I promise we will go very slowly.' With care and reverence he brought her eyes to his. 'You need just say stop, sweetheart, and I shall.'

'And you promise not to hurt me.'

His eyes winced at the pain in her words and huskily he formed his answer as truthfully as he could manage. 'I cannot promise that, my love, but I do promise that I will hurt you the least I am able.' His forefinger traced the line of her lips, silencing the next worry and joining with his thumb to rub a sensuous trail down her throat, tarrying awhile where the line of her jaw met her neck, and then diving lower across full breasts to her stomach and down into the wetness of the junction between her legs. All the time he watched her, intensity boring into denial, caressing her fear with a strength of love she found difficult to question. He was Nicholas Pencarrow, her husband, and he had said he would protect her. Still she was not convinced.

Worried, her body tensed for the assault she thought would follow quickly, relaxing a little as she noticed the laughter lines creasing about his mouth.

'You are not ready?' Her question came with a growing uncertainty. Why did he tarry? At the Crays, when she had been made to watch the other girls, the act would by now be almost over.

'Indeed I am, sweetheart.' His reply came measured and resonant. 'But as yet I can see that you are not.'

'And that would matter to you?'

Incredulous eyes raised to his as she digested the implications of his statement. Did he truly mean for her to believe that he wanted her ready? Was there a truth after all in the ramblings of romantic young girls that forever she had scorned? Her uncertainty floored Nicholas completely.

'Lord, Brenna!' He swore beneath his breath as he brought his wife up against him, holding her so she could not see the extent of anger that welled within him at her simple phrase, for it told him much of the world she had endured.

'Here, sweetheart,' he whispered quietly. 'Let me show you.' His thumb covered her mouth when he saw she might answer, for he wanted no more words or worries, no more conjectures or anger, no more past or future to cloud the beauty of now. Brenna would soon be his and in the taking she would understand finally the consequence of their coupling.

'Feel me, sweetheart,' he whispered, placing her hand across his hardness and guiding it towards the passageway that lay hidden within her, his fingers searching out and finding a nub of hardness within the folds. She felt his caress, the flesh deep within her throbbing with an answering motion, and though she tried to stay still she could not, her hips rounding in a movement of their own, her nails digging into her husband's back with the pressure of his ever-increasing intimacy.

'No more,' she found herself groaning, as she felt herself slipping into an oblivion totally of Nicholas's doing. How could he make this happen and so simply?

His eyes swept across her, locking into her own without waver. 'Tell me truly you want no more, love, and I will stop, though there is much yet that I would teach you.' His thumb did not falter as he talked and the pressure on her hand that held his manhood also increased. 'Feel how I want you, Brenna, and know that you want me too.' He brought her thumb to the entrance of her passage, and she gasped at the wetness that dwelled there.

'This is your body telling mine it is ready to receive me,' he said huskily, having trouble to keep his breathing even in the face of this hastily given lesson to his most unusual wife and sure now that if he did not enter her soon he would come before the minute was out. The explanation denied experience, all his previous lovers well versed in the arts of the boudoir. With will he parted her legs, flinching as he felt the muscles tighten. Would she fight him still? Would he let her deny him? 'Please open for me, sweetheart.' The words were out before he knew it, raw and bleak as he weighed up the odds on his wife's compliance.

And Brenna understood the measure of his restraint with a blazing clearness, for even now, lying without a stitch between them save for a garment that would fire the imagination of even the most dull-witted of lovers, still he gave her the choice. Shaking hands guided his arousal to the place her own hand had just left, and she faced him directly without shame or inhibition.

'I trust you.'

Three simple words and undoubtedly sincere. With care he brought her beneath him and parted her thighs.

'Look at me, Brenna.' The direction brought confused eyes up to his, widening as she saw his intensity and passion and darkening desire. He came into her in a single movement, allowing no time for fear, and buried himself deep within the soft wetness of his wife, groaning with an uncontained fervour.

She was a virgin.

He felt the barrier of her maidenhead with an ache. Twelve years in a brothel, scars to prove her ordeal and yet she was still a virgin. Shaking fingers entwined dark hair as he held her closer and Brenna revelled in his mastery. He was insatiable and strong as he brought her to a throbbing release, her body rippling into exquisite waves, her world splintering into life and joy, fire and bliss.

Their breathing quietened as they came back to earth, slowly and still joined, his hands tracing circles again across the wetness of her inner thigh, his eyes alight with a joy she had never seen there. Brenna pushed herself up on her elbow and gazed down at him, one finger threading back tawny wisps of hair damp with sweat and coming to rest upon his cheek. She smiled as she felt the rough masculinity and the line of his jaw.

He observed her quietly now, his eyes soft with passion. 'Twas his usual habit after lovemaking to leave the bed and dress, the women wanted too much otherwise, wanted words he had never thought to say and could not in all truth whisper. With Brenna he lay fulfilled and still, without a thought to leave, his glance running across her face.

'You didn't tell me.'

'Tell you what?'

Gently he tipped her chin upwards in challenge. 'Between a husband and a wife, sweetheart, nothing needs to be hidden.' He pulled back the sheet, and showed her the blood.

'Oh, that!'

Amusement glinted as he answered in kind, 'Yes, that.'

Dropping her glance from his, she felt her heartbeat quicken. 'They used me only to make the other girls do as they were told. When they didn't, I was beaten.'

'But at Airelies that weekend. You told me…you led me to believe you were…' He didn't finish.

'A whore?' She shrugged as he brushed one finger down her cheek. 'Explanations would have belittled the others, Nicholas, for their choice was as limited as my own. And I was always glad you never asked again.'

He groaned and turned her over, stilled by the scars that lay so evident upon her back. 'I have loved you for ever, sweetheart.'

She felt his lips trace the outlines of the marks, leaving small slithers of coldness across her back, and she turned over and snuggled in, smiling as his arms came to bind them together.

Nicholas could barely move. She had let him take her in with a complete and utter abandon and the promise of more each time. And all his spirits soared aloft, this bride who came cold and icy into a marriage with many conditions was a woman whom he had never known the likes of before, her raw sexuality hidden beneath stillness and morality.

He loved her.

His whole mind burst with a pride he'd never before felt. This night had come fully unexpected and with an ending he could not in his wildest dreams have foreseen. Nun, indeed! Ice Queen! The words he'd heard spoken of her whirled in his brain. And he liked the duplicity, for he knew a side of Brenna that only he would ever understand, the lady of the drawing room turned different in his bed.

Brenna lay inert, unable to speak, unable to make even the smallest of movements and overcome with a tiredness that demanded sleep. This night had been magical and forbidden and she knew without repent that she had acted shamelessly, a side to her character completely untamed in the company of her rampant lion. His shield of arms lay above her bed embroidered in a new tapestry proclaiming her as his property, just another unspoken way the name of Pencarrow was wrapped fully about Stanhope, melding her to him as did their lovemaking, merging who she was into what he had made her.

And with joy now she let him.

She woke to the sun streaming into her room proclaiming the lateness of the hour, and as she stretched she felt the tenderness between her legs, which protested at the ardour of the evening past. Her hand went quickly to the spot and she blushed anew as she felt his wetness, wincing as she touched the swollen flesh still pulsating even across the ache. A smile came unbidden to her face as she remembered the words Nicholas had whispered in the heat of their passion, wild phrases that had only driven her on to demand more from herself and him. She'd been wanton and reckless, none of the reticence she'd for ever fostered on show, and Nicholas had egged her on with an equal ardour.

She looked over to where he lay, pulled away from her on the other side of the bed, the whiteness of the sheet making his golden body look darker and harder, though sleep had the opposite effect on his face. In slumber he seemed younger and softer, his streaked hair falling across his forehead in a tousled fringe, one arm thrown up behind his head in the way she'd often seen children sleep at Beaumont Street. Without warning his eyes opened to her, gaze unfocussed slightly for just a second as he assimilated his wakefulness and a red blush stained her face and neck as she observed all the memories of last night written plainly on his face. With a smile he took her hand and brought her across to him, taking her mouth to his in a kiss that sent her pulses racing anew.

'You look beautiful this morning, Princess.' His words came soft and sincere.

'And you were beautiful last night.'

Nick's heartbeat quickened and with difficulty he clamped down on his lust, feeling his growing size with a groan. Would she be too sore this morning to take him again? She sensed his intent and throbbed for him to guide her, wanting again the sweetness of last night's passion. Without speaking she pressed against him, demanding again something she barely knew the meaning of.

'Nay, it will hurt, sweetheart,' he whispered, holding her still with his free hand.

'Please, I want you,' she whispered back, her body rising to his and moaning as he found the hub of her desire and began to tease it into a response. Everything dissolved in her need for him as her legs opened to his pressure with a will all of their own, and it was well into the afternoon when finally the Duke and his Duchess did come down to eat.

They met the day as lovers, all the world could see it in the way his eyes followed her, and in the way she bent her head to his words and blushed at his scorching glances, and Airelies seemed to dance to their laughter and rejoice in the music Brenna made late in the afternoon on a piano that looked surprisingly like her old one.

She'd hardly even begun the melody he'd asked her to play when she stopped, her ear tilted to the tone of the instrument, delight coming fresh in a wave of disbelief.

'It's my old piano! You bought it for me, Nicholas? From the Keneallys?' Rampant joy sent her scuttling to her knees as she climbed beneath the fingerboard, her hands running over the mahogany at the very back of the panel, searching for the initial she had scrawled in the wood almost twelve years earlier. Finding it, she pulled at his arm, insisting that he join her to see.

Nick squatted and bent his head, a smile well in place as he watched her.

'Here,' she enlightened him with a lilting happiness. She brought his finger up to the letter 'B', which sat in a childish hand beneath the middle C chord. 'It was all I could think of at the time to make the instrument truly mine.' Her nose crinkled as she savoured her foolishness.

'And no surname?' he queried, looking at her with puzzlement.

'No.' She frowned.' At that time I had just disowned Cray and De Lancey was a name I could not claim without too many questions being asked.'

'And Stanhope?'

'It was new.' Her voice was sad. 'They were months when I believed I fitted no place.' Suddenly dimples showed plainly as she reached for a hairpin and boldly scrawled a 'P' behind the 'B'.

Nicholas watched her as she finished the new letter, white in the wood where the old one lay dirtied. 'Brenna Pencarrow,' he said softly, 'do you know how much I love you?'

She shook her head in a mock denial. 'Show me,' she whispered and came up against him with a scorching warmth, lifting her skirts and stepping from silken bloomers, and he took her right there, in the music room down on the floor by the piano, dismissing even the thought of intruding servants to his overriding need to be within her. After they had finished, she looked at him with mischievous guilt written all over her face.

'You make me shameless, Nicholas,' she said as she patted down her skirts.

'And you make me careless,' he returned in a voice filled with an emotion she could only name as astonishment.

Her eyes danced with mirth. 'It is said, your Grace, that you are never that, for long I have heard the stories of a success that leaves little to chance.'

'I was ever a lot of things until I met you, sweetheart.' His mind revelled at their activity over the last few minutes. God, in the music room on the floor! She made him reckless and he liked it. He liked it also that she did not question his needs, meeting his with her own and every bit as strong. The thought made him hard again. He could take her when and where he wanted?

Brenna, seeing his drift, backed away in laughter, rushing into the hallway and up the stairs to their room, and Nick, following in pursuit, locked the door behind him as he caught her.

'Disrobe,' he said huskily, all humour fleeing on contact and, watching him, she did just as he bid, her nakedness bathed in the light of sunshine that streamed through the window.

With care and reverence he knelt and opened her thighs, his tongue licking at its junction and plunging into the honeyed caverns of her very being. And Brenna, clenching his hair in her hands, willed him never to stop.

Chapter Sixteen

The light was almost gone as they walked together through the gardens after dinner, the sound of a gathering wind in the trees upon the evening air.

'Could we not stay here forever,' she whispered, 'and never go back to the city?'

He smiled. He had meant to leave Airelies today, all the appointments in London screaming for his presence, and yet he could not tear himself away. Pencarrow House held people who would be in the way and duties for him that could not be left unattended. For now he needed to be with Brenna, alone in her house amongst all of her memories.

'You wouldn't get bored with me?' he teased, laughing as she pulled his hair in retaliation and holding her close as she overbalanced in the process. His head snapped up suddenly as he heard the noise of leaves crunched by heavy feet, but far too late to stop the two men who now ran upon them, one grabbing Brenna from behind, pinning her arms in his grasp whilst the other levelled a pistol at Nicholas's chest.

Nick shot out his leg even as the bullet whistled harmlessly across his head and went in for the fight, pummelling the surprised man senseless but turning as a voice behind him shouted loudly into the night.

'Any more and I blow her brains out.'

He stopped at once and stood still. The second man held a gun to Brenna's temple and Nick shrank back, arms outstretched, breath heaving as he caught her frightened eyes. 'Don't hurt her, I'll do as you say.'

The weapon came down to face him and the man pulled the trigger even as Brenna screamed, and for a moment all was as it was before, save for the smoke from a gun aimed now uselessly at Nicholas's chest. As Nicholas advanced, the man behind Brenna swore in disbelief and with a final curse he hared off into the night.

Brenna almost lost her balance as she ran towards her husband, for she knew there was something terribly wrong. Nicholas seemed to lose his way and sway, dark gold-green eyes coming to hers in a numbed disbelief at the pain that now swept through his body, and he fell even before she reached him, the ground swallowing him up into darkness.

Hot tears scalded across him as she turned him over, cradling his head in her lap, frightened, weeping aloud in the silence as she pulled away his jacket to find a large gaping hole visible on his left shoulder, blood pumping from an artery and flowing across the ground beside him.

Fear dictated action and she pressed hard upon the wound, screaming into the night for the servants from Airelies, mindless of any new threat to her own person should the one who had just left hear her and return, her free hand running quickly to Nicholas's neck to check the pulse that she could no longer visibly see with her eyes.

'Oh please, God, let him live,' she wailed as she registered an opening door and running feet, the faces of Mrs Fenton and Peter, her nephew, peering down from the closing darkness, expressions horrified when they saw the Duke's condition.

'Get something to lay him on,' Brenna shouted, all her thoughts intact now others had come. 'And hurry,' she stressed, her voice breaking into a terrified sob as she looked at Nicholas; his colour seemed worsened, paler, as if he welcomed death.

'No!' She shook him. 'No, don't you dare die! I love you so much…Nicholas…' She screamed as his eyelids flickered. 'I love you. I love you. Don't die.' The words she'd never said to him were repeated over and over in a panicked liturgy when she thought she might never have the opportunity to say them again.

Bells sounded from the house and lanterns came with running feet beneath them throwing light into the semi-darkness and a door acting as a stretcher was placed under Nick's body, the men lifting him in unison on the count of three. Brenna's heart stopped as he groaned with the pain even through the oblivion, her own hands tightening on the wound at his shoulder.

Haggard faces looked uncertainly at Brenna as they made their way into the house, one man dispatched to take the inert form of the first intruder and lock him in the shed until a constable could be fetched from Worsley.

Upstairs Nick was placed gently on his bed, stripped of its sheets and laid out instead with wadding cloths to catch the blood that still dripped from his body, and, as Brenna instructed Mrs Fenton to remove his boots, Ilona, the healer from the village, hurried in, her

weatherbeaten face assessing the situation with a calmness born of knowledge.

'Keep your hands there, your Grace,' she instructed,
turning to the housekeeper and ordering hot water and
rum, long bandages and cloths with which to clean the
wound. 'Gemma, go to my house for my bag,' she
added, hailing forth a nervous downstairs maid. 'And
make sure you bring the earthenware container on the
mantel, the one with the rose-coloured pattern. It's important we dress the wound properly or else the whole
thing will fester.'

'Will he live?' Brenna could barely phrase the question.

Ilona lifted back the jacket, tearing at the remnants
of both that and a shirt, her fingers prodding at the
gaping hole with a careful watch on the flow of blood.
She shrugged and turned him over, cutting at the back
of his clothing and nodding when she saw the hole
there too. 'This is a good sign, the bullet has at least
left him and, if the fever does not take him, he may
well yet live.'

Brenna shivered. Such words were bare comfort and
fresh tears assaulted her eyes as she stripped away the
clothes Nicholas wore, leaving his hard brown body to
full view, her eyes going to a scar he sported on his
right arm and one she had fondled as he had taken her
to him in the night.

What if he died? The thought was raw in her brain,
and in dread she took his hand and held it, willing
warmth into the coldness, willing life where death
lurked, willing him to know of her presence and fight
all the harder because of it.

The wound was cleaned and sealed, hot scalding
flesh singed with the edge of a silver scabbard, the

smell bringing bile to Brenna's throat and renewed thrashing from Nicholas. He groaned as the knife burnt into him, writhing even beneath the weight of three men brought in especially to hold him down. Brenna's nails pressed painfully into her own palms as she turned away, not bearing to look at the hurt of the one she could never replace.

And then they bandaged him, the doctor arriving just as they had finished, nodding his head at the finesse of Ilona's ministrations.

Alec Jamieson bent his head down to listen to Nicholas's chest, a frown crossing into his eyes. 'Are there other kin who should be notified?'

Brenna blanched. What was he implying? With anxiety she stood. 'You are saying he may…' She petered out, not even willing to express her fears.

The old man tipped up his glasses to observe her. 'Gunshot wounds are always difficult to predict, your Grace, but your husband is a strong and fit man. That counts for much if the fever should take over; it gives him some reserve with which to fight. The important thing now is that he is kept still for he has lost much blood already and we cannot risk the possibility of another rupture.'

'Of course.' Brenna turned as Doctor Jamieson took a vial of medicine from his bag. 'This is for you, to sleep.' He overrode her argument. 'If you do not have any rest yourself you will be utterly useless in doing the best for your husband.'

Brenna nodded, though she did not intend to take the sleeping draught. She knelt at Nicholas's side as he departed and sent the housemaid off to find fresh cloths and water, glad that, for a moment at least, she had Nicholas alone. Worried, she took his hand and held it to her heart, letting him know of her presence, letting him feel her care and love.

The hours passed by slowly. Brenna refused her bed and ate only a little of the supper placed beside her by a hovering Mrs Fenton.

By midnight her head dropped on to her arms and with exhaustion she slept fitfully, awakening again at three when she felt the first thrashings of his fever. Her palm touched his brow and she knew he was burning up, glazed open eyes sightless to what lay before him, words tipping jumbled across his tongue, his hands flung wide as he thrashed with the pain of what was happening to him.

'Stay still, my darling,' she whispered, bringing a damp cloth across his brow and down to his neck, dipping it to the places on his chest that the bandage did not cover. 'Stay still and I will take away the heat.' Her voice crooned endlessly to him, above the toneless ramblings of one who knew not what he said. By morning Brenna's misgivings had grown apace with his fever. He burned with it, a searing blistering sweltering malady that defied even the coldest of compresses and the best of her prayers.

The fever still raged in the early afternoon and Nicholas lay so still that she bent her ear to his chest just to listen that his heart did beat. He lay so still that she could barely believe he would recover.

'Oh, God,' she whispered her voice high with panic. 'Please let him live. Please don't let him die.' Desperate sorrow welled in her throat and she pressed at her mouth to try to still the fear, her glance straying to Nicholas's face as she stroked his forehead.

'If you die, Nicholas, I will have nothing left, nothing to live for, no one to laugh with or tell my secrets too, no one to smile at me as you do or hold me against the darkness.' Despair tripped across sanity as she fell against his body, wrapping herself into his warmth and familiarity. 'If you die, I want to die too, for I can't live without you, not when I have just found you. Oh please, God, please let us stay together, please.' Sobs racked her frame as she struggled to find breath, struggled to find reason and hope. And then she heard a soft whisper and felt a movement against her cheek. Her eyes jerked up to Nicholas's face, widening in amazement as she registered a clear glance born not of fever. 'Nicholas?' she questioned, imploring him to answer her and bending across to hear the words forming on his lips.

'I love you.'

Tears of joy tore down her face as she kneeled closer and whispered back. 'I love you too, Nicholas. Oh, how much I do love you.'

He smiled and weakly clutched at her hand brushing it against his lips. 'I know.' And with that he fell promptly back to sleep.

'He will live! He will live.' Her shout brought out all the other members of the household of Airelies who had been holding their breath at the sorrow of the young mistress and praying in their own way, trying to find the right words to deliver the master safely back to her.

Half an hour later Brenna climbed into the bed with care and lay against Nicholas, unmindful of the sheen of sweat that dampened her nightdress, instead relish-

ing the feeling of the thin batiste being the only thing
separating them.

His eyes flickered open again at the contact, willing
himself from his world of nothingness and watching
his wife as she cuddled into his right-hand side. His
arm tightened on to her, drifting off the moment she
looked up, just a small gesture of belonging before
unconsciousness claimed him yet again.

By the morning he was desperately thirsty and she
scampered from the bed at his husky pleadings for a
drink and poured out some water, bringing his head
up into her arms as she slipped the glass to his mouth.

'Just a little,' she softly instructed, taking it from
him, unsure as to how much he should have. Replacing
his head upon the pillow, she brought a cloth to wipe
his much cooler brow. Thankful eyes came up to her.

'Welcome back, my darling,' she said gladly, soft
hands upon his cheek.

In response he smiled and tried to rise, though the
effort cost him much in strength, and with a groan he
fell back against the pillow. Brenna hurried to stop him
trying again. 'Ilona said you must not move. There was
much blood lost and she said it would take a good
while to recover.' He nodded and stayed still.

'How long since I was shot?'

'Two days ago now.'

Gold-green eyes showed a definite surprise. 'We all
thought you might not live. The minister came and
blessed you yesterday evening.'

His eyebrows shot up. 'That bad?' He lifted his head
slightly, his eyes running across the bandages in place
to try to determine the damage beneath.

Brenna quickly volunteered the information. 'The

shot went in here—' she gestured '—and out at your back. You have a large hole that Ilona, the local healing woman, singed. She could not stitch the breadth of it, you see.'

'And the men?'

'One is in jail and the other ran off. The constable is questioning the first one, but it seems they were merely hired men paid to kill you and take me. It's all the information we have…' She trailed off at his frown.

'Did anyone come down from London, or is this all being dealt with here?' Irritation and worry vied with each other on his face and Brenna hurried to quell his fears.

'The constable from Worsley is a good man, and he has sent in people to watch Airelies while you recover. We are quite safe.'

Nick reined in his impatience and reached for his wife, making a mental note to send for reinforcements from Pencarrow House that very morning. 'I don't want you going outside, Brenna, not to Worsley, not into the gardens, nowhere! Not by yourself. Do you understand?' Pain shot momentarily across him and he forced himself into a quieter pose, all this exertion and thought costing him much in strength. As Brenna eased in beside him, he relaxed and held on to her tightly, slightly puzzled when she worked herself free and raised her head on to one elbow, her warm gaze meeting his questioning one.

'I love you, Nicholas.' The words came soft and true and with all of the warmth that she could muster.

He smiled and brought up his right hand to trace a path across her lips. 'You told me each time you kissed me, Brenna, and all night when first we made love.'

Dimples showed plainly and she laid her head back against his shoulder. 'And I thought you might die without ever knowing. I shouted it at you, you know, when first you were shot.'

He laughed. 'I heard. It was the last memory I had before I woke up and heard you tell me again.' More seriously, he added, 'And it was the one thing that kept me fighting when the fever came full upon me.' He lay still for a moment, his thoughts flickering across the last few months. 'When did you first love me?' he asked quietly, smoothing her hair where it fell across the bandage on his chest.

'The night before the fire,' she returned without hesitation, blushing as he looked down at her. 'I woke up drenched in sweat after dreaming of a handsome green-eyed knight. I worried that you might have seen it in my eyes when you lifted me into your carriage.'

He smiled. 'Now I understand why you did not fight me as I had expected, but you were far more cautious than I, Brenna, for I loved you the first minute I ever saw you and fifty times as much when you stood in the hall at Pencarrow House with blue moonbeams in your hair.'

'That time I first saw you at Pencarrow House?' She could hardly believe what it was he told her, yet it explained the following turn of events as nothing else could have. 'You make up your mind quickly, Nicholas Pencarrow.'

'And I never change it, Brenna Pencarrow.'

Chapter Seventeen

The man opposite Nick shuffled uncomfortably as he watched the Duke sort through his recent report, agitation evident as Nicholas met his eyes.

'We've been back from Airelies for twelve weeks now and you're saying to me that the man has been tried and sent to Newgate without offering one single piece of information as to the perpetrator of this plot, even though it could alleviate his own circumstances?'

'Yes, your Grace.' The reply came without pride. 'Unfortunately the man was the victim of his own greed, so to speak, twice the money forthcoming only upon a completed deed. The partner presumably was the only one who knew any details.'

'We caught the wrong man, you mean. Damn. Surely you can see the predicament that this dead end leaves me in. The third attack on my wife in a year and still no proof as to what or who lies behind it.'

'No, your Grace.'

Nicholas sighed loudly, depositing the sheaf of papers into a file already thick with other reports before hauling himself out of his chair, wincing slightly at the pain still evident across his shoulder, angry that it dogged him so. Lord, he'd tried every avenue, every angle, and still to come up with nothing. The professionalism of the ones responsible worried him. It was no simple put-together plot he dealt with here, but a carefully constructed strategy that one day might very well net the bounty.

Brenna.

His heart tripped painfully at her vulnerability. God, how he hated to be apart. Even now, knowing that she was somewhere in the house, the fear still haunted him every minute, every day. He ran a hand through his hair as he dismissed the nervous investigator, surprised when the man tarried and began to speak.

'Excuse me for asking, your Grace, but would there be anything in your wife's past that could bring on such a problem?'

'No.' Nick's answer came quick and certain and the man reddened instantly.

'Of course not. It's just that Hobbes gave me the job to ask—sometimes people leave out important pieces of a jigsaw.'

'Well, tell him he's barking up the wrong tree,' Nick countered tersely, reaching for the brandy as the man showed himself out.

God, that's the whole problem, Nick thought wearily. I can't tell him anything for fear he'll discover everything. With careful stillness he downed a glass of brandy and crossed to the cabinet to one side of his study. Opening the door to four shiny derringers, he took the largest one in his hands, sighting the shot on a leaf blowing in the autumn wind outside of the window.

'Bang,' he said softly to himself, clearly imagining his invisible opponent. *Just one clue, just one false*

step, and I will have you, he thought, his mind running
to the skirmishes so far. Two attacks at Airelies and
one in London. And before that, nothing. It was linked
somehow to his own near miss at Worsley, he knew,
but why involve Brenna and Michael? And why was
the instruction given to shoot him and take his wife
hostage? A ransom with the main player dead would
make no sense at all. Was it not for money they diced
with death? Then revenge. Who would profit most
from Brenna's discomfort and sadness—someone who
knew of her past? Someone who had been made increasingly angry by the failed attempts so far? His
mind scooted to the man who had shot him at Airelies.
Had he not instructed the other to take care of Brenna
or else the witch would not pay? He'd heard the words
himself as the gun discharged. She? A woman. A
woman who loathed Brenna so much that it was not
for money she sought revenge, but a pure unadulter-
ated hatred. But who could hate his wife with such an
intensity?

Mary Cray.

Lord, the thought struck Nicholas as a thunderbolt.
Mary Cray, with one husband killed and her foster-
daughter gone in the process. Had the incident at
Worsley alerted her to the identity of both Michael and
Brenna, Brenna's profile more visible still in the company of the Pencarrows. His mind flashed to the news-
paper articles and descriptions of his wife. Had Mary
Cray read them from her place in hiding and plotted a
revenge? It all fitted. A woman, and one with a motive
that could seethe and simmer for all these years. How
old would she be now? Perhaps fifty. Where could he
find her?

Nick placed the gun back into his cabinet and called

for his secretary, Winslop, who came, pen and paper in hand, and with a message from Brenna.

'Her Grace asked me to inform you when your report was finished that she had promised Michael she would go with him to the library, sir. Do you wish to accompany her, or shall I send Robertson?'

Nick frowned. Any outings placed an added worry and the possibility of another attack on Brenna. Yet how could he refuse her? The world for Brenna must not become another prison, but, in the face of his new discovery, everything seemed dangerous.

'I'll accompany her, Winslop,' he said grimly, schooling his face to gentler lines as he walked to find her.

Brenna stood in their bedroom before the window, one arm draped in a strangely protective gesture across her stomach. The sun shone on her dress, marking it in differing tones of lightness and there were tears on her face.

'Brenna?'

She moved suddenly, as though startled, and a journal fell from the sill. When he bent to pick it up he noticed Christian names scrawled in lists across the page. And hearts with his initials intertwined with her own.

'A secret?' he asked, puzzled by her reaction.

Uncertainty radiated from her, reminding Nick forcibly of the days when first he had met her, and an expression that he had not thought to see again.

Worried now, he asked quickly, 'What is it, sweetheart?' The cold dread clutching at him abated a little as he noticed her answering smile.

With care Brenna set down the book beneath a cushion and stood beside him, her eyes shining with both hesitation and excitement. 'Remember that time at Airelies, when you were recovering and we went to the belvedere and sat and talked for hours and hours and then we…and after we…we…' She faltered, embarrassed and nervous.

'Made love,' Nick finished the sentence with amusement, astonished when she blushed an even a brighter shade of red and stood watching him with a burgeoning unsureness.

'Yes,' she continued, hating herself for this tongue-tied stupidity given the magnitude of the news she had to impart. 'Well, the thing is, you see…the thing is…I think because of it I am with child.'

'You are what?' The words came like a bellow from Nick, his gaze falling of its own accord to her stomach, his hand coming up to stroke the smooth hardness. 'You're sure?'

'No, not really, for in truth I know little of the subject.' Ruefully she raised the book and Nick saw it to be some sort of text on midwifery.

Dancing delight crossed his face and with a wild shout of pure happiness he hugged her to him, raising her from the ground whilst he spun on his heels. 'A baby. Our baby. Truly?' A mistiness filled his eyes. 'When was it you knew?'

'Ilona bade me recognise the signs last week.'

'You have been sick?' Worry crossed his voice.

'No. It is the blood flows that I have missed.' More unsurely, she added, 'Why, are you supposed to feel sick too?'

Nick looked at her with a growing incredulity. God, she knew as much about the process as he did and the whole thought concerned him immensely. A child, their child, needed to be at no risk due to parental ignorance, and what of Brenna herself? A thin sweat broke out on his upper lip as he took his wife against his body, wrapping his arms about her smallness, wanting to protect her, shelter her. The memories of his own childhood were suddenly and blindingly close and Brenna was smaller than Johanna had been.

'We will have my doctor come to Pencarris tomorrow to give you an examination, and us both some information. And you must rest. And eat well.' His mind ran across every argument for good health in pregnancy that he had ever encountered. 'And walking. I have heard it said walking is beneficial.''

Brenna laughed and snuggled in tighter. How she loved Nicholas and how she wanted this child.

Everything was right.

Everything was perfect.

'I've already seen Dr McInnes. It was he who gave me the book,' she returned, her smile broadening as Nicholas groaned. 'And it's no use saying anything because there is no way I would want to see Clive Weston-Tyler about this.' More quietly she added. 'If you must know, I find him strange.'

'Strange?' His voice filled with an undercurrent of disbelief. 'Sweetheart, medically speaking he's the best there is and if anything ever happened to you...'

She placed a finger against his lips and did not let him finish. 'It won't. This pregnancy so far has gone all to plan according to Ilona, and the labour should be no different. It's woman's work, don't you see, Nicholas, and I long for the chance to show you the complete person that we have made together.'

Put like that, Nick had no rejoinder, though with the

tenderest of care he tipped her face up to his. 'If I lost you...'

'You won't.' His manhood stirred as she ran a finger across his chest, unfastening the linen shirt till it was fully opened and slipping warm up against him. 'We'll be together forever,' she whispered, smiling as he bent behind to ram home the lock on the door, dancing passion blazing forth from his smouldering eyes.

Chapter Eighteen

Nicholas and Brenna lay in bed and made joyful plans for a child almost come. His hand rested on her stomach as she turned towards him beneath down-filled covers.

She revelled in this pregnancy, a tiny baby born of parents who loved each other fully, and even now, when her term was almost complete, still their love-making was as impassioned and desperate as it always had been.

She ran her fingers across his chest and downwards, turning herself against him sideways and opening her legs with direct invitation. Moaning as she felt him enter, she brought one breast to his mouth to suckle like the baby she would soon hold there, surges of blistering wild excitement vacillating right across her as he thrust gently inside. Her nails raked his shoulder as she cried out with the exquisite pain of a longing for him that had never altered, clinging tight as he quickened his urges and straining ever higher as her body broke into waves of pleasure, surge after surge rippling across the tautness of her stomach, on and on in a coupling made in heaven.

They lay watching each other afterwards, his eyes meeting hers in a silent union of mutual worship, the babe between them turning in the quiet, making its presence felt against Nicholas's stomach.

'She grows restless, I think,' he said as the movement rolled on.

'Trying to get comfortable after his rude awakening, no doubt,' she parried.

In worry he raised himself on his elbow and stared down at his beautiful wife. 'I wouldn't hurt her, would I?'

'No, your Grace, he's quite able to look after himself.'

Hard lips came down on her laughing ones, though this time he lay slightly apart and taking his weight fully on his own elbows. Her teasing as to the sex of the child always confounded him. She was sure he wanted a male heir, first in line to the Pencarrow fortunes, but, if he was truthful to himself, what he most desired was a daughter and in exactly the same mould as her mother.

'It's time to rise, my lady, much as I would like it otherwise.' Puzzled eyes came up to his. 'The Winter Fair,' he clarified, quickly looking at the clock on the mantel. 'Already we are late.'

With a sigh she rose and Nick watched with regret as she pushed her long dark hair from her face and stretched to meet the morning. 'At least it is a lovely day for the festival,' she said from the window, the watery sun outside breaking through an early morning fog into a blue and cloudless morning. Nicholas got out of bed and joined her, wrapping his arms about her coldness and smiling as a silver roan came into view with Charles seated on its back, both their breaths trailing steam through the coldness.

'Charles has been busy,' Nick commented. 'He needs a wife to keep him in bed longer.' His hands ran down her body, returning even as she slapped them away. 'A shapely wife like mine would see him abed till a much more respectable hour.'

'And later still if I let you have your way.' Brenna turned into his warmth, shivering slightly and smiling as he reached across for his robe and placed it across her shoulders, content in the silence of the moment before the hurry of the day set upon them again.

Two hours later they came into the village of Penmayne, which was bedecked with gaily coloured stalls, banners slung from every jutting point and ribbons of all hues trailing earthwards.

All about them were people. When the horses had drawn to a halt Nick helped his wife out of the carriage, holding her longer than was normal as her feet touched the ground, so that she felt his body hard down the length of hers.

'Are you never satisfied, your Grace?' she whispered, thinking of their coupling just a few hours before.

'Get back into the carriage and I will show you how much I want you still,' he threw back lustily, frowning as he noticed the welcoming committee descending upon them, and steadying her gently with a warning. 'Here comes the Mayor and his wife, my love. We'll have to postpone our meeting till later.'

All mirth fled at his words, her shamelessness aired in front of Nicholas only, and she became the proper mistress of Pencarris, turning with a gentle smile and quiet eyes to the people before her, and giving them greeting as Nicholas was whisked away to the dais. Left with Caroline Weatherby, Brenna observed the proceedings from below, watching her husband with pride as he stood tall and commanding among the others present. He spoke quickly before cutting the ribbon, giving back the scissors to a woman whom Brenna failed to recognise and who observed him from beneath heavily disguised eyes. Brenna smiled; she was by now almost used to the reaction Nicholas elicited from the opposite sex and their marriage had never changed that, though the lopsided grin turned her heart as his eyes searched only for her.

He waited by the edge of the tent as she walked across to him, James Weatherby and Charles talking at his side, all three of them observing a group of bulls in the paddock opposite who were of formidable size and proportion.

'You are feeling well?' he asked her quietly as the others spoke at length about the livestock, James and Charles most knowledgeable about the qualities of a good animal.

Brenna nodded and squeezed Nick's hand teasing gently. 'For a farmer you seem very quiet.'

'It's ignorance rather than anything else.' He smiled. 'My world lies mostly in the ships of the Pencarrow Line and I've always left the farming side to Charles. That's part of the reason he's come today, he wants to show me a new breed of stock he thinks will work well on our northern properties.'

Brenna sighed. All this noise and movement had made her feel tired and she looked around eagerly for a place in which to rest. A tent to one side of the cake stall caught her attention as it boasted both hot tea and

scones. Nick, diverted by a tenant, bid her wordlessly
to go before him and watched as Caroline Weatherby
accompanied his wife.

A shout came two minutes later from a carriage behind him, and fear thickened in his throat. Caroline
was in the arms of a farmer, the bump on the back of
her head congealed with freshly run blood.

Nicholas was at her side in two seconds, trying to
shake her awake, desperation building as his eyes flew
across the roads that departed Penmayne for any signs
of settling dust or for the back end of a hastily departing landau.

Nothing.

His gaze came back to Caroline, her eyes flickering
as the smelling salts were applied beneath her nose.

'Brenna,' she groaned. 'They've taken Brenna.'

'Who?' Nick growled, white hot anger flashing
through his veins. 'Which bastards have got her?'

'Two men. They have a gun. They said they would
kill her if she struggled.'

Pain caught in Nick's heart as he stood to meet
Charles who was already unlacing the Pencarrow
horses from the coach.

'You take the Northern Road while I go south. With
speed we can beat them easily.' His voice cracked a
little as his gaze centred on his brother, Charles's expression exactly how he knew his own must look.
Damn it, he chastised himself angrily, he couldn't let
the fears be voiced or else he'd be no good to anyone.
Grabbing the roan mare from the hands of his surprised
brother, he was off in the direction of Tonbridge, the
gun pushed into his hands, cocked ready for any kid-
napper he would chance to meet.

* * *

Three hours later Nick knew she had not come this way. His careful searching had come to naught, and it was with a heavy heart that he turned his horse northwards, meeting with Charles an hour later, looking equally dispirited, having arrived at exactly the same conclusions.

Brenna was gone, vanished into thin air like smoke, and none had seen or heard anything of a carriage headed quickly from Penmayne or sheltering along the way in a barn or heavy patch of woods.

Nicholas's fears grew with the darkness that spread over the land, at first as an earth-red glow, deepening into charcoal as the hours ticked on. By six o'clock the night was upon them, a gloomy black and moonless night, an endless lonely windswept night, and a night that frustrated all the searchers further in their attempts to find the beautiful young Duchess of Westbourne.

Nicholas primed his weapons and thought of Brenna. He saddled his stallion Mercury, checking all the leather bracings and thought of Brenna. He sent riders to every village on the road from Penmayne to London and from Penmayne to the southern Coast, and when the reports came back with nary a sign of anything unusual, he thought of Brenna.

Caroline had been lying upon the chintz sofa at the rectory of Penmayne, telling her story and safe in the arms of her husband when Nicholas had returned from his ride south, dust and sweat across his body.

'We were just going towards the tent for a cup of tea when a man I had not seen before walked up to Brenna. He had a gun in his pocket that he told us was pointed directly at Brenna's stomach.'

Nick gritted his teeth and listened as Caroline continued. 'He said another gun was directed towards you, Nicholas.'

Standing back, Nick swiped his hand through his hair, ignoring his grandmother's arm across his back, ignoring everything but the dreadful howling rage that had settled inside him.

'Brenna didn't speak. She just stood in front of me and went…' The last words were delivered with a sob, Caroline's hands clenched to her mouth, eyes awash with tears. 'I should have screamed or done something.'

The pain in her voice pierced the growing numbness in Nicholas and he bent down to Caroline and took her shaking hands in his. 'I will find her, I promise. I will turn this part of the country upside down to find her…' His voice tailed off. Words, he thought even as he said them, words, words, words and all he could do was to sit and wait.

Two days later the morning dawned with the promise of a storm and Nicholas watched the darkening sky with a growing apprehension, the stubble on his cheeks attesting to the fact that he had given no thought to himself as he tried to piece together the puzzle of Brenna's disappearance. Lord, he'd dismember whoever had done this deed piece by piece if they had hurt her. It had to be Mary Cray, his mind reasoned with an alarming clarity, but every search he had made of the area where Brenna had used to live had turned up nothing, an empty hotel, a neighbourhood full of shifting itinerants. It was as if the woman had vanished into thin air, her name appearing nowhere in all the checks Nicholas had run across numerous counties.

And Brenna was gone. Gone from his house, from his bed, from his life, leaving nothing but an empty shell where before had lain everything that he had wanted. Every second thing reminded him of her, her piano, her gardens with the bulbs of next spring just pushing their way through earth tilled to life by her, her combs and brushes on the desk upstairs, long strands of curling black still entwined in the bristles. The smell of violets seemed to whisper of a living presence, assailing him as he walked through their bathroom or lifted her gowns to his face. It comforted him, told him she'd soon be back, hung like a good omen against everything else that was bad.

The barrenness of his thoughts were pulled suddenly back to reality as Harris raced into his study, with Charles one step behind, and Michael in his chair behind him again.

'This came to Pencarrow House this morning, your Grace,' the butler said quickly, handing a note to Nicholas. With shaking hands he broke the sealed wax and began to read.

If you want to see your wife alive again, bring twenty thousand pounds to the gates of Airelies Manor at midnight. Any sign of others and we kill her.

'Oh, God,' Nick groaned, his mind thinking quickly as he tore a large sheet of paper from a roll near the door, brushing what correspondence sat on his desk aside as he laid the sheet down. 'Here, Airelies is here, and the path in and out of the place, here.' The paper filled with different spots of note.

A mistake. Their first mistake, meeting him on a ground where he held all the advantage in knowing the layout, and a place so smothered with trees another's presence could be easily concealed. He grabbed at a book of maps, ripping the right pages from the spine and flattening them out in front of him. 'Here,' he said with certainty, raising his eyes to his brother. 'Here is where we hit them and it had damn well better be good and hard.'

Nicholas assembled a posse during the morning, not large in size but strong on conviction, and that afternoon, as he saddled his horse, he looked up at a sun swathed in clouds and was caught by the strangest feeling that somewhere across the lonely countryside Brenna also glanced heavenwards, and wished that he would come.

Mary Cray stood above Brenna and cracked her hand up hard against the cheek of her long-ago foster-daughter, a cheek still stained with another blow from yesterday, the once-dried blood upon her lip beginning to flow anew.

'You bitch,' she cried, yellow teeth bared as she shouted, 'Think that you can order just what you wish to eat like at some fancy restaurant, like some grand Duchess to see others do their bidding. That water is plenty good enough for the likes of you and, if once you knew the meaning of want, then it's a good thing you learn it all again. Just pick the damn insects out and eat them as we had to do when we raised you, and what for, I'll tell you what for, so's that uncle of yours could come and kill my Brian, and your husband kill my son. I rue the day when I ever agreed to the nonsense your mad mother spouted, for I've paid thrice over in blood ever since and now so shall you.'

Brenna began to shake, her hands shielding her stomach and the form of her unborn child. Why did Nicholas not come? Where was he that he should leave her here to this bullying and shouting madwoman and these eagerly gloating men?

Mary Cray noticed the glance towards her companions and the girl's fear. 'I've let them all know of your charms, but until Nicholas Pencarrow turns up I have a need to keep them off of you; after all, it's whispered in London now that you do have your uses as his wife. Have you not told him of the past? Have you not whispered your secrets to a Duke who may be interested to hear that his wife was brought up in a whorehouse?'

Laughter followed her remark as she withdrew and the heavy wooden door shut upon a windowless room.

Brenna pulled her legs under her and felt the new cut to her lip. Shaking hands then shielded her stomach and she prayed with all her heart that Nicholas would come as she whispered to the child within, 'Not yet, my darling, wait until Daddy comes, wait until he is here to save us.'

Quarter of a mile away, Nicholas caught the first faint smell of smoke and was puzzled. The old gardener's cottage had been vacant since he had resettled Albert into newer accommodation at the rear of the big house and this was the only dwelling within two miles, save for Airelies itself, but that sat in an upwind position. Stopping Mercury, he gestured to the others. 'If we walk from here, it will give us an hour to get into position and another to play the waiting game. And there is a cottage to the west that I want to look over.'

In silence the men did as he asked, though two were requisitioned to take up position on either side of the only routes from Airelies. If it all went wrong, Nicholas needed to know where they had fled to, and this time there'd be no waiting around.

Brenna lay against the side of the wall, her fingers clenching the beam beside her until the knuckles showed white, her teeth biting down the scream that threatened to come any minute, sweat running in small rivers across her brow and down between the valley of her breasts. The baby was coming, she knew it instinctively, and finally she could do nothing to stop it, all the contractions running together now in a lather of movement and a strength that tore the silence from her throat. She screamed as the child began to birth, screamed into the quiet of the night, breaking the stillness into a resounding clatter of noise and bringing Mary Cray into the room in a fever pitch of anger.

'Shut up or I'll kill you now.' The gun she held came about to face Brenna who bit down on her lip and panted with a desperate shaking, her whole body clenched in tight pain. 'Make one more sound and I'll pull the trigger, understand?'

Brenna nodded, tears of anguish slipping unheeded down grimy cheeks. She'd never get out of here alive. Suddenly she knew it and her child was almost born. A shout from outside turned Mary's head around and it all changed within a moment, the anger of the woman transferred from her to the one who advanced slowly in.

'Nicholas!' Brenna whispered as he appeared through the portal, tall enough to have to stoop slightly, his eyes barely believing what they saw.

His wife lay on a dirt floor covered in filthy straw, her dress ripped, and her face filled with a fear he had never seen there before and a pain that seemed to rack her body.

The gun at his hip was trained on the mad woman as he registered in a second that hers was trained upon his wife. He gave her little leeway as he turned as if to speak, blasting away at Mary Cray before she even registered the action, her body falling broken to the floor, red blood staining the brown filthy reeds that were strewn all around.

Nicholas dropped his gun and in two strides was kneeling before Brenna, his words raw and urgent. 'My God, Princess. My God, how have they hurt you?' Shaking hands surveyed her body for fresh signs of blood or a bullet, and bafflement crossed his face as she seemed to pant with a fright born from within. 'Sweetheart,' he shouted. 'It's me.'

Desperate eyes raised pleadingly to his as the tension seemed to leave her body. 'Nicholas,' she sobbed, grabbing his arm and holding it close, 'it's the babe, it comes now and I cannot stop it at all.' A furrow was ploughed into her forehead as she felt the next pain and Nicholas paled visibly.

'There is no doctor.' He went to stand, panicked by something he knew nothing about, the safety of both his wife and child set squarely into his hands, but she held him back, panting again, beseechingly watching through dark and pain-filled eyes. He sat with her then, knowing there was no other, knowing it was him or nobody. The alarm left his face and he whispered gently, 'Tell me, Brenna, tell me what it is that I must do.'

'Hold me,' she sobbed, biting into the material of his jacket as Charles came around the corner, stopping dead as he saw the twisted body of Mary Cray.

'Can you get her out of here, Charlie, and come back as soon as you can. Our baby seems set to arrive at any moment.'

Brenna's cries were louder now, louder and longer and nerve-rackingly regular. Oh, God, why did the child not just come? Nicholas thought, as he removed his jacket and tucked it around the shoulders of his wife, positioning himself behind Brenna, cushioning her tightness and agony and massaging her back, which ached with an unbearable painfulness in the small spaces of quiet.

Charles reappeared in a moment, closing the door behind him and catching his brother's eyes in obvious fright. 'I left our men outside. Everyone else is dead and Kenneth has gone for a doctor. He said he knew where to find one.' His gaze came across Brenna, darkening with anger as he saw the signs of mistreatment, though he held his tongue as Nicholas shook his head as if to dismiss comments until later.

Brenna lifted her head tiredly to Charles and tried to smile her thanks, and, licking her dry lips, she whispered hysterically to Nicholas, 'If I die, promise that you will take me home to Pencarris with you. I want to be with you.'

Alarm surged through him as he clutched her hand. Did she know something he didn't? His eyes went in fright to Charlie and it was as if they were eight and five again and their mother was in the next room dying. Swallowing down panic, he watched as Charles turned towards the door.

'I'll go and fetch the doctor myself, Nick, and if Mrs Fenton is at Airelies I'll bring her too.' He was gone in a second, the sound of footsteps echoing in the silence.

'It seems as if this baby business has Charles running scared, my love.' Nick tried to make light of his own desperate worry.

'He has not read the manuals we have, I fear.' She copied his lead, though her voice petered out as another contraction swamped her with agony.

'Just as well then that we know them backwards.' His hand rubbed at her brow and pushed back a loose strand of hair that fell across her vision. What the hell was supposed to happen next? he wondered, cursing his inability to propel things into any sort of an order and swearing solemnly never to put his precious wife through any such danger again should they by any grace of God actually come out of this one without loss. Hell, this was all his fault—after all, she'd sworn celibacy until he'd persuaded her otherwise.

A rush of breath alerted him to a change in his wife's demeanour, her panting turning to pushing as she knelt forward, striking Nicholas's offered help away and bearing down.

Five minutes later Madeleine Johanna Pencarrow arrived, her father taking her into his arms and seeing not a wrinkled baby, but a beautiful young lady whose dark black hair was already ringed in curls, plastered as they were against bright red skin. The men outside heard her loud cry and a cheer was raised above the silence of the compound.

Brenna held Nicholas's arms and cried. 'I knew you would come,' she said quietly. 'I told the baby to wait until you did so, and I watched the moon through the cracks in the boards and prayed that you would find me.'

Nicholas smiled, his mouth running across her hair, the smell of violets so dear and real and nearly lost that he could scarcely believe his luck. 'I couldn't find you,' he returned huskily. 'They sent no note until this morning.'

''Twas the child they wanted, I think, as well as revenge on me,' Brenna said quietly, and Nicholas's fingers bit into her arms at the realisation of such a close call. 'They knew the Pencarrows would pay well for a lost heir. They did not think you could want me too.'

'They're all dead now, sweetheart, and so is your secret. It can never hurt us again.' His face lifted as Charles, Mrs Fenton and Ilona appeared, anger and joy mixed at seeing their young mistress's condition and then without ado they shooed both men to the door, mumbling about the propriety of men in a birthing room.

Nicholas was not so easily dismissed, however, crossing to his wife and laying the tiny bundle in her waiting arms. 'I will be right outside.'

Brenna's fingers closed around his hand and she nodded, quietly placing the now wailing baby at her breast and watching her husband as he ducked beneath the sagging lintel. She was safe and loved, and the child who suckled with a hungry abandon was perfect in every respect. Twinkling eyes held the wise glance of the healing woman Ilona beside her, who kneaded her stomach with careful practise.

'He can come back in a moment, your Grace. Let us get you fit to move first.'

Fifteen minutes later the women were satisfied with the state of Brenna's dress and health, and, summoning the fretting Duke, they watched as he bent to his wife, holding on to her tightly for a second before he began to speak. 'Come, I will lift you into the carriage, sweetheart. Charles will bring Madeleine,' he added as his brother joined them, placing the now sleeping babe into a downy blanket fetched from Airelies. 'All of Pencarris and Penmayne holds its breath to know that you are safe.'

She laughed and held up her arms to him, hiding her face in his shirt as they came into the light of day, but watching her daughter closely as she followed with Charles.

'It was a girl after all,' Nicholas said softly as they went. 'A girl with all the signs of being just as beautiful as her mother.'

Brenna wriggled and whispered back. 'Maybe next time it will be a son, Nicholas, with chestnut hair and gold-green eyes, and with a penchant for falling in love once and for ever.'

*　*　*　*　*

Savor the breathtaking
romances and thrilling adventures
of Harlequin Historicals

On sale September 2004

THE KNIGHT'S REDEMPTION by Joanne Rock

A young Welshwoman tricks Roarke Barret into marriage
in order to break her family's curse—of spinsterhood.
But Ariana Glamorgan never expects to fall for the
handsome Englishman who is now her husband....

PRINCESS OF FORTUNE by Miranda Jarrett

Captain Lord Thomas Greaves is assigned to guard Italian
princess Isabella di Fortunaro. Sparks fly and passions flare
between the battle-weary captain and the spoiled, beautiful
lady. Can love cross all boundaries?

On sale October 2004

HIGHLAND ROGUE by Deborah Hale

To save her sister from a fortune hunter, Claire Talbot offers
herself as a more tempting target. But can she forget the
feelings she once had for Ewan Geddes, a charming
Highlander who once worked on her father's estate?

THE PENNILESS BRIDE by Nicola Cornick

Home from the Peninsula War, Rob Selbourne discovers
he must marry a chimney sweep's daughter to
fulfill his grandfather's eccentric will. Will Rob
find true happiness in the arms of
the lovely Jemima?

eHARLEQUIN.com

The Ultimate Destination for Women's Fiction

The ultimate destination for women's fiction.
Visit eHarlequin.com today!

GREAT BOOKS:
- We've got something for everyone—and at great low prices!
- Choose from new releases, backlist favorites, Themed Collections and preview upcoming books, too.
- Favorite authors: Debbie Macomber, Diana Palmer, Susan Wiggs and more!

EASY SHOPPING:
- Choose our convenient "bill me" option. No credit card required!
- Easy, secure, 24-hour shopping from the comfort of your own home.
- Sign-up for free membership and get $4 off your first purchase.
- Exclusive online offers: FREE books, bargain outlet savings, hot deals.

EXCLUSIVE FEATURES:
- Try Book Matcher—finding your favorite read has never been easier!
- Save & redeem Bonus Bucks.
- Another reason to love Fridays— Free Book Fridays!

Shop online
at www.eHarlequin.com today!

INTBB204R

eHARLEQUIN.com

The Ultimate Destination for Women's Fiction

Your favorite authors are just a click away
at www.eHarlequin.com!

- Take a sneak peek at the covers and
  read summaries of **Upcoming Books**

- Choose from over 600
  author **profiles!**

- Chat with your favorite authors
  on our **message boards.**

- Are you an author in the making?
  Get advice from published authors
  in **The Inside Scoop!**

**Learn about your favorite authors
in a fun, interactive setting—**

visit www.eHarlequin.com today!

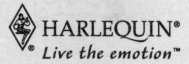

DEBORAH HALE

After writing more than ten award-winning
historical romances for Harlequin Historicals,
Deborah Hale now also writes otherworld
fantasies for LUNA Books. Deborah likes to
think of her word processor as a magic carpet
that can whisk readers away to enchanted times
and places. She hopes they enjoy the ride!
Deborah lives with her own personal hero and
their four children in Nova Scotia, Canada—
a place steeped in history, romance and magic.

Deborah invites you to become better
acquainted with her by visiting her personal
Web site www.deborahhale.com or by chatting
with her in the eHarlequin Community
(www.eHarlequin.com).

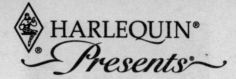
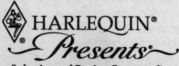